THE STONE

NIGEL TRANTER was born in Glasgow on 23rd November 1909 and educated at George Heriot's School in Edinburgh. After leaving school he trained as an accountant, but took up writing full-time in 1936, a career only partly interrupted by service in the army during the Second World War.

Almost his entire literary output is concerned with Scotland's history. His non-fiction, from his first book—*The Fortalices and Early Mansions of Southern Scotland* (1935)—deals principally with his life-long interest in Scottish architecture. He also wrote over eighty novels, many of them drawn from his unparalleled knowledge of Scottish history. Notable among these are *The Gilded Fleece* (1942), *The Queen's Grace* (1953), *Balefire* (1958), *The Bruce Trilogy* (1969-71) and *The Wallace* (1975). Two of his novels, *The Freebooters* (1950) and *The Stone* (1958), are concerned with the Stone of Destiny, a subject of great interest to Tranter, who was involved in negotiating the return of the Stone after its theft from Westminster Abbey in 1950.

Nigel Tranter died in January 2000.

Other B&W titles by Nigel Tranter

BALEFIRE
BRIDAL PATH
THE GILDED FLEECE
ISLAND TWILIGHT
THE QUEEN'S GRACE
TINKER'S PRIDE
FAST AND LOOSE
THE FLOCKMASTERS
KETTLE OF FISH
HARSH HERITAGE
THE FREEBOOTERS
FOOTBRIDGE TO ENCHANTMENT

THE STONE

NIGEL TRANTER

B&W PUBLISHING

British Library Cataloguing in Publication Data:
A catalogue record for this book is available from
the British Library

Cover photograph:
*The Coronation Chair in Westminster Abbey,
with the Stone in position underneath*
Courtesy of
The Hulton Getty Picture Collection

Cover Design *by* Winfortune *&* Associates

Printed by WS Bookwell, Finland 2000

I

THE man who leaned against the red gnarled bole of the lone Scots pine and gazed out over the fair scene that glowed golden in the flooding radiance of the sinking sun, did not actually crouch, nor yet hide behind that ancient tree. Unquestionably, it would have been a gross exaggeration to have said that his attitude was furtive. Wary perhaps; unobtrusive, no doubt; not anxious to make himself unduly prominent on a scene of quiet pastoral seclusion, certainly. Which was as it should have been, assuredly.

And almost any less modest and retired stance than in the shade of that dark and solitary tree *would* have made the watcher distinctly noticeable and apparent. For only one other individual was evident in all that lovely and verdant sun-filled prospect—though it was a bare four miles from the Fair City of Perth itself. And this other man was by no means flashily advertising his presence either. Down by the riverside, three hundred yards away, he moved slowly, quietly, discreetly amongst the willows and alders of the grassy banks, and the rhythmic raising and flicking of an arm, though regular, was gentle, unremarkable, part of the quiet evening—and only the occasional flash, as the levelling sunlight gleamed on what must be a steel rod, drew attention to the fact that an angler fished assiduously. And not merely fished assiduously but kept glancing as assiduously upstream and downstream, and over his shoulder at the gently rising green foothills that made so pleasing an amphitheatre of that sequestered section of the wide valley. Since only scattered grazing cattle and a few thinly-baaing sheep moved on all those rolling slopes, the watcher up by the tree would have been apparent indeed had he thrust himself out from under its shadow. And he was a modest man, by most standards.

But his glance was not wholly preoccupied with the

1

fisherman. Far from it. Indeed, it made a more or less regular circuit of four distinct spots in that wide vista. Firstly, to where up on a natural terrace amongst the grassy slopes a large mansion sprawled, its long red-stone turreted façade of mid-Victorian Gothic so seemingly out of place in that pastoral setting. But the many windows of Kincaid House turned only dulled blind eyes on the glory of the sunset; no evening smoke rose from any of its innumerable chimneys; and the ivy and shrubbery that once would have been its adornment now luxuriated wildly, threatening wholly to engulf even that aggressive sham-baronial challenge in stone. The watcher, really, had no call to take the dead house into his considerations.

From there his glance slid round to another edifice, nearer at hand a little, that crowned a steep and rocky knoll directly above the twisting river; a less imposing building altogether, this, though challenging too in its own way, for only a single tall fang of crow-stepped gable and a fragment of a circular tower thrust above a heap of weed-grown fallen red masonry. Kincaid Castle was as little likely to offer any threat from its broken apertures as was its great shuttered successor.

The third object of the man's regard, though ridiculous to mention in the same breath as the other two, was also an erection for the shelter of man—and moreover, one with more implication of life about it; a small green-and-khaki bivouac tent nestled in a tiny neuk of the riverbank below the castle, well hidden amongst bushes, and so adequately camouflaged that the observer would never have noticed it had not it been for the sharp angular shadow cast from it by the level rays of the westering sun. He linked that tent with the discreet fisherman, and wondered. And hesitated.

It was not that he was a hesitant man, that onlooker. One glance at his face, dark, long-featured, blue-chinned, keen-eyed, established that. A tall youngish man, bare-headed, dressed in well-worn almost shabby tweeds, without being in any way aggressive, he did not look as though he would not know his own mind. For that matter, of course, neither did he look the sort to skulk with even a semblance of furtiveness,

2

for any cause whatever. Yet appearances can be deceptive. And the appearance of Sir Patrick Kincaid of Kincaid, 17th Baronet of that Ilk, in that place that golden evening of early June, was highly deceptive indeed.

Should he go down, he wondered? Chance it? The fellow was almost certainly poaching. He might scare him off the scene—if he seemed authoritative enough. That would be the best thing. On the other hand, of course, if the man was *not* poaching, was fishing legitimately and with due permission, it could be awkward. Especially if he turned out to be a local. That would be asking for trouble—might spoil everything. That tent, of course, wouldn't seem to indicate a local. But then, it mightn't be this chap's tent at all.

Patrick Kincaid made up his mind—since his time was limited. Keeping the tree-trunk in line between himself and the distant figure by the waterside, he walked straight backwards, unhurriedly, heedfully, until a dip in the slope hid him from any possible view from the river. Then, swinging sharply right-handed, he went long-strided down the hill. He set a few new-clipped sheep bolting out of a hollow on the way, and cursed to himself. But likely that would not be seen, either. Reaching the waterside, he turned upstream.

That stream—and it was only that, and no river really, the Kincaid Water, and but a minor tributary of Tay—though peat-stained and fast-moving from high heather hills only a few miles to the west, wound a dilatory meandering course through the smiling vale. So that it was easy for the man to work his way up its bank without being obvious to anyone at the same level. Moreover, he was something of a deer-stalker, and rather prided himself on being able to utilise cover to advantage. When, therefore, he glimpsed his angler again, at some two hundred yards range, and saw a fairly adequate screen of alders and willows and red earthen banks in between, he decided that he could, with a little care, traverse three-quarters of the intervening distance unseen, and so obtain a fairly close look at this character before committing himself to action, one way or another. And that surely seemed to be advisable.

3

Patrick Kincaid was distinctly crestfallen therefore, when, with still some seventy yards to go, he discovered that his quarry had taken fright. Though that, indeed, barely described the situation. The fellow was no longer fishing—though he had been up till half a minute previously. He gave no impression of ever having been fishing, for that matter. Of rod or other angling gear there was no sign. He lay on his back against a grassy bank, hands clasped behind a vividly red head, a cigarette between his lips, and eyes innocently upturned, intent on all the darting swallows of the heaven. His stalker frowned ruefully.

But the frown cleared. After all, this told him most of what he wanted to know, didn't it? The large individual in front of him most clearly had not wanted to be caught fishing. Therefore he was here without permission. Poaching. He might still be a local, of course.

If so, Patrick decided, he would be well-known, outstanding. The fellow was huge, a giant of a man, brawny, tough-looking, red-faced and redder-headed, his shock of flaming curly hair as good as a beacon to highlight him. He would be approximately Kincaid's own age, in his early thirties. If he lived locally, it ought not to be difficult to identify him, at any rate.

Quite casually the big man turned his head to look directly at the bush behind which the other was hiding. "Aye, man," he said. "Fine night." And though that was a mere murmured remark and no shout, the great voice carried over the intervening seventy yards with ease. It might have been a bull rumbling in its throat.

Distinctly sheepishly Patrick Kincaid picked himself up and moved forward out of his cover. He felt his inadequacy very much upon him. A show of authority now, undoubtedly was what was called for. But—" 'Evening," he said mildly. "Er . . . any luck?"

The other did not stir. "Luck?" he wondered. "What way should I hae ony luck? Luck at what, Mister?"

"Well . . . at fishing, for instance."

"Fishin'? Say—you reckon there's fishes in this bit burn? Trouties? Och, fancy that."

4

Patrick shrugged. If the fellow was going to brazen it out, there was no point in provoking him. That would not serve his purpose. "I just thought that you might have been," he said, rather lamely.

"You the bluidy keeper, Mister?"

Kincaid shook his dark head, and sighed with relief at the same time. If this ruddy giant had been a local, he would not have asked that question. He would have known any game-keepers, surely. So that was all right. He was no menace. It was just a matter of getting him out of the way.

"No," he declared. "I'm no keeper. My name is Kincaid." He cleared his throat, a little self-consciously. "Kincaid of Kincaid." He had a slow, gentle, almost hesitant voice, that belied his looks.

"Kincaid!" The big man sat up now, but unhurriedly. "Hell—*this* is Kincaid, is it no'? Kincaid Water." He jerked his head. "An' yon's Kincaid Hoose, up yonder?"

Patrick nodded. "That is so."

"Jings—you're worse'n a keeper, then! A bluidy laird!"

Kincaid drew a hand over his mouth and chin. "I . . . I wouldn't just call myself that," he said.

"Wud you no'?" The red-headed colossus thrust out a craggy chin pugnaciously. "A bluidy laird!" he repeated. "An' frae London! Frae blasted baistard London!" Rising to his full height, that must have reached at least six-and-a-half feet, he glared down at the by no means diminutive Kincaid as though he might well eat him. "It's aye London! Bluidy London!"

Patrick blinked a little at this unexpected onslaught. If he did not shrink back a pace or two it was not because he did not feel so inclined. "No, no—I'm not from London," he denied. "Nothing of the sort. What makes you think that . . . ?"

"They tell't me back in the pub, there—in Redgorton—that the owner o' this Kincaid place was in London. They said it was some damned London company. Anither blasted absentee-landlord."

"H'rr'mm." Patrick cleared his throat. This was coming rather near to the bone. "I . . . er . . . you don't like London then?" he asked, to change the subject as quickly as might be.

"*Like* it!" the other roared. "Like yon muckle great bluid-suckin' shambles? Yon splurge o' infamy that's fair drainin' the life oot o' puir auld Scotland? Jings!"

"You're a Nationalist, then, I take it?"

"No, I'm no'. Leastways, I'm no' one of thae boys wi' the beards an' the kilts, see. Hell, no! But I ken fine what's wrang wi' Scotland the day. Aye, an' I've did somethin' aboot it, tae!"

"*You* have?"

"Aye, I have. Jings, aye. I'm Roddie Roy MacGregor, an' I dinna care wha kens it!"

"Roddie? Roddie Roy, you said? Not Robbie?"

"Roddie, aye, Roddie Roy MacGregor. That's me. O' the cattle, see. An' the whisky. An' the crofts. D'you no' mind? Or d'you never read the papers, man?"

"Roddie Roy! Of the Gregorach! The Glasgow Freebooters!" Patrick Kincaid's mind slid back a few years to the famous occasion when a group of Glasgow youths, led by a gigantic young riveter from the shipyards, and a medical student back from the wars, had sought to waken up and inspire a lethargic and weary Scotland—and succeeded in doing so, too, to a remarkable degree—by a series of spectacular if highly unorthodox exploits concerned with retaining for Scottish use some of the prime beef, whisky, and other notable products that were being shipped out of the country in spite of the people's own needs. "Of course!" Patrick thrust out his hand. "MacGregor! Roddie Roy—of course! I'm proud to shake your hand, man."

"Oh, aye. Fine that," the big man said, with less certainty. But he extended a great hamlike fist, nevertheless. "What sort o' a laird are you, then, Mister?" he demanded.

"No laird at all, and that's a fact," Sir Patrick Kincaid admitted. "I think St Andrew, your auld Scotland's patron saint himself, must have sent you to poach the Kincaid Water this day, Roddie Roy. Sit down, man, and I'll tell you all about it."

"I dinna get this, look," Roddie Roy declared presently, scratching his somewhat incongruous mop of red curls. "You say you're a sir. You ca' yoursel' Kincaid o' Kincaid. But you're no' the laird o' this place?"

"That's right. I'm Patrick Kincaid, 17th Baronet of that Ilk—Heaven help me! The Kincaid of Kincaid is just part of the title. Doesn't mean a thing—at least, not a thing in law. My family hasn't owned an inch of land here for two hundred years. Since our forfeiture after the Forty-five, in fact."

"Say—d'you tell me that! This forfeiture—you mean they pinched it? The bluidy English Government pinched your land?"

"Well . . . that's hardly the way *I'd* put it. Say that we were on the losing side, and we had to pay for it. Like a lot of others. But that's an old story. And, actually, it's still older history than that that's brought me here tonight." Patrick looked around him at the lengthening shadows in the tapestry of black and gold that the sunset wove out of that valley. "D'you know, this is the first time I've set foot on Kincaid land since my father brought me here as a small boy. I suppose I've always deliberately avoided the place. Foolish, I suppose."

"Oh, yeah." Such considerations did not seem greatly to impress Roddie Roy. "What you here for then noo, Mister? Or Sir . . . or whatever you ca' yoursel'?"

"I think it might be easiest if you just called me Patrick," Kincaid said gravely. "And I'm here for a reason that may well interest you quite a lot, actually. You see, I'm here in connection with the Stone of Destiny."

"The Stane! You mean . . . yon one? The Stane the boys brung up—an' the bluidy polis took back to London? Yon Stane?"

"Yes . . . and no. It's the Stone of Scone."

"But yon's lockit up in Westminster Abbey, man, wi' chains an' Goad kens what, an' you get an electric shock if you sae much as keek at it! Damn them!"

"That's where you're wrong, Roddie. It's not." Kincaid

declared. "*A* Stone is tied up there, yes—but not *the* Stone. Not the genuine Stone of Destiny, the *Lia Fail*, on which the Kings of Scotland were crowned from time immemorial. That Stone lies much nearer home. In fact, to be exact, it lies within perhaps a couple of hundred yards of where we're sitting now!"

MacGregor turned to stare at his companion. He did not say anything, but his glance was eloquent. He would be a hard man to tell a fairy story to, would be that Glasgow ex-riveter.

"It's true. The real Stone is here. Has been, all along. The one at Westminster is a fake. A seven-hundred-year-old fake."

The big man shook his red head. "Jings, man—is it you that's crackers? Or me? Tell me that?"

"Neither. Look—it's a long long story, that goes right back to the time of Edward I of England. The Hammer of the Scots, 1296. I can't tell you it all just now. But you can take it from me that the Stone which Edward Plantagenet stole from Scone Abbey, across the Tay there, and took away south with him, the Stone he thought was the Stone of Destiny, was just a plain unworked block of Old Red Sandstone, dug out of a quarry at Scone specially for him. Precisely the same stone as this ruined castle is built of, and the mansion-house there, too. And the real Stone, the *Lia Fail* as it was called in the Gaelic, a different thing altogether, much bigger, richly carved, and saddle-shaped, was buried somewhere near the Abbey and two years later dug up, brought across the Tay, and hidden again here, for safer keeping. At Kincaid. And here it has lain, untouched, ever since."

"But . . . Hell, man—hoo d'you make that oot? Hoo do *you* ken that? I'm no' sayin' you're a damned leear, mind. But . . ."

"I don't blame you for doubting," the other allowed. "You're not the first, by any means! In fact, I've never got anyone really to believe me, up till now. Though the thing stands to reason. And it's not only *my* theory, which is based on an ancient family tradition. All early written accounts of the true Stone describe it as highly carved, ornate, and shaped to form a hollowed seat. Like a saddle. Whereas we all know that the Stone that Ian Hamilton and his friends managed to abstract from Westminster Abbey a few years ago, and is back there again now, is just an oblong hunk of plain red stone. It wasn't to be expected, was it, that the custodians of the Stone of Destiny, Scotland's most precious relic, would not have sought to keep it from Edward, in the War of Independence? After all, they knew that he was coming for it. They had plenty of warning. So they fooled him with this other stone. Or maybe even he wasn't actually fooled—for he was an astute old scoundrel, the said Edward First—but if he couldn't lay hands on the real thing, at least he could take a Stone south with him, in triumph, that was *said* to be Scotland's Coronation Stone. Who was to know the difference, in London?"

"Aye. I'ph'mm. Maybe. That could be, aye. But . . . hoo d'you ken it's here? At this Kincaid? The right one?"

"It has always been a tradition in my family that it was brought here. You see, my ancestor, Gavin Kincaid, was one of the principals in the business of digging it up, at Scone, and bringing it over the Tay to here, to his home, for safer keeping. The deed is actually commemorated in our coat-of-arms and motto."

"What for did they dig it up, an' shift it again, Mister . . . Patrick?" Roddie Roy obviously was interested in facts rather than theories.

"Well, two years after the Stone was first taken, in 1298, for some reason or other, Edward ordered another and special raid on Scone. He pulled the Abbey apart, stone from stone. Razed it to the ground. Obviously he was looking for something. The tradition is that the Abbot and others got wind of this raid, and what it was coming for, and hastily got the genuine Stone up and away, before Edward's thugs arrived. Gavin Kincaid was a neighbouring laird—Scone is only three miles from here, across Tay—and he brought it to his own castle, and hid it somewhere."

"Aye. It sounds right enough. But—och, Jings, I jist canna credit it, man Patrick!"

"I dare say not. That's been the attitude of practically everyone, up till now. Though some of the greatest historical and antiquarian experts in Scotland believe the Stone at Westminster to be a fake, and the real one still buried somewhere. And up till a couple of days ago, it didn't greatly matter whether you or anybody else credited my story or not. But the situation has changed—changed drastically."

"Eh? Hoo d'you make that oot?"

"Two days ago there was a report in *The Scotsman*—maybe you don't read *The Scotsman*, Roddie? No? Well, there was a report from Oxford, announcing that the Oxford University Historical Research Society had discovered what they considered was adequate proof that the real Stone of Destiny was still buried somewhere in this area, that they knew where to look for it, had got permission from the landowners, and that a field party would be setting out in a day or two to come and dig the thing up. A party from Oxford."

"Bluidy Wars! The devil-damned English again!"

"Precisely! Mind you, I've nothing against the English, as such. Nor against Oxford University, or any of its societies. But you know as well as I do what will happen if those fellows once manage to lay hands on the Stone. It'll be whisked away over the Border, and down to England, either by themselves or, more likely, by the authorities stepping in—and Scotland will never see its Stone again. Nothing surer."

"B'damned, but you're right there! Cooper an' confound them a'," MacGregor bellowed. "That mustna' be!"

"No," the other agreed, quietly. "Not if I can stop it. Not if we can stop it."

They looked at each other in silence for a moment or two, eyes fiercely blue and darkly brown. And both of them nodded.

It was the big man's turn to offer his hand, a hand that might have felled an ox. "I'm wi' you, man Patrick!" he said, deep-voiced. "A' the way. Even to bluidy London—or the jyle itsel'!"

"I rather thought you might be," Kincaid admitted. "I could

hardly have stumbled upon a more satisfactory poacher, could I?"

"What you aimin' to dae, then?" Rod Roy demanded, presently.

"Well, as far as I can see, there's only the two possibilities. Either to find and dig up the thing before the Oxford people get it. Or to try to take it from them when they've found it!" Patrick grimaced. "Needless to say, I'd much prefer the former!"

"Oh, aye," MacGregor rubbed a not-too-closely shaven chin. "Maybe they wouldna' send a sir to the jyle?" he mentioned hopefully.

The other nodded. "I've thought of that. I'm afraid that they would, you know. The Age of Privilege is dead, undoubtedly. You mustn't take the baronetcy very seriously. Nobody else does, I fear! Actually I'm a pretty poor man. I'm a consultant civil engineer—and not one of the eminent ones you read about. Not enough people have got into the way of consulting me, as yet! So anything we do, we'll have to be prepared to take the consequences for!"

"Aye. Och well—it'll no be the first time for Rod Roy MacGregor, onyway! But look, man—d'you no' ken even a wee bittie where to be seekin' for the thing?"

"That's the trouble—I've just nothing to go by, at all. Except that it's here, somewhere. Presumably these Oxford people know something of where to look—though how they have got on to it, I don't know. I've tried to tap their sources. I've a friend who has a young brother at Oxford just now, and we phoned him to see if he could find out anything. He's to telephone me back at my hotel at Perth tonight, if he's been able to discover anything. But I can't say I'm very hopeful. He's not a member of this Historical Research Society, and they're pretty certain to keep that sort of information to themselves."

"Aye. Sure. But, say—hoo d'you ken they're comin' here, at a'? To this Kincaid place? Hoo d'you ken they've got the same story as you?"

"Well, I've no proof, of course. But I think we can be fairly certain. Something in that *Scotsman* report assured me. You see, the spokesman for the Society, a Dr Conrad Lister, making the announcement at the Annual Meeting three nights ago, said a strange thing. He said that, after the genuine Stone was dug up at Scone in 1298 it was floated across the Tay to be buried again at a safer hiding-place nearby. *Floated*, you'll notice. A peculiar word to use about a great block of stone weighing many hundredweights. Peculiar—if it wasn't that our family tradition says that the Stone *was* floated across. On inflated sheepskins. Like the goatskins they still use as floats in the Red Sea and thereabouts. Why they didn't use a boat, don't ask me. Probably the river was being watched and all boats guarded. It was done at dead of night, according to the story. Edward had his spies in Scotland. Anyway, there are three pillow-like objects in the Kincaid coat-of-arms to this day. Officially they are called woolsacks—but they really represent these blown-up sheepskins. And our family motto tells the same tale. It is 'Guard Weel'."

"Issat so. Sort of caissons, eh?" Being in the shipbuilding trade, MacGregor could appreciate such matters. "So you reckon they'll come here—the baistards?"

"I do. Wherever they winkled it out, they've got pretty good information, that's clear," Patrick looked around him. The sun had sunk now, and its last glow had faded, and the lovely half-light of the north was on all the land. "Where would you hide a big lump of stone that you didn't want anybody to know about, Roddie, around here? Remembering the spies."

"Hell—I dinna ken." Rod Roy MacGregor scratched his head. "Some place folks wouldna look, I s'pose. No' in the castle, onyway. The first place they'd seek it."

"I'm with you there," Kincaid agreed. "I should think there's not much use in looking in the ruins there. I was chewing the thing over, up on the hill, before I came down to you here. It would be a big thing to bury, mind, at short notice. I don't think they'd just dig a hole and put it in. That would be difficult to do without trace. At the time, I mean.

12

Spoil to hide, and so on. Knowing that there'd be a pretty thorough search. Natural cavities—caves—would be obvious, too. It's difficult. I'd say they'd want to put it somewhere *near* the castle, so that they could keep an eye on it."

"Aye. Nae doot. But that's no' a deal o' help. We canna jist dig up the whole glen. Hoo long've we got?"

"Till the Oxford folk turn up? I don't know, exactly. The report said they'd be coming to Scotland in two or three days. That was three nights ago. They may be here any time. I just dropped everything at the office, and came."

"It's a right stinker, is it no'. I doot we'll jist hae to let the baistards find it, and then lift it off them. Naethin' else for it."

Patrick shook his head, unhappily. "No. I don't want that if we can possibly avoid it. Only as a last resort. It wouldn't be so easy, either. No doubt there'll be quite a lot of these people."

"Damn that!" the giant scoffed. "I'll can whistle up a bunch o' the boys frae Glesgy as'll lift your Stane for you off any shower o' Englishry ever spawned!"

"Umm. Well . . . maybe. But think of the uproar that would cause! Think of the consequences, man. It would set the whole country by the ears. We'd have the entire police force after us."

"Will we no' hae that, onyway. An' wha cares for the bluidy polis!"

"I'm hoping not. I'm hoping that we can manage this thing with the minimum of fuss. If we can only remove the Stone quickly, before these people can actually lay hands on it, and then hide it again somewhere else, somewhere safely out of the way—then I'm hopeful that there won't be too much fuss. That was my original idea, anyway. Just what my ancestor did, seven hundred years ago, actually."

"Aye—but if you need these Oxford guys to find it for you?"

"I know. That's the snag. But it's just possible that they may give us a clue, themselves. I mean, when they first arrive they may go to have a look at the spot. Before actually starting

13

to unearth the thing. Quite a likely thing. If we could be watching, hidden somewhere . . . ? A lot depends on where it is, of course, and the conditions. But we might just be able to steal a march on these folk, working by night, maybe—and get the Stone away from under their noses. It's a long chance, admittedly."

"You're tellin' me! I'd sooner lift it off them, an' take the consequences, man."

"No. That only if all else fails. And there's always the possibility, of course, that my friend's young brother will phone something worthwhile through tonight, from Oxford."

They fell silent for a little, only too well aware of the magnitude of the task they were setting themselves, its manifold problems and difficulties, and the unwelcome repercussions that were almost bound to follow either success or failure. Sitting there, in the quiet shadowy valley, the entire situation seemed unreal to Patrick, so much less practicable and hopeful than it had appeared when he had decided back in Edinburgh, after a whole day's battle with himself, that he was in duty bound to make the attempt. How it all really appeared to the big ex-riveter at his side, Kincaid could only guess—but for himself, the worst of it was this inaction, the fact that they should be sitting there, probably within a matter of yards of what he so badly wanted to find, and yet could see nothing that they could usefully do about it. Surely it might have been expected that there would be some hint, some indication, something in the lie of the land even? How utterly unhelpful, infuriating, could be mere inanimate matter, scenery, geography.

It was this feeling that presently drove Patrick to suggest that at least they ought to have a look around, make some sort of survey—even though with no expectation of results. It was not too dark. And he had an electric torch.

They started at the ruined castle, for want of a better place—and found no great deal to look into there, in that stronghold of Kincaid's ancestors. Without major excavations into the great heap of fallen weed-grown masonry and rubble, there was nothing to be seen that could hide any large object.

14

The broken corner of what had been a vaulted basement they did uncover, beneath a screen of nettles—but obviously it was the merest fragment, and contained nothing but debris. And the single remaining gable and brief section of round tower offered no scope for exploration.

Underneath, they examined the rocky knoll on which the castle was built, for anything in the nature of a cave or crevice or hollow large enough to have been used to encase the Stone. They found nothing of the sort.

They walked up the valley, for perhaps quarter of a mile, waded across the stream, and came back down the other side. They saw nothing, in the half-dark, that looked in any way hopeful.

As they went, they talked. Patrick learned how it came about that Roddie Roy MacGregor was poaching the Kincaid Water. The ex-riveter had a sister married to a Perth railwayman, and he not infrequently came to stay with her for a long weekend. It seemed that, after the famed Gregorach exploits and adventures of seven years previously, he and some of his gang had settled down to a period of crofting and land reclamation in Wester Ross—and made a success of it too. But in time the draw of the busy Clyde, with its noise and bustle and strident activity, had been too much for the restless questing MacGregor, and after four years of the Highland North he had returned to Glasgow, and started a small boat-building project with two kindred spirits, on a corner of waste riverside ground at Govan. His spell in the Highlands, however, had infected him with the angling disease, and in Perth this stream, the Kincaid Water, had been recommended to him, as accessible yet nicely tucked away, with the big House conveniently empty. He had fished here on three or four occasions, without interference. And this time, so that he could fish both the evening and early morning rises, without having to return to Perth in between, he had brought along his little tent. He had been intending to return to Glasgow on the morrow. But that no longer applied, he assured his companion. He would stay just for as long as there was any need for his services—and to hell with the

15

boatyard! Unless he wanted him to go back right away? He had a motorcycle hidden down near the road there. He could be in Glasgow in two hours . . . ?

Patrick's look of enquiry at this suggestion elicited that what was being proposed was that MacGregor should hasten back to Glasgow forthwith, round up some few of his friends and accomplices—even some of his original Gregorach band that had not settled in the North, it seemed, were still to the fore and not averse to a little bit of excitement now and again—and be back here with them before midday tomorrow.

Grateful as he was for this alarmingly handsome offer, Patrick felt bound to decline it. The time for that was not yet, he thought. He might be glad of all proffered help, later—very glad. But not yet. They must see what guile and cunning might do, first.

They parted soon after that. Patrick had promised to be in his hotel in Perth at eleven o'clock, when young Duncan Keir was to telephone; and it would take him fully quarter of an hour to reach his car, parked in some trees the best part of a mile away. They would meet here again in the morning, fairly early, for another inspection, in daylight. And perhaps he might have some news by then.

They took leave of each other with a hand-clasp, Sir Patrick Kincaid to set off striding through the shadows eastwards, Roddie Roy MacGregor to his modest tent and a fry of brown trout.

16

II

AS Patrick Kincaid crossed the foyer of his hotel to the
reception desk, he had to lean over a row of suitcases
on the floor in order to reach and press the bell for attention.
As he waited for the night porter, his downward glance was
caught by an upturned label on one of the cases—caught and
held. It was inscribed "Miss Alison Craig. Passenger's Luggage
in Advance. Perth, Scotland." And in large capital letters
above, "O.U.H.R.S. OPERATION COLUMBA."

The man peered, and moistened his lips. He stooped quickly,
and turned over the labels on the other cases. Each was headed
with this legend, "O.U.H.R.S. OPERATION COLUMBA." And
all had women's names written—five different names.

Straightening up, Patrick beat a tattoo on the reception
counter with his fingertips. Not in any impatience for the
porter's non-arrival, either. So they were as near as this!
Coming here—to this very hotel! And women! Confound it—
he'd never thought of women being involved, somehow! If
there was to be any unpleasantness—as was almost inevitable
in this business—this surely would complicate the issue more
than somewhat. This was worse, much worse, than he had
anticipated. Women!

The night-porter, arriving to find a very black frown dis-
figuring the already dark enough features of the bell-ringer,
hastened to apologise for the delay. He was cut short.

"It's all right. I'm in no hurry," Patrick assured. "It's just
that I'm expecting a telephone call. From the south. Long
distance. At eleven o'clock." He glanced at his wrist-watch.
"That's in just ten minutes. The caller will ask for Drummond.
Mr P. Drummond." Kincaid's voice, always so slightly hesitant,
was more so than usual as he enunciated the name. "You
have that? Where am I to take the call, please? You don't
have phones in the bedrooms, here."

"No. No—we havena got that far yet, sir," the porter admitted. "Och, there isna' a great demand for telephoning frae folk's beds, jist. But you can take it in the call-box there, Mr Drummond. You'll be grand there. Private, see. I'll switch it through. At eleven, jist?"

"Yes. Thank you. I'll wait. Through in the Lounge, there." Patrick half turned away, and then looked back. "You're . . . h'm . . . going to have quite a bunch of new guests, I see?" And he nodded down towards the luggage at his feet.

"Oh, aye. Students they are, I think. Frae Oxford. Archyologists, they say. Jist lassies, too. It's funny—you wouldna expect lassies to be interested in the like o' that. Would you, sir?"

"No." Patrick agreed strongly. "You would not." And more casually. "When are they coming? These archaeologists. Are they arriving . . . soon?"

"Och, they're here noo, sir. They arrived off the eight-thirty-eight." The porter swung the open Visitors' Book round on the counter, and pointed to the five latest names written therein. "Oxford Univairsity, see. Five o' them. Och, there's mair'n that. These are jist an overflow, like. We jist got the lassies here. The rest o' them—the men—are a' in ither hotels."

"They're here, then? Already!"

"They're awa' to their beds. After a bite o' supper. Och, they've been traivelling a' the day. They're right tired."

"Of course. Quite. Bound to be."

"I dinna see *your* name in the book, Mr Drummond," the porter observed, reading the writing expertly though upside-down. "Maybe you've no' signed-in, yet?"

"No. Er, no—I haven't, as a matter of fact. Not yet." Reluctantly Patrick took the pen that the other so helpfully handed to him, nibbled his lip, and then bent over the Visitors' Book. In a painstakingly back-hand fashion he wrote "P. Drummond, Edinburgh. Room 23. Scots." And felt a criminal as he did it—even though his middle name was Drummond. Never had he done such a thing before. But Kincaid was altogether too unusual and obvious a name to set down there, in the circumstances. Especially next to those of the Oxford women. "I'll be in the Lounge," he said then, abruptly, and stalked off across the foyer.

In the deserted Lounge Patrick Kincaid sat down and sought to collect his wits. So he was to get no time at all—no breathing-space! They were here. And a big party spread over a number of hotels. And women. It was all worse than he had feared. They might well all be out at Kincaid in the morning. What could he do—what could he possibly find out before then? He had talked about guile and cunning to Roddie Roy. A fat lot of that there looked like being, now! Would he have been better to have accepted the big man's offer of a tough bunch of Glasgow keelies? That looked like being the only answer now.

Patrick heard the telephone bell ringing, dead on eleven o'clock, and hurried through to the call-box in the corner of the foyer, waving to the porter.

It was not a good line. And young Duncan Keir seemed to have become infected with an Oxford accent, for his voice came through with a gargling drawl that it had certainly never boasted in Edinburgh. The boy was very guarded and con-spiratorial, asking twice to be assured that it was Mr P. Drummond speaking, and then commencing on an elaborate screed about referring to his firm's previous correspondence of such-and-such a date, on the subject of antique furniture. However, none of this cloak-and-daggerish nonsense for long disguised the fact that he had very little to say. He had been quite unable to find out anything really significant, it seemed. The Historical Research Society kept themselves very much to themselves—and were not accepting any last-minute members for their expedition. Moreover, the rank-and-file student members did not seem to know much about the details of the business, anyway—a few dons and seniors keeping all that in their own hands. As to timing, he had to reveal that the advance guard had already left Oxford.

Patrick interrupted this information a shade tersely.

Keir went on to say that he gathered that most of the party seemed to expect to be home in a week or ten days—so that it appeared that Operation Columba was expected to be

19

successful fairly promptly. Not too much beating about the bush. And did it not strike Mr Drummond that that was a strange name that had been dreamed up for it? Operation Columba. Any idea what the point would be in that?

Patrick agreed that it was a strange name. Was there anything else? No hint of a clue?

Nothing, the boy had had to admit, apologetically.

Ringing off, Patrick moved gloomily away.

"Everything okay, sir?" the night-porter asked, helpfully.

"Oh, yes. Quite," the other lied. "Thanks. Look—can I have an early breakfast in the morning? Really early, I mean?"

"Surely, Mr Drummond. When d'you want it for?"

"Well—say seven o'clock. That too early?"

"No, no. That's fine. Seven o'clock. I'll mark it down, sir. A knock at six-thirty?"

"Yes, please. And . . . I say, what is it these archaeologists are doing here? D'you know?"

"Och, jist the usual. Looking for Roman remains. There's Roman camps an' forts an' things in the Tay valley, y'ken. At Grassy Walls, an' Bertha, an' Colen."

"I see. Roman remains, eh? Interesting."

"Well, sir, for them that likes yon sort o' thing, maybe. I canna say I c'd be bothered wi' it, mysel'."

"Quite. Well—goodnight to you."

Up in his own room, Patrick Kincaid lay late that night, tossing on his bed, and cudgelling his brains. He went over all his problems time and again—with but little profit. But most of all, his mind came back to that word Columba. Why should these people have chosen to designate their expedition by that name? It was strange. It might be utterly unimportant, of course—but surely there must be some reason behind it? Evidently they weren't broadcasting the fact that they had come to find the Stone of Destiny—not here in Scotland, anyway. As was very wise of them. Roman remains, it was to be. But why Columba? These code names, that had become so popular in the War, however light-heartedly selected usually had some relevance. Could it have something to do with Saint Columba and the church he founded? The Pictish Church of the Culdees.

Scone was the Capital of Pictavia, and Columba was bound to have come frequently to Scone from Iona. Could there have been some special cell, or building, that bore his name, in the vicinity? There was a theory, held by some, that the Stone of Destiny itself had been the Saint's own pillow, brought from Iona to Dunstaffnage, and then to Scone. It might have been that story that was elaborated to make it Jacob's pillow, on which he dreamed of the Ladder up to Heaven. But that wasn't much of a help. All distinctly far-fetched, too. And yet, of course, any reason for calling an expedition to dig up the Stone of Destiny Operation Columba must be pretty far-fetched. But there it was, written on their labels.

That question, and others, chased round and round his mind till, at last, he slept.

By soon after eight o'clock next morning, Patrick, his car hidden amongst trees again, was striding it out over the grassy slopes of Kincaid, with the great blue hills to north and west shedding the last of their nightcaps of mist, the larks singing their morning praise all about him, and the dew-decked pastures scintillating in the slantwise sunshine. Though he hurried, he did not make directly for his objective; the farm-house of Kincaid Mains lay on highish ground perhaps half a mile to the south, overlooking certain sections of the valley, and the man felt that it was undesirable that any unwanted activity should be observed from there. So he made a point of keeping out of sight—and wondered just how much of this sort of thing might lie ahead of him.

Roddie Roy's presence was heralded first by the faint, aromatic tang of wood-smoke, and then by the still more delectable fragrance of broiled trout. The big man, Patrick discovered, was sprawled beside his tent beneath the castle's rock, eating a substantial repast of stale bran scones and numerous crisply curling golden fish of varied proportions.

Greeted boisterously, and urged to partake, the newcomer assured that he had already had his breakfast. But informed that that was no excuse for spurning trouties caught within the hour, he capitulated.

21

"Look," he announced, less appreciative of the delicacy than he ought to have been undoubtedly, taking up a nice six-ounce trout. "They're here. They're in Perth, now. A lot of them. And women amongst them. Actually staying in my hotel."

"D'you tell me that?" the other said, munching. "Och, well—the weemin'll be nae bother, anyway."

"I wish I could agree with you! Women will complicate the issue more than ever. But the immediate trouble is that they may be out here at any time now—this very morning, maybe. I came out right away to warn you. It wouldn't do for you to be on the scene when they arrived."

"You needna' hae bothered. I can make mysel' scarce, okay. But, say—did you no' get ony word? What aboot your pal on the telephone?"

"No good. He could tell me nothing that I didn't know already. I've nothing new to go on—no wiser than I was last night. Except that they've given this expedition the name of Operation Columba. I've been trying to puzzle out what that could mean. There must be some reason for it."

"Columbus? That the guy that discovered America?"

"No, no. This is Colum*ba*. The saint, presumably, who brought Christianity to this part of the world. I'm wondering if there could be any old cell, some sort of ruin hereabouts, called after him?"

"Goad kens—I dinna," MacGregor admitted piously.

"It may have little or no meaning at all, of course. Just a name."

"*Does* it mean onythin', then? The word, jist. This Columbus?"

"Colum*ba*, man. Columba itself, of course, is just Latin for dove. That's all. But as a name it's . . ." Patrick stopped suddenly, in mid-sentence. He snapped his fingers. "Of course!" he cried. "Why didn't I think of that? Doves. Pigeons. A doocot! It *could* be a doocot, Roddie."

"Aye," that realist conceded. "Could be. Could be a bluidy henhoose! Or a rabbit-hutch."

"No, no. Don't you see? Every castle and laird's house in

the old days had its own doocot. A separate building. Strongly built, too. With stone nesting-boxes. You must have seen scores of them? Columbarium was the proper name. Pigeons were an important part of the diet. They bred them by the hundred. You know the story about the Fife lairds—how they were so canny and mean that they always erected their doocots at the very edge of their properties, so that the birds would tend to feed mainly on their neighbours' corn!" Patrick leaned forward. "It might be it, Roddie—it *might* just be what we're looking for!"

"Whaur?" MacGregor demanded. "I dinna see ony doocots aboot here."

"No," the other allowed, just a little crestfallen. "That's true. But there may have *been* one. After all, there's not much left of the castle itself, now. There's no reason why its doocot, if there was one, should have survived. But its site—if we could find that. And the Stone might be in it. Come to think of it, the inside of a doocot, hidden away under the droppings of hundreds of pigeons, would be as good a place as any to hide anything that you were particularly anxious should not be found. It's worth trying, anyhow—trying to see if we can locate the site of a doocot."

"Sure. Sure." Roddie conceded, as Patrick started up, all keenness again. "But gie's a minute to finish ma breakfast, will ye no'? An' mind, we didna see ony sign o' anythin' like a doocot, or the site o' one, last night."

"No. But then we were sticking to this valley floor. They preferred to build their doocots on higher ground—I know that much."

So they commenced their search of the slopes and pastures above the windings of the Kincaid Water. They confined themselves to the north side—for it seemed unlikely that the builders would have sited their doocot at the far side of a river that would frequently be an impassable torrent. Anyway, they could see the more gentle southern slopes reasonably well—too well, indeed, for that would apply in both direc- tions, and up there lay the farmhouse of Kincaid Mains, overlooking their area of search. Keeping themselves out of

23

sight of its windows was going to be by no means easy, on this higher ground.

Their search, of course, in all that rolling grassland, was not for anything so obvious as a building or even a ruin, but merely for any excrescence showing through or below the turf that might indicate foundations or man-made interference. And undoubtedly the early morning slanting sunshine helped in this, throwing shadows behind every hummock and corrugation and filling every hollow. Yet, for all that, and despite an extensive and fairly exhaustive quartering of the ground, they found nothing which aroused any hope in them. They came on the grass-grown remains of something much larger, and circular, that had obviously been a stell, or drystone shelter for sheep and cattle, on the lee side of a knoll. But that was all.

And throughout their search Patrick's glance, at least, frequently tended to be directed away from the green hillocks altogether, either southwards towards the whitewashed farm place that crouched in the lap of the braeside opposite, or eastwards to where the road from Perth skirted the property.

Working their way back and forward, their quest inevitably brought them ever closer to the great empty shuttered mansion-house. Its air of desertion and dejection was the more apparent the nearer that they approached. Peeling paint, broken windows, gutters adrift, all aided the rioting vegetation to declare its triumph over the works of man. Patrick Kincaid, too sensitive by half no doubt, could not shake off the feeling of being watched, overlooked, resented here also. Kincaid House glowered in the morning sun.

"A great muckle barracks o' a place," Roddie Roy commented. "Looks like the rats been at it—or the sudgers."

Patrick nodded. It looked indeed as though it might well have been requisitioned by the Army during the war years, and never recovered—as had been the fate of so many similar houses up and down the land. But he felt no particular sorrow over its state. Admittedly the house bore his own name—but this flamboyant monument to Victorian pride and arrogance represented something very alien to the old Kincaids. He indicated as much.

"A monstrosity. Some jute nabob from Dundee built it out of his Calcutta millions, I believe. It would be better as a decent ruin, like *our* old castle. Though there must be a nucleus of good honest stuff about it somewhere, for it's said to be built on to the former seventeenth-century house that succeeded the castle. No sign of it from here."

But Roddie Roy was not looking at the lifeless mansion, but rather away beyond it, and half behind it, to the right. A long stretch of red-stone garden walling showed there, and at its far end, partly hidden by intervening trees, a slanting lean-to roof rose higher. "See yon," he observed. "A coupla doos flew in yonder, the noo. Did you no' see them?"

Patrick stared, eyes narrowed into the level sunlight. "Dammit—you're right!" he declared. "It's a doocot. Come on!"

They hurried round the side of the house, past the derelict stableyard at the rear, and on to the walled garden. At its northern end, back turned to the sad jungle of that garden, as it were, rose a small square building in the local dark red sandstone, with a one-sided stone-tiled roof, moss-grown and broken, and crow-stepped half-gables. In the centre of its ridge was a decorative finial in carved stone, now much weather-worn, and underneath it a row of little archways, like a doll's arcade. And from within came the gentle drowsy *rickety-coo*, *rickety-coo* of roosting pigeons.

"Easy money!" the big man remarked. "Nae bother at a'."

"M'mmm." The other rubbed his chin with the back of his hand. "Yes. Very nice," he said. "But not a great lot of use to us, I'm very much afraid."

"Eh? Hell—what's wrang wi' it?" MacGregor protested "It's a right doocot, is it no'? Wi' right doos in it, too. And it's auld—you can see that. What mair d'you want, man?"

"A still older one, Roddie, I fear. That's a seventeenth century doocot, you see—quite typically so. I studied traditional Scottish architecture a bit, at one time—in fact thought of being an architect once, till I was assured that civil engineering

25

would pay better. That doocot would be built three hundred years after the Stone was brought to Kincaid. Earlier ones were very different."

"Is that a fact? Fancy you kennin' a' that! But, jings, that's no' to say this isna' the doocot thae Oxford guys are aimin' at—if they're efter a doocot at a'. The Stane could of been put in here efter, could it no'? Could ha' been dug up again, an' hidden here?"

"Well . . . yes. I suppose so. That's right enough."

"It's the only doocot here, onyway. I'm for haein' a peek inside."

The door was old and ramshackle, fastened with a few links of rusty chain and an ancient padlock. MacGregor took one look at it, gripped the padlock in both great hands, placed a foot against the door-jamb, and heaved. The staple to which the chain was locked came out like a drawn tooth. A great flapping signalled the event from within.

Throwing open the door, they stepped inside—and promptly fell back again before the cloud of dust, the shower of feathers and grit, the fluttering frantic birds, and above all, the choking musty stench.

"Holy Mick—whatna' stour! Whatna' stink!" Roddie cried. "Worse'n bilge-watter!"

"Haven't been disturbed for years, I'd say. Give them a minute. Till the dust settles. Astonishing to think that these must be the actual descendants of the pigeons that were here in the seventeenth century. Probably the ones before that too."

"Och, every brute's the descendant o' one that lived then is it no'?" the practical Glaswegian pointed out. "Human bein's too—we a' go back further'n the bluidy seventeenth century!"

"I suppose you're right."

When the air had cleared a little they ventured into the doocot again, seeking to do as little breathing as possible. When they got used to the darkness, after the sunlight, it was to discover the interior of the place to be lined with hundreds upon hundreds of stone nesting-boxes. Only some few were broken, but all were coated and covered with a great weight

26

of droppings, nesting material, and the debris of ages. Their feet sank deep into the soft pile of it on the floor, amongst numerous dead birds in various stages of decomposition. But there was no sign of anything that looked as though it might be hiding a great block of stone.

"If it's here, then it's under all this muck on the floor, and we'll have to dig for it," Patrick declared, breathlessly. "Which will be nice!"

"We havena' even got a spade."

"No."

"Jist a minute." The big boat-builder turned and hurried outside. Patrick was glad enough of the excuse to follow him. But Roddie Roy was not seeking merely fresh air. He was making for the stableyard, and in a few moments was back with a long rusty iron rod having a T-handle, one of those great keys used for turning off water at the main. "I seen it against the wall when we were passin' yon stable," he mentioned. "It's no' sae guid as a crowbar, but it'll maybe serve for a bit jabbin' an' proddin'."

That service the key did them, and for perhaps ten gasping and deplorable minutes they prodded and jabbed and sounded every foot of that unpleasant floor—arousing a positive storm of dust and smell in the process. The thing bit deeply, thoroughly. But there was no answering jar of metal on stone. That was not to say that their objective definitely was not hidden there—but major digging with spades would be required to reach it, if it was. Coughing and choking the two men, recognising as much, lurched out into the fresh air again.

"Well, and just what are you two up to, in there?" a voice greeted them, interestedly, a cool feminine voice.

Patrick Kincaid caught his elusive breath, and swallowed, blinking in the strong light. He glanced at the speaker, and then at Roddie Roy—who ran a large hand over a sweaty dust-covered red face, thereby but little improving the effect.

"Jings!" he said. "The weemin, right enough!"

Actually there was only the one woman on the scene, as yet. She was a young woman too, dressed in businesslike

27

fashion in an open-necked red and black checked shirt with uprolled sleeves, and blue jeans thrust into downturned Wellington boots. Not that Patrick, at least, paid a lot of attention to her attire.

"I . . . ah . . . we were just having a look round," he declared, with a little difficulty. "Just interested, you know, in doocots."

"That's a fact," Roddie Roy asseverated heavily. "Aye. Jist that."

"Oh, I see," the girl said. And made it very apparent that she did not see. She both looked and sounded horribly cool and calm and serene, standing there, hand on hip. She was a tall well-made creature who undoubtedly would succeed in appearing entirely feminine whatever her garb. Fair-haired, with clean-cut features and very direct grey eyes, she almost certainly would have been attractive to the men, to any men, under other circumstances. As it was, she aroused no enthusiasm at all.

"Yes," Patrick agreed, nodding vigorously—and was only the more aware of the strong smell of guano that emanated from his perspiring person. "It's a fine day, isn't it. Warm."

"It's early to say—yet!" That was judicial, not to say unsympathetic. "Very early."

"Oh, well . . ." The man consulted his watch carefully. "It's after nine."

"Some folks dinna lie in their beds till a' 'oors," MacGregor added stoutly.

"I would still like to know what you were doing in there?"

Patrick Kincaid bit his lip. This wretched woman's manner was as direct as her glance. She sounded irritatingly authoritative, too—much more so than any Oxford undergraduate was likely to sound. Nor did she look like any sort of female don. Not old enough for that either, probably, nor young enough for the other—though one never knew with women. Not that she had an Oxford-sounding voice, at all.

"We were just looking at the place. Admiring the, er, the nesting-boxes. No harm in that, is there?"

"That depends. On how much damage you do!"

28

"Oh, we've done no damage, Miss . . ." There were no rings on her fingers.

One of those fingers pointed to the doocot's door-jamb, where the violated padlock and chain hung. "You broke open that door," she accused, quite calmly. "That's breaking and entering, you know. It's private property."

"Oh. Umm." Kincaid looked at Roddie Roy.

"Och, it jist came awa' in my hand!" that giant protested.

"You must have been very anxious to get inside. Two grown men—not wee laddies. Why, I wonder?"

It was that phrase "wee laddies" that made up Patrick's mind for him. "*You're* not from Oxford?" That was part assertion, part question. "Are you?"

"Oxford? Me? No—why should I be?"

"You're not to do with this archaeological crowd, or whatever they call themselves, at all?"

"Archy . . . ? Look—what are you talking about? I'm Jean Graham, from Kincaid Mains. We rent the grazings here."

"Oh. I see. That's different, of course. I'm sorry, Miss, er, Graham."

"Different from what? I'd like to know what all this is about? I really would. This Oxford nonsense. And what you're doing poking about there. I've been watching you for some time, from up at the farmhouse. I thought I'd better ride over to see just what you were up to."

"Well, as I said, we're interested in doocots, Miss Graham."

"Excuse me," the girl interrupted. "I don't know who you are, or what you are after. But you sound approximately an educated man, and I'd be obliged if you wouldn't insult my intelligence. I suppose it's possible to be all that interested in doocots that you'll rise up early in the morning to go inspecting them. But you needn't tell me that it drives you to breaking open doors and grubbing amongst . . . amongst great quantities of manure!"

"H'rr'mm." Patrick's eye again sought Roddie Roy's. "Well, it's a bit difficult to explain, Miss Graham."

"Indeed. That remark does not pay me much of a compliment either, Mr . . . ?"

"Er . . . Drummond," Patrick answered, and hated himself for doing so.

"Well, Mr Drummond—out with it. As tenant here—or daughter of the tenant, anyway—I think I have every right to know."

Perhaps Patrick Kincaid was weak. Certainly he was not accustomed to dealing with this sort of situation. Moreover, he was a distinctly impressionable man, for better or for worse. He capitulated.

"Miss Graham," he said. "You have a good Scots name. And a good Scots tongue in your head. May I take it from that that you are, h'm, a, a good Scot? Er, patriotic, and all that?" Never had he sounded such an utter fool in his own ears.

And in her's too, without a doubt. "What on earth are you talking about?" she demanded. "What in the name of goodness has my patriotism to do with you grubbing about inside that doocot?"

"Quite a lot, strangely enough. I know this must all sound quite ridiculous to you, but it's all too serious, I promise you. You see, I have to be assured of your, your loyalty towards Scotland, before I commit myself."

"Loyalty? Good gracious!"

"Och, he jist means are you for the Scotch an' no' for the bluidy English?" Roddie Roy interpreted helpfully.

"No. It's not a question of being against the English, or anybody else," Kincaid insisted. "It's just, well . . ."

"I'm a perfectly good normal Scot, if that's what you mean," Jean Graham interrupted. "What *is* all this leading up to?"

"Good. That's all I wanted to know. The fact is, Miss Graham, that there's a plot to steal the Stone of Destiny. The real Stone, this time—not the one they have down in London. The one that's been buried up here in the Scone district all the time. You'll have heard about that? It's these Oxford people that I was speaking about. They're coming here to dig it up. To Kincaid. They're in Perth now—I saw their baggage last night. They've got to be stopped, somehow. And, you see, we just had a sort of notion, possibly all wrong—that the Stone might be buried in there. Buried in the doocot."

To say that the young woman was looking at Patrick strangely would be a grave understatement. She stared, red lips parted—and her gaze had grown the warier as he went on.

"It's okay, Miss," Roddie Roy reassured. "I ken jist hoo you feel. I was the same way mysel' when he tell't me first. But it's right enough. You'll get used to it."

"Look. Sit down, and I'll tell you the whole story," Patrick invited. "You'd better hear it. I owe you that, at least."

"So you really think this Columba stands for doocot?" Jean Graham commented at length. Whatever else she might be, she made a good listener. This was her first real interjection.

Patrick shrugged. "It may not. It may have nothing to do with that. But for want of a better idea . . . Can you think of anything else?"

"Me? No—I'm afraid not. But then, I haven't really thought about it, at all. In fact, I'm incapable of thought, at this moment." That might have been only a figure of speech, for the serenity did not appear to be greatly ruffled. "And I gather that you don't think now that this doocot is going to come up to expectations?"

"We can't be certain, without digging deep. But it doesn't look too hopeful. You see, it's a seventeenth-century docoot. It seems more probable that if the Stone *was* buried in a doocot, it would be the original one—the one that belonged to the old castle down there. The trouble is, there doesn't seem to *be* any other doocot about. I'm sure there ought to be. This one never belonged to the castle—both its position and its age show that."

Jean Graham eyed him thoughtfully, whatever her disclaimers. "It's strange that you should say that," she mentioned. "Not that I'm accepting all this story about your Stone, you know. I mean, about the one in London not being the real one. That all strikes me as being extremely hypothetical. But . . . well, leave that just now. What's strange is that it's always been a bit of a mystery to me why a certain hillock down there should be called Doocot Knowe, when it's so far away from the only doocot. It's just a local name, of course, and no doubt an old one. But . . ."

"What?" It was Patrick's turn to interrupt, starting up. "Doocot Knowe, you said? But this is wonderful! Is it down near the old castle, somewhere?"

"Well—not far away. I'll show you if you like?"

Two pairs of eager hands reached out to raise Miss Jean Graham to her feet. Calmly she ignored both of them, rose in her own time, and unhurriedly led the way, very much mistress of the situation.

A saddled pony, a Highland garron, was waiting patiently for her at the corner of the House. This she led along also. They went soberly, almost sedately down through the sloping pastures and grassy braes. Patrick could have slapped that plodding horse and pushed its mistress—but at least they no longer had to skulk and keep their eyes on the farmhouse.

"Can you give me any reason, other than just tradition, for believing that the Westminster Stone isn't genuine, Mr Drummond?" the girl asked, as they went. "It seems remarkable that everybody has been deluded for all these hundreds of years. The Government made enough fuss about it when it was removed that time."

"These Oxford Historical Research people must believe it's a fake, anyway."

"Yes. But they've probably just got hold of the same tradition that you have. It may be quite imaginary. False. You've no proof."

"I think I have," Patrick asserted. "I wouldn't be doing all this, risking quite a lot, if I wasn't thoroughly convinced, I assure you. You see, there *is* evidence that's not mere tradition. It's to be found in the various Great Seals of Scotland, issued before Scone Abbey was sacked. Each king had his own seal, and fortunately facsimiles of these still exist. Each shows a king seated on a Coronation Chair—each had a new one made—like the one at Westminster now, only with one very significant difference. They all show the box-like seat which contains the Stone to be the normal height of a chair. The kings are all represented as sitting normally. But the Stone at Westminster is only eleven inches high. And the box made to hold it has to be raised on four carved lions at each corner, as legs, to make it high enough to sit on. All these earlier box-seats are more than twice as high as Edward's one—because they were made to fit a much larger Stone. That is incontrovertible. These seals were most carefully, elaborately, made—quite meticulous in their detail. They leave no doubts on the matter. And, as I said, all the old writings declare the famous Stone of Scone to have been seat-shaped and richly carved."

"I see," Jean Graham said, nibbling her lip. "I see. Edward was easily fooled, then?"

"Not necessarily. He may have been. On the other hand, he may not have been deceived at all. But if he'd announced that, as a conqueror, the famed Hammer of the Scots, he would bring Scotland's most famous relic back with him to London, and then couldn't lay hands on the thing, try as he would—was it so out of keeping with his known ruthless and unscrupulous character to make the best of a bad job and take south what was presented to him, to flaunt it as genuine, even if he *knew* it was a fake? In fact, would it be so wide of the mark to wonder if it was the Abbot of Scone, at all, that quarried this lump of red sandstone for him, but Edward Plantagenet himself? If the real Stone was untraceable, and he had to take something to make good his boasting?"

"Jings—the auld hypocrite!"

The young woman produced her first laugh, in that company. "Mr Drummond," she said, "I don't think you ought to feed me any more of this, at the moment! I feel that I've swallowed quite enough for the time being . . . and it tends to get more indigestible as we go along! Besides—there's Doocot Knowe." And she pointed.

They were down not far from the riverside again, and ahead of them, amongst the jumble of hummocks and braes, seen from this angle, one stood out rather more distinctly and just a little higher than its neighbours, a round gentle dome of turf, perhaps a hundred feet high. Sheep and cattle had made many little terraced tracks around its grassy flanks, but otherwise it appeared to be entirely smooth and rounded. Patrick, looking, sighed.

Leaving the pony at the foot, they climbed to the top of it. No sign of foundations or underlying stone was to be seen there, or from there.

"Och, hell—it's as smooth as a baby's bottom!" MacGregor complained. "No' a sign o' a thing."

"I'm sorry," the young woman said. "But I warned you that it was a mystery why it was called Doocot Knowe."

"There will have been a doocot here once, that's practically certain," Patrick asserted. "Somewhere here." He knelt down, seeking to scan the turf with a sort of worm's eye view, to see if he could pick out any faint undulations. "No good," he reported. "There's just nothing to see. I don't know if . . ."

"Look!" That was Jean Graham. "Quick! Down! Out of sight! They're coming—a whole party of them. Up the waterside." And swiftly as she spoke, the girl, crouching, hurried over to the farther side of the knowe.

Quick as thought the two men followed her, bending low likewise, to fling themselves down on the grass at her side, just safely in dead ground.

"It'll be the Oxford people," the young woman panted. "A whole lot of them. Men and women. Perhaps twenty. I don't think they saw us."

"Good," Patrick said. "Good work." Then, turning to look at her, almost to stare at her, hiding there beside him, he said "Good," again, and in a different tone of voice altogether. He added "Splendid!" too. It dawned on him that he had won another ally.

III

HUDDLED close together, and occasionally peering round the side of their cover, the three of them waited, and watched the progress of the advancing party. It made a long straggling drawn-out line, colourful and variously clad. In the forefront strode a slight dapper middle-aged man in a pale linen suit and Panama hat, and before him, like a tray, he carried an Army-style map-board towards which he gestured with marked frequency. Behind him a curiously assorted company trooped, young, middle-aged, and elderly, dressed in anything from shorts and tennis kit to sweaters and duffle-coats. And as they drew closer, their chatter rose as from a fair.

"I wonder why they're coming this way?" Patrick whispered—though there was surely little need for the precaution. "Obviously they've left their cars at the road and worked up the river. You'd have thought they'd have used the main drive up to the Big House."

"The lodge gates are locked, and we've got the key up at the Mains," Jean Graham informed. "Probably they don't know about the key, yet. Nobody's been up to us for it. Listen to the noise of them! You'd think they owned the place!"

"Hoo aboot goin' doon an' askin' them what the hell they're doin' here?" Roddie suggested. "Like you done to us."

"No, no. That would be foolish. They've got permission anyway," Patrick pointed out.

"Not from us, they haven't," the girl asserted.

"From your landlord. From the Consolidated Lands Investment Corporation, Limited, of Lombardy Street, London."

"They're no landlords of ours!" she returned, with a trace of warmth. "My father bought Kincaid Mains a year or two before the War. At the same time, in fact, that this London

35

investment company bought the policies and some of the other farms. And the Big House, of course, when the estate was broken up. We'd been tenants on Kincaid for generations—but we own the Mains now."

"Good. Fine," Patrick commended. "But where we are here, in the policies, still belongs to the estate. You only rent the grazing? Isn't that right? And the owners have given this Oxford society permission to look for the Stone—so it said in *The Scotsman*."

"Jings—what right hae *they* to gie onybody permission to touch the bluidy Stane o' Destiny!" MacGregor demanded, hotly. "Jist Englishry! It's Scotland's Stane!"

They were edging round on their little hilltop as they spoke, so as to keep out of sight of the party down in the valley.

"I wonder whether this Doocot Knowe is marked on that map of theirs?" Patrick went on.

"I shouldn't think so," Jean shook her head. "We have a six-inch Ordnance map at home, and it isn't on that. It's just a local name, I think."

The explorers reached the ruined castle, and spent some considerable time examining it from all angles. And then under the leadership of the man with the map, they all trooped off up over the grass towards the mansion-house.

"Just a preliminary survey, obviously. Doesn't look as though any of them have been up here before."

"I hope they don't spot old Garve—my pony," the girl said.

"I don't think that's likely. Not where it is."

Soon the invaders were spread out over the slopes, heading for the House on a wide front, and exclaiming as they went.

"Mair like a Sunday-school trip!" Roddie Roy snorted. "I wouldna' reckon they'll be much bother even if they *dae* lay hands on the Stane."

"It's not so much that I'm worried about," Patrick conceded. "It's the authorities. The wretched Home Office in London. They have no real jurisdiction in Scotland, I agree—but you know what they did before, when the Westminster Stone was taken. The pressure they brought to bear on

St Andrews House in Edinburgh, and the police. It was wicked. Those Scotland Yard detectives were sent up here without so much as by-your-leave from the Secretary of State for Scotland. It all had to be put right afterwards. And they'll do the same again, you can bet your last ha'penny on that! If these characters here once bring the real Stone to light, you'll see the powers-that-be will step in and take over. And then off the Stone will go, to London."

"That would be a pity, I think," Jean Graham suggested, quietly.

The two men looked at her, and then exchanged glances.

"Aye, jist so." Roddie Roy nodded ponderously. "Uh-huh. Ooh, aye."

When all the Oxford party was safely out of the way, the trio rose and moved down from Doocot Knowe.

"What'll we dae noo?" MacGregor asked. He was a man for action.

"Well, I'd like to see what these people do up there," Patrick said. "In fact, from now on, I think we'll have to keep them shadowed all the time they're on the property. Otherwise we may miss that vital clue—something that might just possibly give us time to forestall them. But that's a job for one, rather than three."

"Ooh, aye—an' you're real hot at that, man Patrick, are you no'!" Roddie mentioned fleetingly. "Och, a right dab hand at the stalkin'. I'd never've seen you, mysel', yon time, if you hadna' been aye bobbin' up!"

The other chose to ignore that.

"*I've* got work to do, anyway," Jean Graham announced. "My father's away to Dundee. I'll have to get back. But . . ." She paused. "I'll be interested to hear what happens. How the situation develops. You're going to need food, during this watching session. Suppose I brought down a picnic lunch?"

"Miss Graham—you are as practical as you are decorative! Nothing would be more welcome."

She eyed Patrick with that level and direct look of her's. "You do not smell suitably for making pretty speeches, Mr Drummond," she observed, warningly.

37

"Oh!" The man stepped back from her quickly. He had rather forgotten the guano dust. "I . . . I'm sorry."

"I would suggest a wash—in the burn there," and she nodded towards the waterside. "Unless, of course, it would spoil the poaching for your friend! See you later, then. About one, perhaps?" And mounting her pony she set off downstream, presumably making for shallows to ford the Kincaid Water.

Patrick had been going to tell her that Drummond was not his true surname; that he had deceived her. But the moment did not seem to be opportune—and that crack about the smell was not such as to encourage confidences. Moreover, it might be safer to remain incognito for the present, till the situation clarified itself a little.

He let her go, frowning after her.

After the advised wash, Patrick left Roddie Roy at his tent, and made his way discreetly up towards the mansion-house. There were no signs of the expedition members about the front of the House as he approached. Cautiously he worked round the side. From the chatter that came to him faintly now, it was apparent that they were all congregated over in the direction of the walled garden. And at the far end thereof. Patrick knew a moment or two of distinct satisfaction. It looked as though his deductions had been right enough. The doocot was obviously the centre of attraction.

Slipping over to the stableyard, a quadrangle of decaying building, he crossed its grass-grown cobbles to the far northwest corner. It was evident now that their guess as to the property possibly having been requisitioned, had been accurate. Many of the stables and outhouses still bore barely decipherable legends labelling them Q.M. CLOTHING STORE, DECONTAMINATION, N.C.O.'S ONLY, and the like. Everything was broken down and derelict, doors missing, windows empty, slates from the roofing littering the area. Gaining entrance to the corner apartment, that had obviously been a coach-house with harness-loft above, presented no difficulties. Patrick just walked in. The open stairway to the upper floor was lacking some of its treads and in no sound state, but it took the man up nevertheless. And there he cleared and

38

cleaned a small space on a dirty cobwebby window-pane, and was able to peer out directly across at the doocot, a mere hundred yards or so away.

The Oxford researchers were grouped round it still. The man in the linen suiting had discarded his map, and was pointing at various parts of the building and clearly holding forth authoritatively. That no doubt was Dr Conrad Lister, the President of the Society. Not everyone was listening to him avidly. There was much coming and going in and out of the doocot, much grimacing and holding of noses. Patrick could even glimpse some poking about inside with the water-key that he and Roddie had carelessly left at the door.

Patrick wondered how suspicious that key, the burst-open door, and the churned-up droppings on the floor, might have seemed to these people? They certainly did not give the impression of being agitated or concerned about any-thing, now. The general dilapidation of the place, of course, would help to give it all an appearance of normalcy to the unsuspecting. And the guano, being dry and dusty, might not show obvious recent disturbance to the inexpert—and few there, surely, were likely to be very expert on the various aspects of pigeons' droppings. Nothing might have seemed out of the ordinary.

Patrick waited and watched. He watched for quite a long time. Nothing transpired—save that the leader went on lecturing and the rank-and-file began to attack packages of sandwiches, settling down either to listen or to muse. The sight reacted on Kincaid's own stomach. He glanced at his watch and saw that the time was twelve-thirty. The morning had slipped away.

At any rate these people seemed to have decided to settle down here at the doocot. It did not look as though they were interested in the House itself, or any part other than this pigeon-house. They did not appear to have any spades or excavating gear with them. Could he leave them safely, then, assured that there wasn't likely to be any major development for a while.

The question seemed to answer itself, for presently approxi-mately half of the party, the younger half, roused itself and began to move off. From the gesticulations and signings of the others, who clearly were staying put, it was evident that this group was being dispatched to collect something—probably picks and shovels.

The man watched them go, gave them ample time to get clear, and then withdrew himself, as he had come.

Back at the tent by the riverside, he found Roderick Mac-Gregor asleep—for he had fished late and early overnight. Patrick had just finished the waking-up process when Jean Graham arrived back from the farm, on her pony, with a well filled picnic-basket. To the pair of them he disclosed his information.

"It seems to me," he told them, "that we've got it pretty well confirmed now that I was right about Columba referring to pigeons and doocots. The question now seems to be—have they information that leads them to believe that the Stone is hidden in that doocot up there—the seventeenth-century one? Or just in *some* doocot? They seem quite confident about the one they're at—but that may be because they just don't know that there was any other. They may not be so very knowledgeable about Scottish domestic architecture as to be able to date that one accurately."

"Quite likely," the girl agreed. "I don't suppose one in a thousand knows about that sort of thing. Especially if they're English."

"Probably not. Well, then—it's a toss-up as to whether the Stone is actually in that one, or this one."

"What d'you mean—this one?" Roddie Roy demanded.

"Well, shall we say, in the original one that belonged to the castle? And it's surely reasonable to assume that it would be sited on Doocot Knowe."

"A gey lot o' assumin', man Patrick!"

"Maybe. But the assumptions are reasonable. I'd say. And we've nothing else to go on. I'd say, too, that the toss-up is more likely to be in favour of *our* site than theirs." He turned to gaze over towards Doocot Knowe, just a small section of which could be observed from the tent. "If only we could see inside that hummock!"

"You really think it's in there, Mr Drummond?" Jean asked, handing over a cup of vacuum-flask coffee.

"My thanks. I think there's a good chance of it, anyway. If only we had a free hand, I'd have the whole of the top of that knowe dug up, to see if we could locate foundations. But unfortunately we can't do that. Confound these people!"

"We could dae it, an' be damned to them!" Roddie cried. "If *they* can go diggin' for oor Stane, so can we, can we no'? It's supposed to be a free country yet, is it no'?"

"They'd be round us like a flock of magpies! We'd stand out up there for everyone to see."

"Weel, dae it in the dark, then. At nicht."

"But, Roddie—you don't realise the size of job it would be! Two of us digging there—once we'd got spades and picks—would take ages to make any real impression. The top of the knowe will cover at least a third of an acre. And remember the size of the thing—the Stone itself, I mean. The one at Westminster weighed four or five hundredweights, I believe; this one will probably run to half as much again."

"A' the easier to find, then."

"Perhaps. But it would take a lot of handling, for two men. I'm not usually called a pessimist, but I'd say it was asking a bit too much to hope that we'd find the doocot, dig up the Stone, and get it safely away from the scene, all in one short night's work! And there would be no hiding the fact of what we'd been doing, remember; once it was daylight again, it would be crystal-clear that there had been excavations up on that hillock. It would shout aloud. We wouldn't get peace to wait for the next night."

"Could we no' disguise it, some way?"

"On the top of a hill? In a hollow, I daresay, something might be possible. But up there . . ."

"Sheep," Roddie suggested. "There's plenties o' sheep here. If there was sheep a' ower the knowie, the earth an' diggin's wouldna' be sae likely to be seen."

"How could we keep sheep up there?"

"Och, well—some way, surely. Or, maybe, we could set up a bit camp on the top. Tents, see . . ."

41

"Hurdles." That was Jean Graham speaking, thoughtfully. "It might be possible to pen a flock of sheep up there, with hurdles. Even an electric fence. For a day or two. I think it might be done."

"There y'are, see."

Patrick looked at the girl, grateful surprise and doubts balancing themselves in his mind. "Would that not seem mighty queer? Almost *drawing* attention to the place?" he asked. "A flock of sheep penned around one single hilltop?"

"It might—to a farmer," she admitted. "But not necessarily to these Oxford University people, They are not to know how we handle our sheep, up in barbarous Scotland! And it is shearing time. If questioned, it could be said that it was to avoid the flies, that they were being kept on high ground— while they were being treated for tick. Nonsense, of course— but it might well be accepted. Or so that they could be seen all the time from up at the farmhouse. We could say that the foxes had been at the lambs, even—which would be no lie. I'm sure we could produce an excuse that would *sound* reasonable to strangers."

"Too right we could!" MacGregor declared, strongly. "Och, they'd swallow mair'n that, man."

"Well . . ." Jean Graham was making an impact on Patrick Kincaid much beyond the mere evidences of an agile mind and a fine sense of partisanship. He was staring, rather.

"I could provide spades and picks and so on, up at the farm," she added.

"Fine that. A' laid on," the big man commended. "But, see—it's jist as I said, back at the beginnin'. We're needin' mair fellas. Mair hands to dae the diggin', an' the liftin'. An' to keep an eye on thae English . . . an' maybe to lift the Stane off of them, if *they* get it. If the bluidy thing's the weight you say, I canna promise jist to lug it aroond under my oxter! Time I was awa' to Glesgy, for some o' the boys."

Patrick rubbed his chin. Instinctively he was afraid of letting this thing get out of hand, of getting any bigger than was absolutely necessary. The thought of the impact of a gang of unruly Glasgow toughs by no means enticed him. Who could tell where it all might end, once such became involved? Yet there was truth in what MacGregor said. They were going to need manpower, it seemed, whatever happened. And manpower that was not tied down by an exaggerated respectability, that was prepared to take risks, big risks. And, of course, Roddie Roy and his famed Gregorach had already proved themselves, and in stalwart fashion. Looked at one way, it could be the greatest stroke of luck.

Jean Graham interrupted his train of thought. "I suppose I could bring in one or two of our farm people, to give a hand," she said. "They're decent ordinary folk, and loyal."

"No. Not that!" Patrick was very definite on this. "Already I'm involving you, Miss Graham, much too deeply for my peace of mind. I'm not going to have your farm-workers brought in as accomplices. Besides, once the balloon goes up, suspicion would turn on local folk right away. They'd be chivvied and questioned. We might lose more than we gained. No—we'd be better with Roddie's Glasgow keelies! But not too many of them, Roddie—we've got to keep the thing under control if we can. The fewer folk involved, the better. Numbers always draw attention to themselves. Three or four would be ample, I'd say."

"Och, aye—I ken a' that fine. What's the time? I'll be in Glesgy by four, then. Gie's twa—three 'oors to get roond some o' the guys, an' I'll be back here by nine or ten. That suit you? It'll just be gettin' dark."

"But can you rout people out of their normal lives, in that time?"

"Hell, aye—what for no'? Wait till they hear tell o' this ploy, an' they'll jump at it, jist."

And so it was decided. Roddie would depart on his motor-cycle straight away. Jean Graham would return to her duties on the farm—where, it seemed, she lived alone with her father, as a housekeeper—and without making a fuss about it, sort out the digging implements and hurdles. And Patrick would resume his vigil up at the stableyard. They would meet again in the late evening.

IV

THE Oxford researchers spent a hot and smelly afternoon, delving amongst the accumulated pigeon-droppings of centuries. It was dry work even to watch them from a safe distance. Whether they toiled in the name of Science or of Saint George, they surely earned much merit. Not that they went at it feverishly or with unseemly haste. Though the fatigue-party had provided them with a notably large selection of fine brand-new shining tools, only two of the historians were apt to be inside the doocot at a time—and frequently not even that. And for not over-lengthy spells. But, knowing the conditions, the watching Scot was on this occasion not inclined to be unduly critical.

By four o'clock, when Roddie Roy ought to have reached Glasgow if he drove a motorcycle as he did most other things, the spells of digging had grown shorter and the breaks longer, and odd explorers were roaming around—dangerously, as far as Patrick was concerned—looking for a water-main on which to use the great key. Just before five the entire party packed up, the tools were stacked against the side of the doocot, and all trooped off. The riverside, and water, undoubtedly would be the first stop on the road back to Perth. No locking-up process was attempted and no sort of guard or caretaking picket was left behind. In ones and twos the pigeons returned.

After a due interval, Patrick ventured out of his hiding-place, to inspect progress made. A large and somewhat ragged trench had been dug diagonally across the floor of the doocot, deepest in the middle and tailing off somewhat towards the ends. The spoil had been heaped up in one corner, and was getting out of hand, some of it already beginning to trickle back into the trench. In the centre a depth of fully three feet had been reached—and what was being brought up now, fairly clearly, was genuine earth and not just ancient impacted guano. Some lumps of the local red sandstone had also been unearthed, but these were obviously loose pieces and not fragments recently broken off some larger mass. Of any such great block there was as yet no sign. The stench was appalling.

Patrick borrowed a pick-axe and did a little probing on his own account, along the line of the trench. Stone there was under there, intermittently, but so far as he could gauge, nothing substantial. Of course the trench did not cover more than a tenth of the floor area. A great deal more hard labour, with much deeper digging, would have to be put into the site before it could be said with any certainty that the Stone was not buried there. All this spoil would have to be cleared outside, first, too. There was work here for Oxford's busy scholars for quite some time to come.

Contentedly enough Patrick Kincaid strolled back to Roddie Roy's tent.

With nothing special to do for an hour or two, he presently walked down to his hidden car, and drove the four miles into Perth. There he had a substantial meal, before checking out of his hotel. He carried the very few belongings that he had with him in a rucksack on his back. In his old Harris Tweed suit and the still older and bleached trench-coat that he hung over his arm, he was satisfied that he would be taken for a holiday-maker, one more walker through this popular gateway to the Highlands.

He bought a selection of newspapers, hoping that just possibly Dr Lister might have held a Press conference or issued some sort of statement. But there was no mention of the expedition, or of the Stone of Destiny, in any of the papers, even in the *Dundee Courier*, the nearest daily. The local sheet was a weekly, and would not be out for a couple of days.

With a little difficulty Patrick found a shop still open to sell him a few more batteries for his electric torch—which he conceived might prove useful. Thereafter he spent an hour in the Reference Department of the Public Library, Topography and History sections, before returning to his car.

The sun was setting beyond the western hills in a blaze of scarlet and gold and purest green, when the man got back to the Kincaid Water—just about an hour later than when he had arrived the previous evening. Walking up the splashy murmurous riverside, he was suddenly hailed from higher ground on the south bank, across the water. It was a woman's voice, and she sounded urgent.

"Mr Drummond!" she called. "Up here. Come on up here. Quickly. Hurry up. This way . . ."

"Coming," Patrick acknowledged, and with a nice disregard for footwear and trousering, went splashing straight across the shallows and up the bank beyond, to a shoulder of the braeside on which Jean Graham stood.

"I didn't mean you were to soak yourself," she greeted him. "There are stepping-stones just a little farther up, when the water's low. But I've been waiting for you for ages. I was afraid you'd never be here in time."

"Eh? In time for what? It can't be more than eight."

"Look at the knowe. Doocot Knowe," she said, pointing.

He peered, shading his eyes against the last of the sunset. "I don't see anything special . . ."

"Over on the left. See that levelish bit, just below the summit on that side? A sort of shelf. It's terribly faint now, admittedly. But you can still see it, if you know where to look. Almost a complete circle . . ."

"Yes! Yes . . . by George, you're right! I see it. Just below that."

"Will that be it? The doocot? It was much clearer, before the sun sank so low. When the actual slanting rays were striking it. Quite round, it was."

"Of course! Of course—nearly all the early doocots were circular in shape. This is magnificent! Good for you, Jean Graham!"

"What amazes me is that I've never noticed it before. Because I've never really looked for it before, I suppose. I saw it from our sitting-room window, actually. About half an hour ago. Oh, more. I'd been glancing over at the knowe, off and on, thinking about it all, when suddenly I noticed this marking. It was very faint at first—like the shadow of a ring. Then it gradually got darker, clearer."

"As the sun levelled," Patrick nodded, "throwing the slight projections into relief."

"I suppose so. I came hurrying down to the tent, to tell you. You weren't there. And I couldn't see it—the ring—from down in the valley, at all. I got into a panic that I'd lost it—for I hadn't taken any exact note of its position, you see. So I moved back and back, in this direction, crossing the water, trying to get into the line of it again. Till up here it came into view again—much paler, but still visible. I waited. I thought you'd never get here. Not in time . . ."

They hurried downhill and across to reach and climb the knowe. While waiting, Jean had taken careful note of the precise position, as far as she could, and though there was no indication of any foundations or protuberance on the spot, they were able to stick in a couple of pegs, as markers, to ensure that they would dig in the right place, later.

"We could start digging right away, if we had the tools," the young woman suggested. "There's nobody going to be watching us, now. I gathered together a selection of shovels and spades. They're up in the cart-shed. I could only find one pick."

"I've a better idea," Patrick said. "The less of your stuff that get's used in this business, the better. There's almost bound to be a show-down sooner or later, and enquiries. I don't want you to be involved any more than is absolutely necessary—and your people will be the first to be questioned, I'd say. We'll use the Oxford folk's gear. They've left it all up at the doocot, there—with no sort of watch on it. I'm pretty sure none of them will be back for more manure-turning tonight—and since we're on the same quest as they are, perhaps they won't grudge us the use of their fine new gear! We'll go right up now and get some."

"If you think that's best . . ."

They made their way up over the colour-stained slopes, reconnoitred the House area and found it deserted as ever, and had another look into the doocot, to the alarm of the roosting pigeons. Patrick collected two picks and two shovels, while the girl insisted in shouldering a couple of spades.

They were almost back to Doocot Knowe when the man stopped, head raised. "Listen!" he said.

Faint but clear, from down the valley, came the stirring if vengeful strains of "MacGregor's Gathering", sung with considerable vigour and feeling, if a certain lack of precision:

"While there's leaves in the forest and foam on the river,
MacGregor despite them shall flourish for ever!"

Deep and powerfully vibrant, through and above the efforts of lesser lungs, a great voice boomed the challenge on the quiet evening air.

"The Gregorach would seem to have arrived," the young woman commented.

"Undoubtedly. And I hope . . . I hope Roddie Roy's not drunk!" her companion added uneasily.

Drunk or sober, Roderick MacGregor compelled the watchers' tribute of swift-drawn breath when he rounded the last bend of the Kincaid Water and came striding towards his tent. He had discarded the more discreet garb of the Lowlander and donned a kilt that, though old and stained, nevertheless still retained sufficient of the red and green of the MacGregor sett to match and enhance the flaming thatch of his hair. And not only the hair of his head, for he had discarded more than his trousers, and the unbuttoned khaki shirt that hung loose and open revealed a tremendous torso furred and felted in red. His massive muscular legs scarcely could be termed bare, so thickly hirsute were they. On his feet were huge steel-shod boots over which thick socks were downturned. In one hand he casually bore a heavy iron crowbar—that ought to have been a broadsword, assuredly— and in the other a black bottle which he beat to the measure of his singing and pacing. And behind him trooped four nondescript and comparatively puny specimens of manhood, having almost to trot to keep up with the hugely striding giant. Their supporting chorus, in the circumstances, was the more valiant for being thin, discordant, and quite breathless.

"Mercy . . . on us!" Patrick got out.

The girl said nothing, but her eyes were busy.

"Hey—here y'are, Patrick man!" Roddie Roy roared, waving the crowbar as though it was a pencil, as he caught sight of the pair in front. "Here's the fellas, like I tell't you. Och, they're no that much to look at, mind—but they'll dae fine for bluidy diggin' an' luggin'. Hell—one o' them was a bluidy undertaker's assistant, one time, at the Western Necropolis!" And he bellowed his mirth to the surrounding hillocks. "The best I could dae, at short notice!"

"Yes. Of course. Excellent, I'm sure. Fine. I'm very much obliged . . . to you all." Patrick decided that Roddie was not drunk, only drink-taken as the saying was, and in notable spirits. "Good evening, chaps," he said to the newcomers. "I must say it's a pretty good show, really, rallying round in such a short time. On such a difficult and thankless sort of a job as this, too."

That drew no comments from the reinforcements. Actually they were all considering and assessing the young woman, rather than the speaker. Of the four, two were in their thirties, and two were youngsters. Roddie did not trouble to introduce them. One of the older men was small and dark and ferrety, his companion sandy, lanky, almost gangling, and badly in need of a shave. Of the others, one was only a short step removed from Teddy-boy, with a bottle protruding out of both pockets of his over-long jacket, while the other was a crew-cut young ruffian with a freckled face, a cast in one eye, and a permanent leer. None seemed to have brought with them any sort of baggage. They looked precisely what they were—the products of the slums of a great industrial city, no longer short of money but utterly lacking, unlike their women-folk, in any of even the most superficial graces that were now within their reach. Yet there they were, breathless and a little tipsy, come right across Scotland at a moment's notice, at the behest of this uncouth colossus, in order voluntarily to take part in risky, unpaid, and far from attractive toil—it was to be assumed, approximately for their country's sake. And singing a degenerate but authentic version of one of their country's ancient traditional airs as they came. They gave Patrick pause for thought. The crew-cut patriot pursed his thick lips and managed, at the third attempt, to blow a panting wolf-whistle.

"Shurrup, you!" MacGregor ordered, casually. "Say—you got some real fancy picks an' spades, there! See's a hud o' one. Jings—a right guid-payin' fairm you must hae, upbye, lassie! I could of done wi' these back on the croft at Findart. Stainless steel, b'damn!"

"They're not Miss Graham's—they're the Oxford party's gear. I thought we might suitably borrow them . . ."

"Say—that's mair like it, Patrick! That's the spirit! Pinched the stuff! You're comin' on, man. Noo we'll get some place. To hell wi' namby-pamby sissy-jessie stuff! Och, we'll tear this bit glen apart, see, frae end to end, till we find yon doocot. An' then . . ."

"No need, Roddie—Miss Graham's found it for us. It's high up on the south-west flank of the knowe—Doocot Knowe, right enough."

"Jings—is that a fact? Hey, Jeannie—guid for you, tae!" And swinging round, he took a single great stride, dropping his bottle and crowbar, and swept the young woman right off her feet, tossing her bodily into the air with the greatest of ease. "Hooray!" he cried. "Up the Grahams! Gie it big licks!"

"My goodness," she gasped. "Stop it! What way is this . . . to treat anyone?"

Though she was set down thereafter, her protest went quite ignored. Straight away the big man turned from her, to pick up and heft one of the pick-axes that Patrick had been carrying. "Jist the job!" he declared. "Fits me grand. C'mon—let's get crackin'!" And he waved his chosen implement in the general direction of Doocot Knowe.

"Och, tae hell, Roddie! No' the noo!"

"Whit's a' the bloomin' rush, big boy?"

"Gie's a meenit, man Rod—I've no' had my supper!"

"Shurrup!" MacGregor requested. "Can it! You came here to dig, did you no'? Weel, then—you'll bluidy-weel dig! C'mon."

"Oh, there's no such great hurry as all that, Roddie," Patrick protested. "Give our friends a moment or two to get settled . . ."

"Hell—nae hurry is there no'! An' me fair beltin' the guts oot o' my bike to get to Glesgy in time, an' wheechle roond a' this bunch o' safties! D'you tell me noo that we've got plenty o' time to dae a' the diggin' we need?"

"No. No—I wouldn't say that. But . . ."

"Weel, then, tae hell wi' it! Let's get crackin'." And waiting for no more talk, the big fellow picked up a further selection of tools and stamped off for the knowe.

Mutterings and glowerings did not prevent the others from trailing after him.

Roddie Roy MacGregor had come back a transformed man it seemed. At first, Patrick wondered if it might be the effect of the liquor that he had obviously swallowed. But he quickly dismissed that theory. After all, the fellow must have had a tremendous drive, and power, and flair for leadership, if all the stories that the Press had printed about the Gregorach, that time, were true. This probably was the real man emerging, the man hidden beneath the guise of the quietly poaching angler and the well-doing Clydeside boat-builder. Perhaps this other self was released when he discarded his humdrum Lowland clothes and donned the tartans of his freebooting MacGregor forebears? Patrick Kincaid eyed his brawny back a little doubtfully, as he climbed that knowe. Was Roddie Roy going to set the pace from now on? Had the big fellow got the bit between his teeth? Somehow had the reins slipped from his own hands? And what would the result be, if that situation was allowed to develop? Raising the devil was a notoriously risky process.

At the top of the knowe the pegs had only to be pointed out, for Roddie Roy to throw off his apology for a shirt, and spit vigorously on his hands. "Whaur d'we start?" he demanded.

Patrick looked around him. The twilight enfolded the land now, and though the eye still could cover great distances, the wells of shadow were overflowing amongst the knolls and braes, so that there was little certainty of detail and outline. Nothing stood out clearly to catch the eye.

"I suppose it's all right to start," he said. "Some of the farm people might notice us—but that's about all."

"Fortunately our row of farm cottages are gable-end on to this valley," the girl assured. "Our people wouldn't cause any bother, anyway. They can hardly have missed seeing all these Oxford types parading about the place. If they noticed anybody working here now, they'd be pretty sure to assume that it was the same lot. And since it's on the estate, and not on the Mains property, it's nothing to do with them."

"I didna' ask when to start, but *whaur*!" MacGregor announced.

"Yes. All right." The circular area that Patrick declared to be the doocot's foundations, measured about fifteen feet across within the walling, as far as he could guess. "The way they're doing it up at the other place is probably as good as any," he said. "Dig a trench right across the centre. Only, here we'll make sure that all the spoil is dumped *outside* the digging perimeter right away, so that we don't cover up half the area, and have to shift it all again later. Some sort of baskets would be useful for shifting it—I should have thought of that. And it will have to be heaped up neatly, so as not to attract any more attention than can be helped."

"Och, aye. Yous ones can see to that," Roddie cried. "Me an' Alicky'll get bashin'. You tae, Tosh. Get a hud o' a bluidy spade, man!" With the point of his pick the big man scored two roughly parallel lines across the grass, to Patrick's directions, about three feet apart. "There y'are. Gie it the works!"

"Watch the turf," the other urged. "We want it stripped off carefully. To use as camouflage."

Digging commenced.

Despite the gusto and vehemence put into it—by some, at any rate, of the labour force—it soon became apparent that the excavation was going to be a long and arduous process. After the first layers of turf and top-soil were removed, in fact, it became quarrying rather than delving. Though no

52

doubt much of the masonry of the former doocot had been carted away at one time or another for dyke-building and bottoming, a great quantity remained fallen in on the site. The stones were of all shapes and sizes, but massive sections and lumps of the walling still lay adhering, as they had fallen, a tribute to the ancient oyster-shell mortaring. Dealing with this was slow heavy work—especially as it was stone that they were looking for, and if damage to the hoped-for relic was to be avoided, every contact of the pick-axe with stone had to be treated gingerly. Roddie's fine frenzy of energy was continually frustrated.

Presently Jean Graham went off, accompanied by the little dark man Jakey, to collect some of the farm's open potato-picking baskets, for transferring the soil. Patrick would have much preferred to have gone with her himself, but he felt that he must not leave the site at this stage. And half a dozen baskets would make a lot of difference to their progress here.

They were working by the shaded light of Patrick's electric torch by the time that Jean got back—and had achieved no spectacular results in the interim. Three figures loomed up out of the shadows, instead of two, a quiet elderly grizzled man accompanying the basket-carriers, who eyed the proceedings thoughtfully, obviously in no hurry to comment.

"Father's back from Dundee," the girl explained. "He . . . he wants to see what goes on."

Patrick straightened up from the back-breaking job of moving stonework from here to there, wiped a palm on the seat of his trousers, and held out his hand. "Naturally. I must say, I'm glad to see you, sir," he said. "I've been distinctly uncomfortable about getting your daughter involved in all this. Without your knowledge, I mean."

"Indeed," Mr Graham said.

"Yes. It's quite a big thing to land on anyone, I agree . . ."

"Mr Drummond didn't involve me in anything," the young woman intervened. "I involved myself."

"I can believe that," her father nodded gravely.

"Well . . . in a way that's true, of course. But the fact

remains that it's the kind of business that could cause all concerned a bit of trouble, one way or another. In your absence, sir, I wouldn't have liked to commit you or yours too deeply."

"You are very thoughtful, Mr Drummond," the older man acknowledged. "But, of course, it isn't exactly *your* Stone, is it?"

"Oh, no. No, of course not. But I think we've all got *some* responsibility in the matter."

"Precisely. That's the way it seems to me, too." The farmer spoke with a quiet unhurried and reflective voice. "And, being so near at hand, I suppose I might claim to have as much responsibility as anyone. Even as much as you, perhaps, Mr Drummond—if it comes to that."

"Well . . ." Patrick looked at the other uncertainly. In the semi-darkness it was difficult to gauge the man's expression.

"So I think you should let us do our own worrying, young man," the newcomer ended. "And you wouldn't want to monopolise the Stone, would you? No sign of it yet, I gather?"

Relieved, Patrick smiled. "No, I'm afraid not. We've only just started, really. Give us time. I gather then, sir, that you don't think that we're just complete fools, in all this?"

"On your foolishness or otherwise I'll reserve judgment, meantime! But I've always felt that that old Abbot of Scone wouldn't be so much of a fool, away back in the old days, as to allow the English just to march in and take away the most precious thing in Scotland from his Abbey, without some attempt at hiding it. I've never believed the Stone at Westminster to be the genuine article. There's always been a local tradition here, you know, that the real Stone is still buried in the Scone district. But I must admit I'd never thought of it so near at hand. On *this* side of Tay."

"No. That's a tradition too—but not so well known. But I'm glad that you approve. Of what we're trying to do, I mean."

"He had no option," Jean informed. She moved over, to peer downwards. "Is it heavy work, in there?"

"It's no' that it's a' that heavy," Roddie Roy declared.

"It's jist that you canna get right crackin'. An' there's ower mony stanes."

It was well after midnight before the diggers were able to claim that they had won through that belt of fallen stones. They had been digging up mainly flat squared slate-like pieces for some time, and undoubtedly these would be nesting-box material which would have been apt to tumble in first. Below was a layer of what seemed like beaten clay, but which probably was no more than caked and impacted droppings. When this was pointed out, MacGregor, who had been taking a turn at spoil clearing, dropped his basket, seized a pick-axe out of a feebler grasp, and leapt into the trench again.

"Stand aside!" he cried. "Noo we're gettin' some place. Oot the road, man, an' gie's room."

"It might be quite a bit yet," Patrick warned. "After all, when they buried the Stone in the first place, they'd be apt to put it well below ground. All this debris we've been shifting has been added since then. If *you'd* been hiding the thing, Roddie, how far would you have put it down?"

"Two, three feet, maybe. Och, I'd soon be doon that far if it wasna for this wee bit narrow trench you've gi'en us to dig in! A decent-sized hole woulda been far better to dig in, man. It's a right scunner, doon here. You canna get right goin'. Here, shine that torch so's I can see what I'm bluidy well doin'."

An hour later, panting, sweating, and sore-backed, the excavators gradually came to a halt, as by mutual consent. They had worked their way down to fully another three feet in the centre of the trench, though somewhat less towards the ends, without finding anything to encourage them. At one point their hopes had soared, when the pick had struck continually at something larger and much more solid than the many loose stones that were still being unearthed. But careful scraping and clearing had revealed the knobbly and quite unsymmetrical surface to be merely a portion of the living rock of the knowe. Not only was this a disappointment; it was worrying. If the core of this hillock came so near to the surface elsewhere, then there might have been little space in which to bury so large an object as the relic that they sought.

Wearily, disgustedly, Roddie MacGregor tossed down his spade. "Hell—I reckon we're on the wrong track!" he snorted. "Maybe we should be awa' upbye at yon ither doocot, diggin' there. Maybe the Englishry has the rights o' it."

"It may be the other doocot, certainly—but that isn't to say that the Stone is inside it either," James Graham pointed out. "It may be merely at or near the doocot, somewhere."

"The Oxford people think that it's inside *their* one, anyway," Patrick returned. "They're digging it up, inside. And that's all we have to go by, really. I don't see that we can do anything other than we're doing. Just work away at this. There's a big area to uncover here yet, after all."

"Jings!" the youth Tosh complained, briefly but eloquently.

"An' a' the blasted beer's feenished!" his Teddy-boy colleague bemoaned.

"Shurrup!" Roddie mentioned, in the interests of morale.

"Food," Jean Graham suggested, brightly. "That's what's needed now. The inner man calls out for sustenance, I think. Tea. You should all just come away up to the house, and we'll see what can be found. And a break would do you all good."

"No." Patrick shook his head. "Thank you—no. Responsibility and all that is all very well. But I'm not going to have you actually harbouring us on your place. What we're doing, I suppose, is technically a breach of the law. I'm not going to have you people charged with harbouring law-breakers on your premises."

"But that's nonsense . . ."

"Och, we've nae time for it onyway, lassie," Roddie Roy announced, decidedly. "It isna dark that long, mind. I could dae wi' a sangwidge fine. But we'll need to hae it here. Awa' up an' fetch us some mair o' your sangwidges, Jeannie—an' we'll get on wi' the job, see."

"Och, hae a heart, Roddie . . ."

"Pit a sock in it, you! We didna come a' the way frae Glesgy to play bools an' sup beer. You hud your tongue! Here—see's that pick again. We'll hae another bang at it. But

56

nae mair wee trenches. They cramp you, see. You canna get a right whang at it. C'mon."

Roddie Roy had his way, of course. Jean went off for the provisions, and her father, deciding that he could be of little use at the site, elected to accompany her and go to his bed. The diggers started to enlarge and open up the trench in what was to be an ever-extending semi-circle northwards and eastwards—away from the direction in which the outcropping rock that they had discovered seemed to extend. They dug and scraped and carried, now, in a dour and determined silence.

Jean Graham heard that silence interrupted, shattered, just after she had crossed the stepping-stones of the Kincaid Water, with her picnic-basket, and started the climb towards Doocot Knowe once more. It was a shout, a bellow, in Roddie Roy's great voice, vibrant on the night air. It sounded very like a shout of triumph.

Hastening up the hill, she came breathless to the summit area. A considerable commotion was in progress there—a very different atmosphere prevailing from that she had left. She had actually to tug at Patrick's bent shoulder, in order to draw attention to her presence.

"What is it?" she demanded.

"Oh, it's you! Look—I think perhaps we might be on to something here. It's a possibility, anyway."

"Possibility my bluidy foot!" MacGregor roared. "This is it, see. The Stane. What else could it be, man? We've got it!"

"It *might* be something else," Patrick maintained, but with little conviction. There was no keeping the excitement out of his normally so strangely hesitant voice. "See—we've uncovered a corner of worked stone. Well down below the droppings level. Part of a large block, obviously. There's only a few inches of it uncovered, as yet. If that mutt, whoever it is, would keep his great head out of the light, you could see it! But the three faces are all dressed. Squared, you know—at right angles. The chances of that being accidental are pretty slender."

57

"Och, skip it!" Roddie requested from down in the cavity, where he was working away with his bare hands. "What's the guid o' talkin' that way? It's dressed stane. Awa' deep under the floor o' an auld doocot. An' a big lump o' it, that's sure. Dinna be daft, man—it couldna' be onythin' else."

"Well . . ."

The discovery had been made about nine inches below the guano level, some four feet north of the original trench, and well off-centre. A furious and more or less indiscriminate assault by MacGregor's pick-axe had revealed the existence of a large mass of very solid stone—an example of the triumph of sheer haphazard enthusiasm over method and reason.

Careful hands now burrowed and scraped around the block—Patrick would allow no pick and spade work close to the stone, for fear of damage. Presently they had the upper surface clear—and exultation mounted as it became incontrovertible that what they were uncovering was indeed a great squared block, with an uppermost face roughly 28 inches long by 20 inches wide. This surface was not flat, however. Much soil, caked and adhering, had to be scooped away heedfully before the true aspect of it could be established—and much more earth came away from the centre than from the outer rims. When it was all disposed of, the yellow beam of the electric torch shone on an oblong face, with the lateral ends curved over into something like carved rolls—volutes, as Patrick called them—and the centre hollowed out into the likeness of a shallow wide bowl, in smooth flowing lines. The stone itself was dark, almost black-seeming in the torch-light, and non-granular, feeling hard, almost glazed to the touch.

"Weel, damn the lot o' yous—there it is!" Roddie Mac-Gregor shouted, standing back and wiping a furry forearm across his perspiring brow. "There's the bluidy Stane that auld deevil o' an English king couldna' find! There it's—Scotland's ain Stane! Jings—get a load o' that! Up the Gregorach!"

"Yes," Patrick Kincaid swallowed. "Yes. There can be no doubt, now. That's it. That's the Stone." His voice shook to another uncontrollable tremor. "Very nice. Good show."

The young woman turned to him impulsively, and grasped his arm. "Splendid!" she exclaimed. "Wonderful, Patrick. Mr Drummond! I'm so glad. Your faith justified."

"Yes. Thanks. It's most . . . encouraging. But, look—I'm sorry. I'm afraid . . . well, my name isn't . . ."

"Hell—listen to the guy! Moanin' an' girnin' the noo!" Roddie cried disgustedly. "Encouragin', is it? Say—it's fair magneeficent!" And grabbing them both together and to himself in his enormous bear's-hug, the giant went waltzing round the Stone with them, willy-nilly, crushing any untimely and foolish revelations by Patrick Kincaid still-born by main force, and submerging even his victims' gaspings in his shouting.

He did not wholly drown the man Jakey however, who had a most shrill and penetrating voice. "The Lord Goad be thankit!" he whinnied high. "Blessit be the name o' the Lord!"

"Yippee!" a less reverent colleague substantiated.

"Och, niwer heed him," MacGregor advised, at the pitch of his lungs, abruptly releasing his prisoners. "He's hairmless. Jakey used to be in the Pairty—a Commynist. But he got religion, an' noo he's just aboot heid bummer o' the Salvation Airmy!"

"May Goad forgie you your ill tongue, Roderick Mac-Gregor—for I winna'!" Jakey screeched.

"Aw, can it!" the ruminative Alicky Shand requested. "The baith o' yous. What do we dae noo—aboot the Stane?"

"Sensible man," Patrick commended, a little breathlessly. "As well we don't anticipate there's anybody about, except for the farm people! We'd be heard a mile off. Let's get on with the job. We haven't got all night. It's nearly three now. The sun rises before five. And we've a lot to do . . ."

V

THE clearing away of the soil that encased the sides of the Stone took longer than might have been expected. Though it could be loosened, round about, with pick and spade, the actual removing had to be done by hand. And the deep-set position of the block meant that only two scrapers could conveniently work at it at a time. Patrick set the remainder of the party reluctantly to carting back and packing in the spoil that they had so laboriously removed from the original trench. That was urgent work, also.

Gradually the sides of the Stone were revealed. They were carved over-all, in intricate patterns that Patrick asserted to be Celtic.

"That disposes of the theory that it was originally a Roman altar, at any rate," he declared. "That was one of the theories about it."

"Wasn't there a story that it was the stone that Jacob used as a pillow when he was dreaming about the ladder up to Heaven?" the girl asked. "Something about it being brought from Egypt to Spain, wasn't it?"

He nodded. "The legend was that the Egyptians took it from the Israelites, and one of the Pharaoh's daughters, called Scota, who married a son of the King of Greece, took it with her, first to Spain and then to Ireland. She it was who was supposed to give the Scots their name. But that sounds like just one of those tales that used to gather round any venerable relic in the old days. Probably the Stone *did* come from Ireland, though, with Columba and the missionaries. Certainly it was at Dunstaffnage in Argyll, the capital of old Dalriada, and was brought from there to Scone, the Pictish capital, by Kenneth MacAlpine when he united the two kingdoms and formed a united Scotland. That would be around 840, I suppose."

"MacAlpine?" Roddie Roy interrupted. "Did you say Mac-

Alpine, man Patrick? Jings—then he was a MacGregor! We're Clan Alpine, are we no'?"

"You're not far out, Roddie. Though you've got it the wrong way round. The MacGregors are the senior branch of Clan Alpine. But it's right enough—they descend from King Alpin. The first Gregor is said to have been the younger brother of King Kenneth MacAlpine, who brought the Stone to Scone."

"Weel, I'll be damned an' coopered!"

"There was a Culdee monastery of the Celtic Church at Scone," Patrick went on. "And looking at this Stone, now, I'd say that it was probably originally a font, a baptismal basin. Possibly Saint Columba's own—which might partially account for its holiness."

"It certainly looks like something of that sort," Jean Graham agreed. "Look how intricate that carving is! All that elaborate pleating design. And the herringbone borders round it. It's almost like weaving, in stone, isn't it. Even caked with earth, as it is, you can see how fine it is. It seems to me remarkably well-preserved, considering its age."

"No' much wear an' tear lyin' under the doocot for hundreds o' years," Roddie pointed out. "Jings—it's hot, is it no', wi' a' this bendin' an' scartin' . . ."

Patrick was running his hand over the carvings. "It's because the stone is so hard that it's lasted so well. I'd say, by the feel of it, that it's one of the plutonic stones—heat fused, you know. Iron hard. That's the stuff of meteorites. And I've heard that many of these ancient relics *were* made out of meteorites—the ancients considered them very holy, having come down from Heaven. It's certainly nothing like the soft Old Red Sandstone that thing at Westminster is made of. This one won't break in two when we shift it, anyway! I wonder what tools they used to work on such hard material as this? It's all typically Celtic workmanship."

All four sides of the Stone were differently carved with intricate and comprehensive designs of broad-ribbon interlacing, diagonal key patterns, and elaborate spirals culminating in raised bosses, within borders of a kind of dog-tooth tracery that Jean had called herringbone. Only the upper surface was plain, save for the basin-shaped depression and the volutes at the ends—that might well, indeed, have been formed as handles to lift the heavy block.

Roddie Roy echoed Patrick's unspoken thought. "It's goin' to weigh somethin', yon, I'm thinkin'."

"The same idea occurred to me!" the other nodded grimly. "We're going to have to do some more thinking."

But they went on with the job in hand meantime, and at length the Stone stood clear right to its base, in the hole that they had scraped around it. Now it was seen to be about eighteen inches high, darkly vigorous in concept, well proportioned, solid yet of graceful lines.

"It's lovely," the girl breathed. "Or, no—that's not the right word, at all. It's handsome, rather. Fascinating. Maybe even just a little bit sinister, seen like that."

"But how are we to get it out of there?" Patrick wondered. "Take a hold, Roddie."

The two men each gripped a stone scroll at either end of the block, and heaved. Nothing happened. They tried again, with all their strength. Roddie Roy's end moved, perhaps half an inch; Patrick's not at all.

"Jings!" the big man exclaimed. "It must weigh a bluidy ton!"

"All of six or seven hundredweight, at least," Patrick panted. "It's a lot more dense than that other one. And half as heavy again. It could weigh twice as much."

"Hell—gettin' it oot o' that hole's goin' to be nae joke, then! You canna get a crowbar, even, in there for leverage."

"No."

"Here—gie's a hand wi' this, yous ones," MacGregor commanded. "Three at each end."

But even with the full manpower, the six of them could do no more than lift the massive Stone a few inches up from its bed. They could gain no purchase, having to lift directly upwards, all the strain bearing on their wrists. They would never manage thus, for there was no room for any more lifters to operate.

Various suggestions were tried, with consistent non-success. It was decided at length that there was nothing for it but more digging—to dig down one side of the hole into a sort of ramp up which the Stone could be dragged or manhandled. Rope would be a help. And rollers . . .

Patrick consulted his watch, anxiously.

As they bent to the latest labour, and Jean and Jakey were about to set off once more for the farm, in search of ropes and something to serve as rollers, James Graham turned up again. He wore a waterproof over his pyjamas, with the legs tucked into gum-boots. He had heard shouting, assumed that it portended some discovery, and had had to come to see what it was all about.

Patrick shone the torch full on the Stone, for the farmer's benefit—with satisfactory results. His congratulations were like himself, quiet, reflective, and sincere.

But it was not congratulations that the excavators desired.

"Look, Mr Graham," Patrick said. "I'm beginning to think that the finding of this thing is going to be the easiest part of it, in the end! It weighs the very devil! Getting it out of this hole itself is proving a big enough job. How we're going to get it any farther, for the moment beats me!"

"Yes—that's one of the things I was wondering about," the older man conceded. "What were you intending to do with the Stone once you got it?"

"Well, the whole idea was to keep it out of English hands. To see that it doesn't get carted off either to Oxford or to London. The scheme is to get it well away from this vicinity, and bury it—or hide it—somewhere else. Meantime, at any rate. And if possible, without any fuss and publicity. My car is one of those shooting-brake affairs. It should carry the Stone well enough—if we can get it that far. The point is—how to get it down to the nearest road?"

"Wi' a tractor, you could winch it oot," MacGregor suggested. "Could you get a tractor up here, Mister?"

"I'm afraid not. Not an ordinary one, anyway. It would take a crawler. One of those caterpillar-track affairs. And I don't have one of those, of course."

"Hell—we ken a' aboot them things, do we no'. Alicky! D'you mind yon time on Skye? Jings—yon was a ploy! They're right noisy deevils o' things to pinch, them. But, say, Mister—any Hydro schemes aboot here? They're the boys for the crawlers, them."

"Not hereabouts, no. This is much too valuable land for that sort of thing."

"Anyway, we've no time to go hunting for them," Patrick pointed out. "The cocks will be crowing any time now. We're going to have broad daylight on us before we know where we are! And there's an almighty lot to do before we can afford to have these Oxford characters snooping around here again."

"When do you expect the first of them on the scene?" the girl asked. "It would be about ten o'clock this morning—or rather, yesterday morning!—when they turned up, wouldn't it?"

"We can't rely on them being as late as that—now they've started the job. Admittedly they've to come from Perth. We've got to get this site disguised, camouflaged, somehow, before then, too."

"I told Father about the idea of penning sheep up here, round the top of the knowe," Jean informed. "He thinks that it might be just possible. But is it absolutely necessary, now? I mean, once we've got the Stone away?"

Patrick bit his lip. "Maybe not. Certainly it would be much better if we didn't have to do it. For one thing, your farm people would have to be told what it was all about. *They* couldn't be expected to accept the sight of a flock of sheep penned up here, without questioning. And there's the time factor, too. If we can get the Stone away, and the holes filled in, and the turf back, in time, it wouldn't be too obvious, perhaps? We couldn't hide the fact that there's been something going on here, from close inspection, of course—but it's just possible that it might escape notice from folk not looking for anything of the sort. If only there was some *small* thing that we could camouflage it with—something that wouldn't look too out of place and actually draw attention to the site?"

64

"My wee tent—like I said," Roddie proposed. "If it was sittin' up here, on top o' whaur we been diggin', it would maybe look a' right. They wouldna' likely come right up an' peer at it. Jings—I'd soon send them aboot their business if they did!"

"That might be all right for these Oxford types. But what about a keeper? I expect there'll be a gamekeeper about here, somewhere?"

"There is, yes," the farmer nodded. "And he would be apt to turn you off, here, if he saw your tent. Just what he would do."

"That's no good, then. We certainly don't want *him* snooping about here, either. It's a poser, isn't it?"

"*I* think that it would do if we just dumped a few rolls of wire-netting and some fencing-posts about here," Jean said. "It would break up the line—which seems to be all that's needed. We could put some on one or two of the other knowes, too—for it to look less obvious?"

"Yes. Yes—I believe that would serve. Probably the best thing," Patrick agreed. "What's more, that wouldn't need to involve you, up at the farm. I mean, you're pretty sure to have lots of that sort of thing lying about up there somewhere? We could just go up and take it—theoretically without your knowledge. We could hardly pen your sheep for you, unawares! There may well be enquiries into all this, whatever we do—and while the rest of us can disperse to the four winds, you and your daughter, sir, will be left on the spot, with the questions to answer. We must cover up there, as far as we can."

"I appreciate your forethought," the older man nodded, gravely. "Though I doubt whether all your precautions would absolve us, if it came to the bit! However, we'll meet that one when it comes. Now, about the other thing—the moving of this Stone. I'm wondering if a slype wouldn't be the answer?"

"A what?"

"A slype. It's a sort of horse-drawn sledge that we use for shifting hay in the field."

"I know now, yes. I've seen them. It sounds just the job. Could you get one up here?"

"I think so. Jean's garron could drag it up here, I expect. It's a sure-footed brute. Once we got the thing over the burn. That would be the trickiest bit."

"We'd have to seem to borrow them, too—without your knowledge," Patrick said, a shade uncertainly. "It's going to look, well, just a bit improbable, perhaps. I don't altogether like it. But, on the other hand, I don't see what else we can do."

"Nobody's asking you to do anything else!" the young woman declared, just a little tartly. "We're quite capable of looking after ourselves, thank you!"

"Guid for you, lassie!" Roddie commended. "Gie him the works. He's a right auld maid aboot some things, him!"

"I didn't mean that, of course. But . . ."

"Some of us have to use a little forethought. For the sake of all concerned." Sir Patrick Kincaid sounded distinctly dignified and baronetish.

"Aw, skip it! Use your bit spade instead, man. Save your breath to cool your parritch! There's ower much blether aboot this ploy, see." And MacGregor returned to the attack on soil and stones with commendable vigour, considering the circumstances.

"There are times when it may pay to use one's head, as well as mere brawn!" Patrick began heavily, when James Graham intervened.

"I think, on this occasion, there may be something in what our Glasgow friend suggests," he said, gently but firmly. "The first priority seems to be to get the Stone mobile. Other things can be discussed later. If a couple of you were to come up to the steading with me, we'd get the garron harnessed to the slype, and some fence-wire and stobs aboard."

"And some rope," his daughter added. "I don't know what we can use as rollers?"

"Come along, then. We may need some more help to get the outfit across the burn there."

"Very good, sir. I . . . h'm . . . I will come myself."

"Fine. Very sensible. Two fingers of whisky will probably put a different complexion on the whole affair, at this stage," James Graham opined. "You coming, Jean?"

It was astonishing how much longer everything took than might have been expected, that morning. Nothing seemed to be simple, straightforward, easy. The farm's two slypes, not having been required since last hay harvest, were found to be hemmed in and all but hidden under miscellaneous gear in the cart-shed—and great was the removal of awkward and unwieldy farm implements before one of them could be brought out into what was now only too surely the light of day. The garron, though reputedly a stolid brute, presumably was alarmed by the early hour's activities, and refused for some considerable time to allow itself to be caught in its field, creating dire panic in the meantime amongst the dozen milk cows that shared its pasture. Then suitable harness had to be found and coaxed on to the reluctant and suspicious steed. Even most of the rolls of wire-netting, and the wooden stobs, for camouflage, were found to have been taken only two days previously to another part of the property to fence in a plantation, demanding a slow and roundabout journey. Patrick Kincaid fretted, and kept eyeing his wrist-watch.

It was well after seven o'clock before they brought that sledge down to the Kincaid Water, a massive dragging jolting thing that caught in every cavity and excrescence and root. James Graham led them quite some distance downstream with it, in an effort to find a reasonably smooth approach combined with shallows suitable for fording. Then commenced a major battle. The garron did not want to cross the twenty or so feet of the stream, attached to that heavy and objectionable contraption. The slype itself seemed to be equally determined to remain on the south bank. Pushed and manhandled into the water at last, it promptly wedged itself between two large stones and there stuck, the horse very patently accepting the situation. Soaked and exasperated, the party heaved and splashed and floundered. Eventually Jean was dispatched upstream to fetch Roddie Roy and all available manpower, as reinforcements.

Spurred on by the big man, they more or less carried that contrivance bodily across the river in the end, to an accompaniment of much slipping and cursing, stumbling and panting, MacGregor's great muscles all but bursting apart with the strain, and the garron sheering and sidling away in disapproval.

"One thing," Patrick gasped, as they sank down with the thing on the north bank at last, "we'll never get it back . . . over here . . . with the Stone on board!"

No one contested that—though much the shortest route to the road lay that way.

The journey upstream again was worse, much worse, than that downstream, for the banks were steeper and more broken on this side, and grown with willows and alders. After a little of it, they turned away from the waterside altogether, to take their chances amongst the grassy braes.

They did better there, but it was a slow process even so. By the time that they reached the steep ascent to Doocot Knowe itself, certain facts were apparent to all of them. Roddie Roy put all their thoughts into words, for them.

"We're bluidy-weel no' goin' to get that Stane far, the day, wi' this caper," he declared. "We'd be catched wi' it, oot in the open."

"I'm afraid you're right," Patrick agreed. "There just isn't the time."

"I've been thinking," James Graham said. "There's only one thing to do. And that's to get the Stone up to the Big House there. And inside it, somewhere. Till nightfall again. It's only three or four hundred yards."

"Jings—right under the nebs o' the English!"

"That can't be helped. Then, at night, you could bring your car up the drive. It's a bit overgrown, but quite passable. We've got the key to the gates."

"It's risky, father. Terribly risky."

"Of course it is. But anything you do will be risky, won't it?"

"I suppose so. But . . . anyway, the Big House is all locked up. And we haven't keys for *that*."

"There's outhouses open."

"The stableyard isn't locked," Patrick said. "We could hide it in there somewhere, maybe. You know, I'm beginning to think it's a chance. Perhaps our only chance, now. It's not the sort of place these people would search, I should think—broken-down stabling and coach-houses that had been requisitioned by the Army. Nobody'd look for the Stone in there."

"But they might *stumble* on it."

"We'd have to take that chance."

"Hell—will we!" Roddie cried. "We'll bide wi' it. An' see what happens if the geysers try for to take it frae us!"

"No, no. That's the sort of thing we're trying to avoid. We'd have to keep a watch on it, of course . . . I think that'll have to be the answer."

Getting the slype up the steep slope of Doocot Knowe was heavy work, but less of a problem than had been most of its journey. The ascent was fairly smooth, and it was merely a case of homeric pulling and pushing, the garron redeeming itself notably.

At the top, flushed and breathless, they found the Stone actually clear of its cavity and sitting up on the ramp of earth and stones that had been built for it. When the diggers had been able to drag and edge it, instead of having to lift it directly upwards, they had managed to move it more readily. Now, looping ropes round the handle-like volutes, and using three fence-stobs as another ramp or gang-plank, they dragged it up on to the slype without a great deal of trouble. Tying it thereon, they covered it with some loose hay that they had brought for the purpose.

"Well, here goes," Patrick said. "All of you, give a hand to keep the thing under control going down this hill. That will be the worst bit. Then some of us will have to come back, to finish filling in the hole and camouflage the place somewhat. I'll stay with that party—for Roddie's brawn will definitely be most needed with the Stone. We'll have to bring the spades and picks up, too. We'll all meet at the stableyard again, as quickly as possible."

With drag-ropes attached both to the slype and the Stone itself, they eased the sledge and its precious cargo slantwise down the steep slope, pulling back on the ropes like tug-of-war teams. There were a few difficult moments, when the thing almost got out of hand, and one alarming occasion when, slithering over a slight drop, it all but pulled the stocky horse off its feet. But at length it was down, and only the fairly gentle grassy braes lay between it and the deserted mansion-house. The time, however, was turned eight-thirty.

With Jakey, Alicky and the youth Tosh, Patrick turned back up the knowe. They had no time for any elaborate covering of their traces thereupon. It was merely a question of shovelling back all the soil and stones that they could readily scrape up, patching it all over with as much green turf as was available, and strewing wire and fence-posts haphazardly on top. All the time that they were so engaged, Patrick's gaze kept searching the neighbourhood.

When they were finished at Doocot Knowe, they divided into pairs to hurry with the remaining rolls of wire and the stobs, to deposit them similarly on the summits of two neighbouring knolls. They could see the slype party well up on the way to the terrace on which Kincaid House stood; two tiny figures were hoeing turnips in a field high above and behind the farm-steading; but apart from that, no human activity stirred over the entire scene. So far, so good.

Collecting the picks and shovels, the four men hastened in the wake of the slype. Its tracks were very obvious on the pasture—but that need not necessarily seem suspicious, surely?

The Stone was just turning into the stableyard as Patrick's party caught up with it. Hurrying on, they stacked their borrowed tools beside the others against the doocot wall, carefully wiping off any fresh soil left adhering. Back at the stables, they found that Roddie Roy had already selected a hiding-place for the Stone—a former hay-shed in which the military had stored, and abandoned, a great number of curved sections of corrugated-iron for the making of Nissen huts.

"Under a heap o' them," MacGregor pointed out. "Naebody'll go pokin' aboot that lot."

It certainly seemed as safe a spot as any. They made no delay about the business, dragging aside enough of the iron to form a cavity, then unloading the Stone, using as gangway the corrugated sheeting itself, along which the great block ran easily, rusty as the iron was. The sheets, tossed back, covered it over again. It was all absurdly simple, the whole proceeding taking only a few minutes.

"Now, off with that slype," Patrick urged. "Are you going to try to get it back to your place roughly the same way as you brought it, sir?"

"No, I should say not," James Graham assured. "We'll leave it hidden somewhere off the drive there, and bring the tractor for it some other time. I won't need it till hay harvest—the best part of a month yet. What about yourselves?"

"Well, we could all do with a spot of sleep, I suppose—especially if we're going to have another big night. We'll have to keep watch, of course—we'll take turn about at that. The loft where I hid before, above the coach-house, might be as good a place as any. You can keep an eye both on the doocot and this shed, from there."

"What about food?" the ever practical Jean wondered.

"I daresay most of us could slip down to Perth, in my car, in the afternoon sometime."

"Nonsense! I'll smuggle a basket over to you. After all, *I* don't have to hide and creep about here! I've a lot more right to be here than these Oxford people. I can come up and ask them what they're doing, for that matter! I can see that they don't go traipsing about our grazings! I can . . ."

"You could do better with a good sleep, like everybody else, I think," Patrick asserted, and mustered his first grin for quite some time. "We'll manage fine. The only thing is—we'll need the key of the lodge gates, to get my car up here, at night. Shall I come over to the Mains for it?"

"I'll bring it over—with the food," the girl said.

Heavy-eyed in the face of the stripling sun, and yawning even at the praise of all the carolling larks, they left it at that.

VI

PATRICK Kincaid slept less than his due share, that day.
It was entirely his own fault, and no one else's failure. He
merely found himself unprepared to accept the assurance of
others that all was well. His weariness, in other words, was
not so compulsive as his restlessness. It was a long day, in
consequence. The Oxford researchers arrived just about
half an hour after Patrick's group had gone to ground in the
coach-house loft. They apparently had noted nothing amiss
on the way up, nor amongst the tools, and went to work
with a fair celerity, considering the nature of the task. About
mid-forenoon the noise of a motor engine brought Patrick
back to his window spy-hole, to see a lorry unloading three
wheel-barrows. Evidently they had acquired the key, and the
lodge gates were open. The scheme of operations was now
changed to a wholesale carting away of great quantities of
pigeon-droppings in the barrows, out of the doocot to a dump
established a suitable distance off, downwind. An unpleasant
but necessary job if further and comprehensive digging was
to proceed. It took them till midday and their picnic lunch.

It was hot again, and in the afternoon a certain amount of
the fire had gone out of the exercise. And the excavation
proper was proceeding again, with only intermittent barrow
work—which meant that only two or three persons were at
work at a time. These conditions tended to favour idle looking
around and casual sauntering. More than once individuals
and little groups came into the stableyard and wandered
about, looking in through broken windows and open door-
ways, and exclaiming. On one occasion two young people
actually entered the coach-house—and in some agitation
Patrick felt bound to awake Roddie who, without really
snoring, breathed somewhat heavily in his sleep. However,
the pair were of different sexes, and certain whisperings from

below, punctuated by girlish gigglings, were succeeded by a long period of silence—in which the young man Tosh had to be restrained from creeping over to peer down and report progress. Eventually, elaborately casual, the couple strolled outside again, and back to duty. There were more subjects for field research than one, apparently, even amongst Oxford's historians.

The effects of continued lack of success at the doocot were becoming evident as the day wore on. There was an ever increasing percentage of talk and argument, as against actual digging and carting. Patrick could not avoid a certain amount of fellow-feeling for the disappointed excavators. Jean Graham came riding up, quite openly, in the late afternoon, and leaving her garron hitched to a door-handle close to the coach-house, went strolling off to chat with the scholars. The hungry hiders promptly slipped down the very decrepit stairway from their sanctuary, to rob the horse of its burden—a grain sack, inside which were a number of cellophane-wrapped parcels, of sandwiches, hard-boiled eggs, lettuce, a cold boiled fowl, and two bottles of milk. The men had reason to congratulate themselves anew on their choice of allies. By the time that the young woman came back, and after a quick look round, hurried up to the loft, only the chicken-bones remained.

She was able to assure the company that all was well. Nobody had been observed anywhere near Doocot Knowe. The Oxford people had been pleasant enough to talk to— but had not admitted that they were looking for the Stone of Destiny. Their spokesman, like Patrick before him, had merely indicated that they were interested in doocots—or columbariums, as he called them—and that they had permission to excavate. It was perhaps significant, though, that he had asked whether there might happen to be any other pigeon-houses on the property.

Patrick was perturbed at that. It must mean, he said, that they were beginning to doubt the accuracy of their present site—which in turn would be bound to cause them to look elsewhere, to make further enquiries. It was only a question of time, then, before they found out about Doocot Knowe.

And once they found it, nothing could prevent them realising that the place had been raided, and recently.

Complications loomed.

Jean had further to inform them that emissaries of the historians had arrived at the Mains during the morning, asking for the key for the lodge gates, so that they could drive right up to the site, on the authority of the estate's lawyers in Perth. Her father had had to hand it over, but claimed that he had occasion to use the drive himself now and then, and had arranged that the gates should be left open meantime. So that was all right.

The girl wanted to know when they planned to move off, so that she could be there. When Patrick assured her that there was no need for her to be present, she declared, almost indignantly, that she *wanted* to be there, to see the Stone actually leave Kincaid, after seven hundred years. She agreed that it would be sensible to wait till fairly late. But not too late. She would put in an appearance about ten o'clock.

Soon after Jean left, the Oxford party packed up for the day. They went off in less cheerful spirits than on the previous day, undoubtedly. Once again they left no guard. When they were safely gone, Patrick and Roddie went down to inspect their handiwork. They found practically the entire floor of the doocot dug away to a depth of over two feet below outside ground level, with deeper pits here and there. Also some sizeable lumps of natural stone laboriously unearthed. And, against the wall in one corner, lay Dr Conrad Lister's map-board.

Interestedly they examined this. It mounted a large-scale map, six-inch to the mile Ordnance Survey. A cross in red crayon, at the end of the square of the walled garden, marked this doocot. A question-mark was drawn beside the ruins of the old castle, and another some way upstream at a site marked "Mill—remains of." That was all. A number of names of fields, parks, and woodlands were printed in on the map—but not Doocot Knowe, nor indeed any of the knolls.

"H.M. Ordnance Survey have failed them I doubt," Patrick observed. "*We've* had all the luck."

They replaced the map, and returned to their sleeping colleagues.

Later in the evening, leaving Jakey on guard, the other five made their way down to the waterside. They were glad to note that Doocot Knowe did not seem to draw any attention to itself, and the dumps of fencing material looked perfectly normal. They packed up Roddie's tent and few belongings, and then proceeded on, inconspicuously, down to the road. There they got Patrick's shooting-brake out of its hiding place in the trees—leaving the Gregorach's own three motorcycles still hidden—and in it drove off to the hamlet of Redgorton, in the little hostelry whereof Patrick did his duty and bought them all a drink. He found it a fairly costly proceeding, with the Glasgow contingent's capacity quite phenomenal, and had the greatest difficulty in prising them loose from the bar around nine-thirty. He was not too happy about this business, but felt that as a gesture it was very much called-for. He hoped that the proprietor would not find it all too markedly peculiar.

Driving back, in embarrassingly hearty song, along the side road that led to Glen Almond, they found the gateway to Kincaid House without difficulty, the lodge-house shuttered and empty, and the rusty wrought-iron gates standing wide and somewhat askew. They turned in, Patrick at least glad to be off the public highway with his notice-attracting passengers—and glad also to note that there were no other houses in sight on this stretch of road. The drive proved to be grassy and weed-grown, but two broadish tracks ran up it, and, though narrowed down, the surface was still fairly good. It made a long avenue, climbing quite considerably for fully half a mile. There were one or two places where trees had fallen, and had been only partly dragged aside or sawn away, much constricting the carriageway.

Back at the stableyard they found Jean already arrived. All agreed that there was no point in delay, and that they might as well get the Stone embarked right away.

The corrugated-iron sheeting greatly facilitated the loading process. Indeed, Patrick wondered how they would have managed to get the thing up into his brake without the smooth sloping runways that they provided—for even with their aid, a great deal of pushing and hauling was required. In consequence, for future use, it was decided that a couple of the sheets could very profitably be taken along in the car—where, raised on their sides, they would serve as quite good cover for the Stone, into the bargain. It would mean that the end doors of the brake would not quite shut—but that was a detail.

With the precious relic safely stowed, flanked by the iron sheets and covered with Roddie's tent in its bag and his blankets, they stood back to consider the result.

"It'll do, I think," Patrick nodded. "Doesn't look too strange. Might be a tradesman's van, of some sort. Perhaps I'd be wise to get some more air into the tyres, soon."

"Och, we can tak it ony place in that," Roddie asserted "We're right mobile noo."

"And where are you going with it?" Jean wondered. "What are you going to do with it, now you've got it?"

"Well . . ." Patrick ran a hand over his dark unruly hair. "I suppose it *is* about time that I thought of that!" he admitted. "I have thought about it after a fashion, of course. It doesn't greatly matter, you see, where it goes, provided certain requirements are fulfilled. It needs to be somewhere sufficiently remote—and yet where we can lay hands on it again without too much difficulty. And the less populous country we can take it through, on the way, the better. And somewhere that nobody's going to discover it by chance. And I think, you know, that it oughtn't to be too far away from here. Still in this Tay valley area somewhere."

"What for that?" MacGregor demanded.

"Well—I don't know. It just seems more suitable, somehow. The Stone has been here for well over a thousand years, within a mile or two of Scone. It was brought about 850. I feel that it should stay in the vicinity of the Tay, at least. Though I agree that's not vitally important."

"Jings—you've said it! What's the guid o' that? Tak it right across Scotland, man. Tak it back, maybe, to Argyll, whaur it come frae. To Dun. . . . What was yon place?"

"Dunstaffnage. Near Oban. I suppose that's a possibility. But . . ."

"No, I agree with Patrick," the girl said. "It's right that it should stay around here, somewhere. It *is* the Stone of Scone, after all. And there's plenty of places, surely, where it would be safe enough. Lonely remote places, but not far off. The big hills aren't far away." She turned to look into the west, towards the towering giants of the Highland Line, unseen now but seldom forgotten in that country. "Why not take it into upper Glen Almond? That would be simple and suitable. It's not far—no more than fourteen or fifteen miles. And it's as wild and lonely a spot as you'll get—yet with a road of sorts running up it."

"You mean, up beyond the Sma' Glen? Behind Crieff, there?"

"Yes. The Almond is one of the main tributaries of Tay. This road that you get on to at the lodge gates runs right up the lower Almond valley, to join the Crieff-Aberfeldy road through the Sma' Glen. That's about ten miles. The Sma' Glen is just a part of Glen Almond, linking the upper and lower valleys. The upper part extends for . . . oh, another dozen miles, I should say. With only a dirt road, that comes to a dead end at the head of the narrow glen. Wild and remote enough for anyone up there—though there is some hydroelectric work going on somewhere."

"Sounds just the thing." Patrick nodded. "I know where you mean—though I've never been up there. Good—that's settled, then. We'll take the Stone up there, and hide it somewhere. We ought to have it there in not much more than an hour. . . ."

"I could come along, perhaps, too—and show you the way?" she suggested, tentatively.

He shook his head. "No, I don't think so. Better not. It's going to be a tight squeeze for the six of us in the car, anyway, with the Stone. And there's no need. We can find our way easily enough."

Jean shrugged. Obviously she had expected that. "Just as you wish," she said, a little flatly. "But . . . I'd have liked to see where it ended up."

"We'll let you know where we put it. We've got to come back here anyway, to pick up the motorbikes. We don't want all those roaring along, to advertise our presence! I'll come up to the Mains, when I get back, to tell you how we got on. All right? And to say thank you. You've been . . . just goodness itself. Helpful. Understanding. I . . . well, I'm more grateful than I can say. And appreciative of everything."

"Och, aye," Roddie Roy wound up for him. "Fine, that. Let's get crackin'."

"Exactly," the young woman agreed. "I'll come down to the foot of the drive with you, at least."

They piled into the brake, packing themselves tightly, with Jean having to sit on Roddie's huge hairy knees, and drove off, the car sitting low on its springs but bearing up gallantly.

Patrick took the drive slowly, with no lights lit. Caution was essential, in more ways than one, for any breakdown or mishap might well prove fatal for their plans. He approached the narrows and bends of the overgrown avenue gently, changing down into low gear—for with the weight that was being carried, the brakes might not react too efficiently. They were fully halfway down when, however, the driver applied those brakes abruptly, savagely.

"Look!" he jerked. "Damn and confound it!"

They had just negotiated one bend, and ahead, a couple of hundred yards off, was another. In the shadow of the trees, and dark as it was, they might not have seen that far clearly. But see it now they could, only too plainly. The bend was outlined and silhouetted by a glow of yellow light, a glow that was steadily growing brighter and larger, illuminating the trees.

"Oh, goodness—something's coming!" the girl cried. "Another car!"

"Jings—that's torn it!"

"Wha'll they be? Thae Oxford jokers?"

"Here we go, boys—catched wi' oor pants doon!"

Slowly, heavily, the brake swayed to a halt, with Patrick already staring over his shoulder, trying to see behind him past the packed back seat and the bulky cargo of stone and corrugated iron. He slammed his gears into reverse.

"You'll never do it, Patrick!" Jean exclaimed. "Not with these bends. Not in the dark."

"Get out and guide me, Roddie," Kincaid snapped.

"It's nae guid, man. Even if you manage roond, you'll no' be quick enough. They'll be on to you." But even as he spoke, MacGregor had unseated the girl from his knees, flung open the door, and jumped out of the already backwards-moving vehicle.

"Only thing to do. Must try it. Maybe we can back off the drive somewhere, in time . . ." The rest was drowned in the roar of his accelerated engine, as the car swung and veered erratically and dangerously whence they had come.

Roddie raced round, and ran beside Patrick's open window shouting directions. "Straighten up, man! Sharp! Aye. Noo—as you go. Keep it that way. Aye . . . aye . . . na, na—you're ower much this side. Noo—hard roond. Roond, damn it! Goad—that was a near one! Aye—straight noo. As you go. Keep it up. You're daein' fine. Na—ower a wee. Ower, I say. To the left—aye, *your* left. You're gettin' off these tracks. Noo—roond again. Jings—no' sae hard! Here . . . !" And thrusting a hand inside the window, the big man himself jerked the wheel round, all but falling over his own feet as he did so, with the backward motion of the car. "Hell—that was close! You near hit yon tree. Noo—there's a bigger bend yet . . ."

"There'd better be!" Patrick panted. "By the look of their lights, they'll be on us in a few seconds."

"Don't, Patrick!" Jean warned him. "It's no use. You can't do it. There'll just be an accident . . ."

"Hard roond, noo!" Roddie yelled.

They could actually see the level twin beams of the oncoming climbing car as the brake bucked and lurched drunkenly round the bend caused by the sprawling bulk of a fallen tree. Patrick peered behind him again. There seemed to be something of a gap in the barrier of trees and bushes that flanked the drive, at his side.

"Look—in there, Roddie!" he cried. "What's it like? Can I back in? Is it flat enough?"

"Weel . . . maybe. Kind of. There's nae big trees, onyway. Some wee bushes . . ."

"Never mind that. Here goes! Hang on, everybody!" And throwing the steering-wheel hard over in a full circle, he sent his car swinging violently round in a tight arc towards this other side, accelerator hard down. Pitching and rolling the brake took the grassy verge, heaved and bumped on through something that yielded while hitting back, and then seemed to hesitate. Then, with a sickening jolt the entire rear end seemed to drop. There was a spine-jarring crash, followed by an ominous crunching. The car stopped dead, the engine stalling, with the radiator in the air and the front wheels still on the edge of the drive. There must have been a ditch, amongst all that undergrowth. And without pause, with the screech and clang of metal, the corrugated iron, impelled by the heavy Stone, shifted, sliding against the off rear upright of the car. There was the smash and tinkle of broken glass as the Stone knocked out the window there, and came to rest again, on the very point of toppling right out of the damaged vehicle.

Then silence.

Patrick recovered his wits first. He found that the girl had been flung on top of him, and that he had an instinctive protecting arm around her person. Jakey, somehow, was down on the floor amongst the gears and feet.

"You all right?" he gasped.

"Yes. Yes—I think so. Are you?"

"Yes. The rest of you? Are you okay? Everybody?"

There was a confused but intense profanity coming from the jumble of bodies and limbs at the back. It sounded healthy enough.

"Quick, then—everybody out of it! Jump for it. That side—away from the light. Go on—hurry! You, too, Jean. Before we're lit up. No—do as I say. Don't argue. We don't want identifications. Quick! I'll stay. I'll say something . . ." Leaning over, he got the far door open again, and practically pushed the young woman out, kicking unkindly at the recumbent

Jakey to go the same way. He could hear a scuffling and cursing behind, which seemed to indicate a similar exodus.

"Here they come!"

The spreading golden beams of the powerful headlights swept round the bend, making a fairyland of colour and shadow out of the scene. Swinging inexorably on, they blazed full upon the stranded shooting-brake. There was a sudden screech of brakes, and the oncoming car drew to a juddering abrupt halt a bare twenty yards away.

Dazzled by the glare, Patrick turned to look behind him—to see, if he could, whether all his party were safely out. One man certainly was not—the youth Tosh, sitting somewhat dazedly askew in the rear seat, blinking into the brilliance.

"Damnation!" Patrick swore tersely. But it was not the presence of the gaping Tosh that so upset him. It was the sight of the Stone of Destiny itself, devoid of all its coverings, that had rolled or fallen away from it, picked out, stark, black, and handsome, in the clearest detail, in the blazing radiance.

He heard the doors of the other car open, and slam shut. That would mean that the newcomers had got out to investigate—he could see little, himself, in the glare. Sighing, Patrick opened his own door, and climbed out into the long grasses. This, undoubtedly, was where he faced the music.

"I say—are you all right?" That urgent enquiry was couched in a distressingly authentic Oxford accent. "You're not hurt? How on earth did you get in there?"

"No. No—I'm all right," Patrick returned, a little breathlessly. "Nothing to worry about. I just backed a little too far." His eyes were becoming accustomed to the glare, now, and he could see that the man addressing him was young and bearded. One of the researchers had worn a beard—the one who had come into the coach-house with the girl, that time.

"Oh, good. I must say, your car looks pretty rum like that, though. Gave us quite a start. I . . . ."

"Michael! Look at that car!" That was a woman's voice. A girl emerged from the shadows beyond the beams of the headlights, pointing. There was no doubt about it—she was the same pony-tailed blonde who had been with the bearded

81

student in the coach-house. Equally, there was no doubting the alarm in her high-pitched voice—or the reason therefor. She had sharper eyes than her escort, evidently. "Look at what's in it! They've got it! It's the Stone! Our Stone!"

Peering, the bearded fellow started forward towards the brake. "My God!" he cried. "So it is. At least, it looks damned like it!"

"It can't be anything else," the girl declared, her voice shrilling with excitement. "They've found it! They're taking it away. They've dug it up. And now . . . now they're bolting with it!"

"Oh, I say!" The man Michael paused in his striding, uncertainly, to stare from the Stone to Patrick, and back again.

"Is this true? I mean, what are you doing with that Stone?"

Patrick was thinking hard and fast, racking his somewhat bemused wits for something to say, something at least to mitigate the dire results of this sudden disaster. If only he had kept Jean beside him; pretended to be a courting couple—with the others out of sight. They could have waved at this wretched couple to dip their lights in decency—and so perhaps prevented the Stone from being spotlighted. Though the brake looked so obviously ditched. Anyway, no point in thinking about that now. The girl had reached the stranded car, and was staring in. And from within, Tosh, who still sat there, was shaking a fist at her.

"They're thieves!" the young woman cried. "They've been watching us. They've been digging up our columbarium, while we were away. And now they're stealing our Stone."

"Not at all," Patrick returned, rather inadequately. "What's all this hysterical talk?"

"That *is* the Stone of Scone you've got there," the bearded Michael asserted. "You can't deny that. What are you doing with it?"

"I don't see any reason why I should have to give an account of myself to *you*!" Patrick put on his haughtiest and most authoritative voice. "Who are you, young man? And what are you doing here? On ground that doesn't belong to you?"

"I . . . we're members of the Oxford University Historical Research Society. We've come specially to find this Stone of Scone. The real one. We're here to dig for it."

"You're *what*? What on earth are you talking about?" Patrick extemporised sternly. "Oxford, did you say? What has Oxford to do with Scotland's Stone of Destiny? What right have you to talk about coming up here and digging up this precious relic? And on private property, too!"

"We've got permission, I assure you, sir."

"Tush! Permission from whom? Have you got permission from the Secretary of State for Scotland?"

"Eh? Well, I, I don't know about that, sir. But we've got permission from the owner of the land."

"Let me see it, please."

"Oh, *I* haven't got it, I mean, not personally. Dr Lister—our President, you know—has it."

"Then what are you doing here?" Patrick barked, in tones that few would have recognised as his own quietly diffident voice. "On private property. Without authority. And speaking insolently to people on the spot, into the bargain!"

"Oh, I assure you, sir, I didn't mean any insolence. Nothing like that. It's just . . ."

"Don't listen to him, Michael!" the young woman interrupted. Obviously she was less impressed by authoritarian tones than was her companion. Obvious also that her voice, when excited, spoke of Lancashire rather than of Oxford. "He's stolen the Stone, and he's just trying to bluff it out. Can't you see?"

"Young woman—I'd remind you that accusations of that sort are actionable in court!" Patrick said pedantically. "Any more of that sort of talk, and I'll have to demand your name and address, with a view to taking proceedings against you!"

"Don't be daft!" the girl returned, but with less assurance.

"This is Scotland, remember—and Scots law safeguards its citizens rather better than does English law, from this sort of abuse!" Patrick said. That was scarcely true and quite unfair, of course—but the situation warranted desperate measures.

"I think you should leave this to me, Celia," the young man suggested, not too happily.

"I think that would be wise," Patrick nodded grimly. "And you, young man, for your part, would be wise to go right back to wherever you came from, and not venture on private property again without written authority!"

"We came on Dr Lister's authority. To get his map case." That was the girl again.

"*Written* authority?"

"Look, sir—I don't understand all these legalities, I must admit," the man Michael began reasonably. "But I think you ought to tell us what you're doing with the Stone. After all, to trace it was the whole object of our expedition. If you've found it—well, that can't be helped. But . . . well, we must know about it. Where you got it, and what's happening to it?"

"How so? What business is it of yours?"

"I tell you, it's our session's field work! We've done a lot of research into this."

"I'm sorry if you feel all your research is wasted. But nobody asked you to do it, did they? Not here in Scotland, anyway. And this Stone is one of Scotland's most prized possessions."

Quite evidently nonplussed, the other shook his head. Then he moved over to have a whispered conversation with the girl. "Excuse me," he mentioned, his manners at least unfailing.

Patrick could not afford that luxury. "Come along," he said peremptorily. "I'm afraid I must ask you to leave this property. At once!"

"And *your* authority?" The girl again.

"My name is Drummond! That, I should imagine, is sufficient authority for anyone."

Blankly they looked at him. "Drummond?"

"Yes." He moistened his lips. "I am the Stone's Custodian. Now—go, please."

Staring at him, puzzlement, incredulity, and an ingrained respect for authority most patently fighting it out within him, the younger man moved towards his car. At first it looked as

84

though the girl would not go. But at length, under Patrick's hard glare, she followed on.

"I'm not satisfied," she announced, to the night at large. "There's something phoney going on here, if you ask me! That car . . ."

The rest was lost in the whirr of the car's engine. It whirred noisily—and went on whirring. Again and again the young man worked it—without other result than the noise. He got out, and went forward to raise the bonnet.

"What's wrong, Michael?"

"I don't know. She was all right before. Can't see, in this light." He gestured to her. "Get in, will you, and try the starter again."

The thing whirred a few times more, with like results.

"Have you run out of petrol, Michael?"

"No. We were low—but not so low as all that. I don't know what it can be."

"You're on a hill, you know. Maybe the petrol is running to the back of the tank?"

"Can I help?" Patrick asked, with a sort of cold solicitude.

"Well . . . I don't know what it can be, sir. I'm not much of a mechanic, I'm afraid."

"Nor am I. It sounds pretty dry to me. You're sure about the petrol?"

The man moved back, to inspect the instrument-panel. "The indicator says there's still some left."

"You can't trust those things—they're always going wrong. Shall I give you a push?"

"All right. We could try it. In reverse."

There was no call for a great deal of pushing, for the car had been climbing a distinct slope, and it ran backwards almost too readily. But no amount of jerking into gear had the effect of starting the engine. And the driver was very nervous about his rearward progress downhill—as well he might be, since he could not see where he was going on a narrow twisting drive. The girl was sent behind to guide them—but proved less than efficient at the job.

It did not take long for the inevitable to happen. At one of the many narrows, the car was not straightened up in time, and rammed its tail into the mixed foliage of the verge. No damage was done—but no amount of united effort would push the heavy vehicle forward again. Not that Patrick tried very hard.

"It's no good," the unfortunate Michael panted. "We shan't move her."

"How shall we get back to Perth?" the young woman demanded, much less sure of herself now.

"That's easy," Patrick assured. "Walk down to the foot of this drive. Then along the road to the right for half a mile, to the crossroads. Then left, and thumb a lift. If you don't get picked up there, you soon will at the main road. You'll be back in Perth in an hour. Less. You can fetch a mechanic—and some petrol—in the morning."

"M'mmm. Yes, I suppose so. I suppose that's about all we *can* do. You don't happen to have an electric torch with you, sir? We forgot one. We might have just a quick glance at the engine."

"No," Patrick said baldly.

"Oh, well . . ."

"Straight down, and turn to your right."

"Yes. Well . . . goodnight. And, er, thank you." That sounded doubtful.

"Don't mention it!"

The girl said nothing.

Switching off the car's lighting, and lifting out a handbag, the pair of them turned away and went disconsolately off down the dark drive.

Back at his own brake, Patrick found the shadowy figures of his colleagues popping up like rabbits around it. The youth Tosh seemed to have recovered from the effects of his jolting and climbed out. All things considered, they were surprisingly cheerful.

"Guid work, man," the largest shadow greeted him, heartily. "You done fine. Jist fine. You gi'en that couple a flea in their lugs! Stalled them grand."

"Aye, man—yon was real nice."

"*I* wouldn't say so!" Patrick shook his head "I didn't enjoy doing it, I can tell you. Speaking to those two youngsters like that. Just babes, as they were. Threatening them . . ."

"Och, dinna be stupid, man. You did what had to be done."

"I suppose so, yes. And what about you? What did *you* do?" That was an accusation.

"Me? Och, naethin' much. I jist sent Jakey to jouk roond, while you were argy-bargyin', to snip a bit wire on yon car Naethin' to it, in the dark—an' Jakey a right dab hand at that sort o' thing. They'll no' be back for a whilie, that couple."

"You were magnificent, Patrick," Jean Graham commended quietly. "I don't know how you did it. Listening to you I was almost convinced, myself, that you were the laird of us all! Or some outraged official. But did you have to give them your name, like that? Surely there was no need for that?"

"Well . . . h'rr'mm . . . I don't know. Perhaps not. But . . ."

"Och, jigger that!" Roddie Roy intervened urgently. "The main thing was to get them awa'. To gie us time to dae somethin' aboot the Stane. An', Jings—we're in a right mess noo, tae!"

"Yes, I'm afraid we are. I'm sorry—terribly sorry. It was just one of those things."

"It was no fault of yours," the girl cried. "You couldn't help it! I think you worked wonders, considering. But what on earth are we going to do now? Is your car smashed up, d'you think?"

"It sounded pretty ominous to me."

"Transmission a' to hell!" Jakey, who was a mechanic, commented flatly. "Propeller shaft bent, likely. A salvage-waggon job."

"It's not to be that, at any rate!" the owner asserted. "That car can identify me—and I don't want to be identified . . . yet! Let's see if we can get it out of this confounded ditch. We'll have to move the Stone out first, of course. We'll never lift it with that weight in . . ."

Patrick's torch, that he had so ungallantly refused to the

other travellers in need, came in useful now. They managed to disentangle the corrugated iron, the tentage, and the blankets, and, though the rear doors of the brake were slightly buckled as well as having their glass broken, they were not jammed. They slid the Stone to the ground on the iron sheeting. Patrick tried the engine. It ran perfectly in neutral, but by no means could he get the gears to engage. It seemed that Jakey was right, and that the car's drop had damaged the propeller shaft.

All six men heaving together, they succeeded in lifting the brake up out of the overgrown ditch into which its rear had plunged, and on to the drive again. Its back was not broken, it still ran—but its engine conveyed no drive to its wheels.

"And now what?" Jean asked.

Patrick shrugged. "I can't pretend that the situation isn't pretty sticky," he admitted. "The long-range position's utterly altered, I'm afraid. And the short-range one is going to be no joke, either. Those youngsters were not too difficult to fool. But their seniors will be a mighty different story. I'm willing to bet that their leader, this Dr Lister, will come straight back here looking for us, the moment he hears their story. Or, not quite straight—he'll call in at the Police Station, on the way!"

"Oh, Patrick!"

"Sure. You've said it!" Roddie Roy agreed. "The polis'll be efter us in a coupla oors. An' the hale o' Scotland'll ken a' aboot it the morn's morn!" He sounded almost gleeful at the prospect.

"Jings!"

"The Lord's will be done, jist!"

"I fear you're right. The thing I wanted to avoid—police and publicity—is bound to follow now. These people aren't going to take this lying down." Patrick nodded gloomily. "And you can guess what a furore there will be, once this gets into the papers! But the moment that couple set eyes on the Stone, the thing was inevitable. It was most damnably unfortunate, the whole thing."

"Och, cheer up, man, we'll beat them yet!" MacGregor cried, thumping Kincaid on the back with a sledge-hammer blow. "We'll beat the hale bang-jing o' them—polis an' a',

I've did it before. They're easy, man—nae imagination, see. We'll get a tractor frae the lassie—twa tractors. One for the Stane, an' one for the bluidy car—an' get them baith oot o' this."

"Yes, of course. We've got three tractors," Jean declared. "We'll get them."

"Running you and your father in deeper than ever . . ."

"Nonsense! No deeper than anybody else. Where are we going to take them—the car and the Stone, I mean? To the Mains?"

"No—not there, at any rate. But we can think about that while we're collecting the tractors. Every minute may count. It will take us how long to get to the farm? Twenty minutes, if we hurry?"

"Yes. About that."

"Jings—wi' a perfectly guid car standin' there idle! Jakey'll fix yon bit wire as quick as he snipped it. Eh, Jakey?"

"Sure."

"D'you think we ought to do that? Take a loan of other people's property?"

"Hell, man—get rid o' thae kid gloves o' yours, will you no'! It's us against the rest, noo—against the polis, an' London, against the bluidy State! C'mon."

VII

THEY were back in the drive, with the purloined car and two of the farm's tractors, one towing a trailer, within thirty-five minutes. James Graham drove one of the tractors himself, and Jakey the other. It had begun to rain.

They were becoming expert at handling the Stone, now, on its corrugated-iron runners, and it only required a few minutes to load it on to the trailer and cover it with a tarpaulin that they had brought along. The other tractor's tow-bar was attached to the front of the shooting-brake. They were ready to move. Roddie was to back the Oxford car into its former position once the tractors were safely past.

"Well, what's the decision?" the farmer asked. "Where do we take the Stone? As I said, your station-wagon can be towed up to that old steading of ours on the Muir—there's a cart-road all the way—where your fellows can see what they can do for it. You can take the Stone there too, of course, meantime?"

"No," Patrick shook his head. "I prefer the other idea—the old church. The steading sounds fine for the car. If necessary, if we're trapped with it, we can bolt and leave the car—once the number-plates are off. It was second-hand anyway, when I got it, and they're going to have difficulty tracing the engine number to me. But the Stone is different. We can't bolt from that. It just must not be found. And this old church sounds as safe as anywhere, to me—for the time being, that is. Till we can get mobile again."

The church had been Jean's idea. Kincaid had been a parish once, though it was now amalgamated with the neighbouring parish of Pitcorthly. Its old Parish Kirk still existed, down near the road, in an overgrown graveyard, though shut up and used only two or three times a year. And underneath it was a crypt—burial-vault, so it was said, of the old Kincaids.

Patrick had had much ado to keep a straight face when the girl had told him that. It was possible to get into the crypt, for, as frequently happens, the place had also been used for the storage of the gravedigger's tools and equipment and other gear, and the great rusty iron key hung in the vestry. What more suitable hiding-place was there likely to be?

It was the very suitability of the thing that worried Patrick a little. Was it not *too* suitable, too apt altogether? The very sort of place that would ask to be searched, eventually? That word eventually, was probably the vital one. The place might well serve excellently meanwhile. After all, the opposition could not know that his car was seriously damaged. When they found it and the Stone both gone, the natural thing to assume would be that they had driven away again. So that there would be no reason to believe that the Stone was still in the Kincaid locality, at all; rather the reverse. The crypt might serve for a little, then. And undoubtedly the fact of it being the tomb of his ancestors added considerable piquancy to the suggestion.

"All right. Jean will guide you down to the Kirk," James Graham said. "I'll tow the car, with your mechanic-chap steering it. And maybe another one, in case we need help. How long would you say we've got?"

"It's hard to say. Depends on a few things. How long those two took to get to Perth. Whether their Dr Lister had gone to bed, or not. After all, the accident happened about ten-fifteen. They couldn't be in Perth much before eleven-fifteen, even if they were very lucky with a lift. Once he hears, Lister's reaction will be pretty swift, I'd imagine. But if he went to the police, he'd have a good lot of explaining to do. It would all make a long story. And not the sort of thing that a local sergeant on night shift would take important decisions about off his own bat, probably. I'd say, if I were such a sergeant, I'd just send a constable, or maybe two, with Lister to see what it was all about, and leave any real decisions to my superiors in the morning."

"Yes—that sounds reasonable."

"In which case, say it took three-quarters of an hour to get both Lister and the police moving, and fifteen minutes more to get here, driving fast—that would give us till about twelve-fifteen. And it's just on eleven-thirty now."

"If they dinna bother about the polis, they could be here sooner," Roddie pointed out.

"That's true."

"Jings, then—it's high time we cut oot the havers, an' got crackin' or they'll be on top o' us. You aye talk ower much, man Patrick. That's a' that's wrang wi' you!"

"I know," the other admitted, humbly enough. "I'm sorry."

"He talked to good effect, a little while ago, I'd remind you!" Jean Graham asserted stoutly. "He got us all out of a pretty nasty jam, by good talking."

"Ooh, aye."

"I got you *into* the jam, first, by bad driving and general foolishness! But Roddie's right—high time we were gone. Who's driving our tractor?"

"I will. I'm used to it," the girl said.

"Good," her father nodded. "I'll go first. Let's hope there's no traffic. This lot might take a bit of explaining! Not that it's likely, on our side road at this time of night. See you all later, up at the Mains."

"Oh, no—I don't think we should all come there."

"I'll bring them along, father."

The farmer took Jakey and the Teddy-boy, while the others piled on to Jean's tractor and the trailer, and down the drive they went in procession. They seemed to make a lot of noise. It was now raining hard.

Turning out of the drive and into the road keyed them all up. But it was a very minor side route, merely linking the Glen Almond and Bankfoot roads, themselves secondary highways. They had only a short distance of it to cover, and one house to pass—the former Manse of Kincaid, now occupied by a retired couple and set well back in its own grounds.

The leading tractor turned off first, after about four hundred yards, up the farm road to the Mains. Then, a little way farther, after crossing the bridge over the Kincaid Water, Jean swung her entourage in at a short carriageway, embowered in dark dripping trees, at the opposite side of the road.

Patrick peered downwards. "Wait!" he called out. "Tracks. Got to watch our tracks. What's the surface?"

Jean drew up. "It's sort of old tarmac here, I think. But farther on, into the kirkyard itself, it will be just dirt. Or at least, old gravel."

"I don't like it," the man said. "Our heavy wheel-marks will show. Especially on gravel and dirt. Muddy with the rain. And there may be plenty of folk looking for tracks in unlikely places before long! How far does the gravel extend? I mean, up to the church?"

"Oh, quite a bit. Seventy or eighty yards, I'd imagine."

"M'mmm. Look—what's the geography of this place? Does it all project into a field? Or a glebe, round the church-yard?"

"Yes. There's a glebe on the left, between us and the Manse permanent pasture. Some bullocks in it. And one of our fields on the right, and right behind. Turnips."

"How close does it come to the church, at the back? This field?"

"Fairly close. Forty or fifty yards, I suppose. You think we should go in from that side?"

"Yes. If there's a gate into your field reasonably handy. Tractor tracks will never be noticed going into a turnip field; whereas into a disused churchyard they certainly might!"

"That means humpin' the Stane fifty yairds on oor backs." the laconic Alicky pointed out.

"An' ower a fence, or a wall, likely," Roddie Roy added.

"A stone wall, it is," the girl informed. "It's broken down a bit, though. We're always having to barricade it up, when we've beasts in that field, to keep them out of the kirkyard."

"Och, we'll manage, nivver fear!" MacGregor cried. "C'mon—let's get a move on!"

"Can you back out of here, without much trouble, Jean? It's only a few yards."

The young woman managed that expertly, and they had another unnerving hundred yards or so of the road before

93

they reached the field gate. Roddie jumped down to open it, they swung in, and he closed it behind them. Then along the headrig, at the edge of the tilth, parallel to the road and with only a low hedge in between, back the way that they had come, the trailer jolting over the uneven ground. Thankfully they saw the black mass of the trees surrounding the church loom up again before them, as they turned inwards along the dimly-seen line of a stone wall.

With the barrier of the kirkyard's trees hiding them from the road, the girl pulled up and switched off the noisy engine. "Thank goodness for that!" she said. "There's a break in the wall here—the nearest to the church, I'd think. There are others, though. Anyway, we're safe from sight, here."

They dismounted, and examined the scene. Kincaid Church and its graveyard stood on a very slight eminence, surrounded by a wall that enclosed two or three acres of neglected grass and weathered moss-grown tombstones. The wall, at least, would be little trouble, for its tumbledown gaps had been only roughly patched with hurdles and old gates, and nothing would be easier than to level a way through and then patch it up again afterwards.

It was decided to have a look at the church and the crypt before unloading the Stone. To ensure that they did not make an obvious track by trampling down the fairly long grass, they prospected a route carefully, behind Patrick's torch. They calculated that less than fifty yards of manhandling would carry the Stone to the church.

"And hoo are we goin' to hump the thing even that far?" Alicky demanded again. "On thae bits o' iron? They'll near cut the hands off us."

"No—I think we may do better than that," Patrick answered. "If I know anything about graveyards, there'll be one of those wooden stretcher-affairs that grave-diggers use for piling soil on, carrying coffins, and so on. One of those will suit us better."

"Gee, man—you think o' everything!" Roddie admired. "Jist the job!"

"I should think we'd find one in the crypt," the girl agreed.

The church proved to be a squat, plain, small-windowed building, in the local dark red sandstone, distinctly secretive-seeming and unforthcoming. But at its eastern end was a rounded and ornate chancel, with much handsome though weather-worn arcading and stone moulding, out of which rose a little parapeted tower, graceful but sturdy. Obviously this was pre-Reformation work. And underneath this part was the crypt, Jean told them.

She took them round the side, and, parting weeds and grasses, showed them the small iron grating, at ground level, almost corroded away, that presumably let light and air into the place. "You get in round here," she explained. "Down these steps. They made a boiler-room out of a bit of it, you see, for the heating of the church."

"Sacrilege!" Patrick exclaimed.

"Oh, well—I don't suppose the old Kincaids would mind. Keep them warm, too, though, of course, if all we hear is true, they may be warm enough where they are, as it is!"

"Haw, haw!" Roddie laughed. "Put that in your pipe an' smoke it! Aye, then—whaur's the key?"

"The keys are all just inside the vestry window. The whole place is locked up, but the vestry window opens a few inches, and you can get the keys if you know where to feel for them."

"Jings—you got it a' taped!"

"Well, it's an old haunt of mine. We sort of look after the place. Father's an elder, you see—of the combined churches. Used to be leading elder here. It's only been shut up for about ten years. It's the shortage of ministers, and rural depopulation. A pity. I was christened in this church. My people are all buried here. And . . . if I ever marry, I hope I'll be wed here!"

"Indeed. Er . . . highly creditable!" Patrick observed, thoughtfully.

"Here's the key."

The door opened creakingly, and down the steps they trooped into the dank earthy-smelling atmosphere of the crypt. Its heavy silence descended upon them like a physical thing, so that they spoke only in whispers—even the ebullient

MacGregor. Something fluttered, like cold stroking fingers, over some of their faces.

"Just bats," said Jean, gulping.

Patrick switched on his torch. Its beam showed dozens of the creatures darting and wheeling in frantic efforts to escape through door and grating, beneath the low arch of a stone-vaulted ceiling that was stained with damp and moss. There were recesses cut into the lateral walls, to contain two massive stone coffins, one cracked and broken, covered by huge stone lids in the form of recumbent effigies of knights in armour, much worn and defaced, their shields on their breasts. Resting on stone stands on the floor itself were five or six large dark chests, or caskets of metal, only one of them actually coffin-shaped, on which heraldic devices were carved and embossed, under the cobwebs and corrosion. There was a drip-drip from the stone-vaulting to a black puddle in mid-floor.

"Aw, Jings!" Tosh observed, in a whisper. "Whatna dump!"

"Nice," Roddie commented, but beneath his breath also. "Real cosy. Nae kiddin'." He stepped forward, however, to run his hand over one of the great metal caskets. "Lead!" he declared. "Solid bluidy lead! There's some cash in this lot!"

"Roddie!" Jean protested. "Those contain somebody's mortal remains!"

"Och, what o' it? They're no' needin' the lead, ony mair. An' I guess thae geysers would've been the first to swipe the lead off ither folks, if there'd been a market for it! Eh, Patrick?"

"I'm not committing myself," the other said. "We'll argue that one some other time. For the moment, this appears to be just the place for the Stone. It can stand between these coffins, as snug as you like." He swung the beam of his torch in a circuit of the place. "There you are—what did I tell you?"

Against the dripping wall, near the door, were digging implements, some containers for flowers, sundry boarding for shoring up the sides of graves, and two door-like stretchers such as he had described.

"Handles an' a'!" MacGregor pointed. "Grand! Let's go."

One of those stretchers made all the difference to the business of carrying the Stone—though it made a mighty heavy load for four men, even so. But it was possible—and Roddie Roy was no ordinary man. With only a little levelling of the wall, and no single halt for rest, they staggered with it right to the steps of the crypt. Gulping and breathless, they set it down between two of the lead coffins.

"There y'are. Nae bother," Roddie panted.

"Listen!" That was Jean.

Above their laboured breathing, the five of them could hear the sound of a car—more than one car. Hurrying out and up the steps, they stared westwards through the rain and the trees. They were in time to see the first car pass. Or, at least, to see its headlights. And the lights of three others following at uneven intervals.

"Four of them," Patrick mentioned. He glanced at his watch. "Ten past twelve."

"You werena' sae far oot, eh?"

"No. Just five minutes. They didn't waste any time."

"We'll have to wait, now, till they're gone," the girl said. "We can't risk starting up the tractor."

That was accepted. They went back into the crypt, and tidied everything up. Patrick sketched a salute towards the Stone. "Rest there . . . amongst, well, amongst your former guardians!" he said, a little self-consciously.

They locked the door, but kept the key instead of replacing it inside the vestry. Shielding the torch carefully, they sought for and endeavoured to erase any traces of their passage, in stamped down grass or footmarks. The rain, unpleasant as it was, would help here. Then they partially rebuilt the levelled wall, under the dripping trees.

It was nearly half an hour after they had gone up, that the cars were heard coming back again. There were five of them this time. The lame duckling had rejoined the flock.

"I wonder what they make of it all, now?" Patrick murmured, as they watched the five sets of lights go past. "There will have been some head-scratching about that car's breakdown, at least!"

"Perhaps they won't believe them—believe the couple's story?" Jean suggested.

"I don't think we can reckon on that. If it had been only one person, perhaps—but not with two of them. The marks of my car in that ditch will be plain for all to see, too. And broken glass."

"They're no' lookin' for us, or the Stane, the noo, onyway," Roddie pointed out, as the car-lights swept on southwards, towards Perth.

"No. Very sensible, too, in the dark and the rain."

"Which lets us get away, likewise—up to the Mains," the girl added. "Now—no arguing, Patrick. It's all settled. A bowl of hot soup, I think, is what's needed. Any objections? No? Then all aboard, gentlemen—and we'll go get it."

"Lassie—I like you!" the MacGregor observed, simply. "You got the right ideas, maist o' the time!"

Up in the cheerful farm kitchen, a pleasant place of gleaming tableware reflecting the bright firelight, white walls and dark rafters, and a stone-flagged floor, they found James Graham and the other two already comfortably installed, sitting down at a corner of the great scrubbed table to cold mutton, bread and cheese, and steaming cocoa. Hot Scotch broth, however, would do very nicely, as a second line of defence.

Their mission had been entirely uneventful, it seemed. They had driven up, about a mile, by farm tracks, on to the high ground to the south-west, known as the Muir, where what had long ago been a small rough-grazing farm had been absorbed into the Mains property. The cottage was a mere two stark gables now, but the little steading had been maintained in some state of preservation to provide storage for lime, winter feed for the cattle on the hill, and such-like. There they had left Patrick's brake in the one-time cart-shed, after removing the number-plates and anything else detachable that might aid identification. In the morning, Jakey and Alicky—who worked intermittently as a lorry driver—would see what they might be able to do about repairs.

Patrick was the only one who did not scorn the offer of an

98

old jacket or coat of the farmer's, to replace his wet one. But, the eating over and the talk flagging, even he would not hear of the suggestion of a bed upstairs—or even in the bothy for occasional field-workers that was situated behind the byre. They would all go and sleep in the hay-barn. Then there would be no question of the farmer having to admit that he had taken them under his roof; they could obviously have slipped into the barn for shelter on their own. Moreover, there were few more comfortable and desirable couches than sweet clover hay—and none of the party professed any tendency to hay fever. Though Jean protested, Patrick was adamant about this; anyway, he was not going to detach himself from the others, and obviously they could not all be put up in spare beds.

Presently, yawning, they all trooped out into the wet darkness. Patrick said goodnight to the young woman.

"Quite an evening," he said. "A bit of a disaster, really—though it all might have been so much worse. That it is not, is largely thanks to you, Jean. You and your father. You've been splendid—just magnificent."

"Rubbish! We've done no more than practically anybody else in Scotland would have done, given the chance."

"I wonder? I would like to think that, in a way. Admittedly, when the other Stone, the Westminster one, was brought back up here, a few years ago, nobody who was asked to hide it refused, or failed to measure up, or gave it away—even with Scotland Yard and all the police on its track, and the papers offering fortunes. Still . . . ah, well—we'll be seeing what Scotland's reaction to this situation will be, all too soon, I'm afraid. The thing's no longer a secret. And if the previous performance is anything to go by, the Stone of Destiny will be red-hot news, and the Press will go haywire over it. I can foresee pandemonium descending on this rural backwater of yours. I'm sorry—I really am. I feel terribly responsible."

"Oh, I don't think it will be so bad as all that. Do you expect it will be in all the papers tomorrow?"

"Not tomorrow, no. That's too soon. The story won't really break till the morning, I think. It might get into some of the evening papers, in the big cities. But the real splash will come the next day, I imagine."

"You think the Oxford people will actually tell the Press? Want them to know?"

"I think they will. They'll be mad, you know—furious at all their hopes being dashed, their plans frustrated, their research wasted. They'll look on it as *their* Stone, and they'll want it brought to light at all costs, I expect. And maximum publicity is the obvious thing. Anyway, even if they wanted to keep it quiet, this story would leak. Somebody would let it out; one of the party, or a policeman, or even somebody in one of the hotels."

"Oh, well—it can't be helped. We'll just have to try to meet the situation as it arises."

"Yes. But . . . well, I'm sorry. It won't be pleasant for you. And the last thing I would want is to be responsible for unloading any unpleasantness on you. I . . . it's just that . . . well, I feel rather the same way as our large friend Roddie MacGregor. About you, I mean."

"Dear me!" she said. "You are an impressionable lot, I must say! I'll have to watch out, obviously! Have a pleasant night in the hay, Mr Drummond!"

"The name isn't Drummond," he declared heavily. "At least . . ."

"Well, Patrick then. Goodnight, Patrick," she said.

VIII

DESPITE the fragrant embrace of the hay, they made a short night of it, and an early start in the morning. There was much to do, if they were to keep a pace or two ahead of events. Roddie and Jakey and Alicky set off for the Muir, to try to get the brake running again. Patrick wanted to keep a watch on the kirkyard, and also, if possible, on the general area round about, the road, the drive, and the vicinity of the House. Jean suggested that the church tower would make as good a look-out post as any, for from its parapet it was possible to see a good distance both up and down the road, and certainly as far as the lodge gates.

The rain had stopped, and in the quiet grey morning, with the mists only reluctantly beginning to rise from the great hills to north and west, Patrick and the two youths took their devious and inconspicuous way down, by hedges and broken ground, to the valley of the Kincaid Water, and so to the road. All was clear; there did not seem to be a single track of tyres on the slowly drying surface. They approached the church as previously, and were glad to note that, apart from the tractor's tracks in the field itself, there were no noticeable signs of their nocturnal activities. In daylight, they found that by jumping on to a heap of stones, presumably accumulated during gravedigging activities, and so on to a moss-grown path, they could save any tell-tale trampling of long grasses.

The tower had its own door, and the key was amongst those to be found inside the vestry window. Shutting the door behind them, the trio climbed the worn ancient steps of a twisting corkscrew stairway, lit through tiny unglazed slits, to the stone-flagged parapet walk. Within this the lichened roof rose steeply. There was ample cover for an individual to hide behind the crenellated parapet, so long as he knelt or crouched.

101

The view, though slightly obscured by trees, was reasonably extensive. They could see for perhaps a mile southwards intermittent patches of the road, in the Perth direction. Northwards was not so clear, but the lodge gates to Kincaid House were visible, and even one short stretch of the climbing drive beyond.

Leaving Tosh and the Teddy-boy, who, it seemed, rejoiced in the title of The Pluke, on watch here, with fairly definite instructions, Patrick, after a glance into the crypt to see that all was well there, slipped back across the road and into the trees at the other side. It was in here that the three Glasgow motorcycles were hidden, and he wanted to assure himself that they were not likely to be discovered. He found them fairly well camouflaged, but decided that it probably would be wise to have them shifted soon to somewhere more remote. Then he moved on to the Kincaid Water again. He followed the stream up only a short distance before striking off to the right, through woodland. In a few moments he was wet through from undergrowth and dripping branches.

He reached the drive to the House a couple of hundred yards below the spot of the previous night's mishap. Carefully assuring himself that there was nobody about, he examined the area. There could be no hiding the place where his car had taken its plunge; but at least there was nothing to identify anybody, nothing to provide any more information than the bearded student could already supply—at least, not that Patrick could perceive. He saw nothing that he might usefully do to improve the situation.

In cover, skirting the drive all the way, he moved on, up to the House, the stable-yard, the walled garden. All seemed to be deserted, just as they had been before—save that the map-case was gone from inside the doocot. There was nothing else to remark.

The man was returning to the drive when he heard the sound of cars. Promptly he hid himself in the shrubbery. But soon the noise ceased. Clearly the cars had stopped at the scene of last night's encounter.

Keeping well within the trees, Patrick worked his way

down. The bends in that drive would force him to go fairly close before he could see what went on. Actually he heard voices before he saw anything. Warned, he crept on with enhanced caution. Parting the leafage in front of him, he peered out.

There were three cars this time—and the first two were large and black and official-looking. Eight people were grouped about, five of them policemen—an inspector, a sergeant, and three constables. Of the remaining three, one was Dr Lister, one was the bearded Michael, and the third was a middle-aged stranger.

The policemen were busy, two constables using a measuring-tape, the inspector poking about with a walking-stick, and the sergeant writing in the inevitable black notebook. They seemed stolid and deliberate compared with the others, who were talking volubly and gesticulating.

Patrick had not been watching for long when another and smaller car came up. A young man got out, dressed in sports jacket, checked shirt, and corduroys, under a trench-coat that hung open. Though he might have been another student, it did not require the notebook and pencil that he produced almost automatically to inform the watcher that here was the Fourth Estate—every casually confident line of him shouted Press. Patrick quickly stepped back from his peep-hole. He had seen enough.

He made his way circumspectly back to the church—and had to wait in hiding for two cars, with Edinburgh and Glasgow number-plates, to pass, before he could cross the road unseen, their drivers proceeding slowly, and peering out from side to side as they went. This quiet by-road was growing popular.

Up on the church tower again, he related to Tosh and The Pluke what he had seen, and heard their report that seven cars had actually gone up the road, every one turning in at the lodge gates. None had shown any interest in the church area, however. There had been no traffic in the other direction.

All forenoon they waited up in their eyrie. The two youths slept most of the time—and, once the sun broke through and

103

dried his clothing, Patrick had some difficulty in keeping his own eyes consistently open. However, his ears did not fail him, and he believed that he did not miss anything of the frequent comings and goings of motor-cars that provided the entire interest of the morning. There was plenty of that.

Jean Graham arrived in the early afternoon, bearing food and a grave face. She had been up at the Muir first, she told them, and the trio up there were very gloomy about the shooting-brake. It looked as though an entire new component would be needed. Not only was the propeller-shaft useless, but the whole back axle assembly appeared to be damaged. They were working away at it, but were doubtful about how much they could achieve. But that was not the worst of it. Their business had got on to the radio—on the One O'clock News. It had been a fairly brief but badly garbled story— Jean had been up at the Muir when it came on, but her father had heard it. It said that a relic, claimed by some to be the true Stone of Scone, had been stolen from Kincaid House, near Scone, after it had been found there by the Oxford Society whose research had brought it to light. The identity of the thieves was not known, though the police were understood to be acting on certain information received. The announcement had ended by declaring that a double day-and-night watch was being put on the genuine Coronation Stone in Westminster Abbey, as a precaution.

"Well, I'm damned!" Patrick exclaimed. "Of all the utter balderdash! That will be London, of course? At one o'clock? Not the Scottish Home Service?"

"I suppose so. But it's bad. So utterly unfair."

"Whit did ye expect?" Tosh demanded.

"Oh, I don't know. But nothing so, so foolish, inaccurate, and one-sided as that, at any rate!" she replied. "What do you think that bit means, Patrick, about the police acting on information received?"

"Just bluff, I should say. What information can they have received, as yet? They're still at the measuring-tape and notebook stage." And he told her what he had seen up on the drive.

But Jean remained preoccupied with the radio announcement. It seemed to have an almost psychological effect on her. No doubt, like so many others, she had been conditioned during long years to accept what came over the ether, in the coolly cultured and scarcely human voices of the News Bulletin announcers, as authoritative, impartial, beyond question. To find herself at odds with this oracle upset her.

Patrick, however, was much more concerned about her news of his brake. If it was going to prove difficult or impossible to repair, they were presented with a serious two-fold problem. Firstly, they would have to find alternative means of transporting the Stone out of this danger area; and secondly, the disabled brake itself could be a menace to their security, if found, since it was an unusual type of vehicle—a traditional varnished timber shooting-brake body grafted on to a fairly mature but powerful Humber chassis—and could be identified by the man Michael.

Soon after the girl's departure, he left the youths to their unexciting vigil, and made his way up to the high ground behind the Mains, where he arrived at the steading of the former hill-farm. He found Roddie and his two colleagues smeared to the elbows in oil and dirt, with the brake raised up on a variety of improvised jacks, in the one-time cart-shed, surrounded by bits and pieces. They were far from cheerful. Despite difficult working conditions and inadequate tools, they had managed to get the back axle removed and dismembered, and the entire transmission system taken down. They pointed out in the accusatory fashion beloved of all mechanics, where steel and machinery had given, bent, and fractured, under the fierce impact of the drop into that ditch with all the Stone's great weight thrown in. Some leaves of the rear springing were gone, also—but that was of minor importance. It seemed as though there was nothing for it but to try to get new parts to replace the damaged ones, they said.

"Where?" Patrick demanded. "Where—in time to be of any use?"

MacGregor shrugged. "Glesgy," he said. "We could ay try

105

roond the dumps. Roond the scrap-yairds. For an auld Humber model, the likes o' this."

"What chance is there of finding such a thing?"

"I dinna ken that. There was plenties o' thae models aboot, one time. The Airmy used them for staff-cars, you'll mind. But it might take time to find, right enough."

"A waste o' time, tae!" Jakey opined, wiping his hands on the seat of his trousers. "You could go days at it. Better to get anither car, a' thegither."

"It isn't so easy as that," Patrick pointed out. "There's not many cars would hold that Stone, for one thing. Mr Graham offered the use of his—but the Stone would neither go inside nor in the boot. That would apply in most normal cars—apart altogether from the weight. It would have to be a van, or a pick-up, of some sort. And how are we going to get our hands on such a thing—without bringing somebody else into the business? And remember, the police are in the game now. We'd have to ask whoever owned it to become an accomplice in a felony, ask him to put himself straight into serious trouble with the police. We can't do that."

"Maybe we could lift a van? Pinch it?" Roddie suggested. "Jist for a wee whilie. One night would maybe do the job. That would keep the owner in the clear."

"And have the police searching for a stolen van, as well as everything else? No, thank you."

"I could maybe bring oot my lorry? Frae Glesgy," Alicky Shand proposed. "It'd shift it, a'right."

"It's not your own lorry, is it?"

"Hell, no! It belongs to the Cooper-ative."

"And what would *they* say, if you were caught using it? After all, to bring a lorry here from Glasgow, do what we had to do, and then return it, would take a long time—even if everything went well. More than any one night, certainly. It would be bound to be missed."

"Och, aye. They'd jist gi'e me the sack, likely. But I've had the sack afore, an' no' deed o' it!"

"No, thank you," Patrick said definitely. "You can wash that one out, too. And are you forgetting that we can't just

106

leave this brake here to be discovered? This place is remote enough—but it's pretty obvious, too. If there was any real searching started, I don't see it escaping. And then, not only might they trace its ownership, but it would implicate the Grahams. Also, they would know that the Stone was still in the vicinity, somewhere."

Silence greeted that, a silence that was maintained for some time.

It was Patrick who answered his own problem, at length. "Rather than have all that happen, I'd prefer that we loaded the Stone aboard again, and *towed* the brake away from here, behind a tractor. At night. Taking the risk of being caught. We'd have to pretend to steal Mr Graham's tractor. We mightn't get as far as upper Glen Almond—but if we could get the thing out of this area, that would be something."

"You reckon it's goin' to get sort o' hot, here?"

"I think it's hot now—but it will get much hotter! Once the Press really get their teeth into this. It's them I'm worried about, more than the police."

"Aye, then—maybe you're right. Maybe that's the best way."

"Say—you guys forgettin' hoo long it'll take to put a' this lot thegither again?" Jakey squeaked. "We been a' these 'oors takin' it doon. Wi'oot a workshop an' right tools, we'll no' put it back ony quicker, I tell you. You'll no' hae this lot runnin' on wheels till the morn, see."

"Oh. Umm. You sure of that?"

"Sure I'm sure. What d'you take us for? It's the Lord Goad works the miracles—no' me!"

There seemed to be no answer to that. Jakey no doubt was a reasonably competent mechanic, but without proper facilities and equally skilled assistance, he was terribly handicapped. Moreover, he had already been working solidly for seven or eight hours. And there was no light in this semi-ruinous building.

Patrick shrugged, and sighed. "Well, we'll just have to do the best we can. Be as quick as we can. I don't see anything else for it. And, look—I'm a bit worried about those

motorcycles of yours. I think you'll have to shift them somewhere safer. Pretty soon . . ."

Patrick, finding himself to be of little use up at the Muir,
went down to the Mains eventually to hear the Six O'clock
News. He was considerably shaken to discover, at the farmhouse, that two newspapermen had already been there. Jean
had managed to avoid them, leaving them to her father
to deal with. They had been very pressing, asking innumerable questions. They had wanted to know whether Mr
Graham or any of his people knew anything of the extraordinary happenings of the previous night? Whether they had
seen any suspicious-looking strangers about? Whether there
were any rumours circulating locally? Whether they had
known previously about this alternative Stone of Destiny?
And, significantly, how they felt about the whole business—
especially about an English party searching for this Stone,
and about its destination, once found. James Graham, it
seemed, had stalled as best he could, playing the dullard, and
only haltingly conceded that he thought it a little strange for
Englishmen to be involved at all. He had allowed himself the
hope that, when it was found, the Stone would perhaps be
permitted to remain at Scone, where it belonged—possibly in
the parish church there. What the reporters would make of
all that, of course, the farmer had no idea.

Patrick Kincaid, on the other hand, who had some knowledge of the Press and Pressmen, *had* a fairly shrewd idea.

On the radio, the BBC News from London gave the same
brief announcement as at midday. But in the Scottish News
that followed at 6.15 there was some amplification. Giving
the item first place, it said that the Oxford Society had
uncovered ancient documents which led them to believe that
the Stone taken south by Edward the First of England was not
in fact the true Coronation Stone of Scotland, and that the
original relic had remained buried in the dovecot of Kincaid,
near Perth, where it had been taken from Scone and interred
for safety during the War of Independence seven hundred years
ago. Whether this was so or not remained open to question,

108

but excavations had been going on at the site. The Society's information, however, appeared to have been tapped by unauthorised persons, and a raid had been made on the site at Kincaid after work had ceased for the night yesterday. It seemed that the offenders had been very well informed as to the progress of the work, for they had struck just when all the hard labour was done and the Stone was about to be uncovered. They had apparently dug it up themselves, and were in process of removing it in a station-wagon type of car when they were intercepted by two of the expedition members who had returned for an item of equipment. In trying to escape, the culprits had backed the station-wagon into a ditch, and it was believed, seriously damaged the vehicle. There had been an altercation, and Mr Michael Dumont, a third-year classics student, with a companion, had clearly seen the stolen Stone in their car's headlights. They described it as large, dark, ornate and obviously very heavy. They had hurried to get help from Perth, but by the time that they had returned both station-wagon and Stone were gone. The authorities believed, however, that the relic and the vehicle were probably still in the Kincaid vicinity, for experts who had examined the scene of the accident were confident that serious damage could scarcely have been avoided to the absconding vehicle, owing to the depth of the drop and the weight being carried. There was much broken glass left lying, and signs which indicated that the car had had to be towed away. In consequence, all roads in the vicinity were being watched, and extra police were being brought in from other areas. Owing to the constitutional and possibly political implications that might be involved in the theft, the Scottish Office in Edinburgh and the Home Department in London were concerned, and were being kept informed. Any members of the public, or local residents, who had information that might prove of value to the police, were requested to communicate with the Chief Constable of Perthshire, or any local police station.

As James Graham switched off the radio-set, the three listeners eyed each other directly, grimly. Patrick's breath came out in a long sigh.

"I don't like the sound of that!" he said. "I don't like it, at all."

"It's horrible! Disgusting!" the girl cried. "So biased. So untrue. I mean, in the way it puts it all. Making thieves and cheats and criminals of us!"

"It's not good," her father admitted. "I don't like that bit about the Scottish Office and the Home Department. What's the Home Department, in London, got to do with it, anyway?"

"They were the villains of the piece last time—when those boys took the other Stone from Westminster."

"Yes—but then they had some excuse. For being involved, I mean, not for the way that they acted. That Stone was taken from London, after all—whatever the merits of it being there. But this time they've no call to interfere, at all."

"I suppose their attitude will be that anything that affects the Crown concerns them. And this does, to some extent. This Stone makes the one at Westminster, the one they've been crowning the kings on there for centuries, a dud. The powers-that-be, down there, aren't going to like that!"

"But they can't do anything about it," Jean objected. "It's there. A fact. They can like it or lump it! What could they do?"

"They could play down the whole thing. Pooh-pooh it. Refuse to give it official recognition. Declare *our* Stone to be the fake! But much more likely, I'd imagine, would be for them just to come up and grab it, one way or another, and take it down to Westminster. Either substitute it for the other one, or install it side-by-side. So as to be safe. If they get half a chance." Patrick shook his head. "But I've recognised that, all along. That's the main reason why I've acted as I have done. That's not what worries me about this broadcast—it's the announcement that all the roads are watched. That they realise that my car must be damaged, and that we're probably trapped in this area. That's really serious. Somebody's smarter than I gave them credit for!"

"Yes. It puts us in rather a spot, doesn't it," the older man acceded, quietly.

110

"What are we going to do now, Patrick?" the young woman demanded. "There must be *something* that we can do?"

"I suppose so, yes. But at the moment I can't think of a thing! And I don't imagine we've got long, either. They're not going to content themselves with just watching the roads. If they think that it's still hereabouts, they're going to start searching for that Stone, systematically. And the church—isolated, unused, and with an underground crypt—is just asking to be searched! It was ideal so long as there was no deliberate local search. But now . . ."

"We'll have to use our wits—that's apparent," James Graham said, puffing at his pipe. "I wonder?" He raised one grizzled eyebrow. "D'you think that we could smuggle it out under a load of hay, say? Behind a tractor?"

"That's an idea . . ."

"You'd never get away with it," Patrick asserted. "It's too obvious. You might get off without being searched in the neighbourhood of your own farm, here. But farther afield it would be suspect, right away. Trailer-loads of hay are just not carted about on long journeys."

"A cattle-float?" Jean suggested. "A big lorry loaded with cattle, and the Stone in the middle?"

"I'm afraid that's open to the same objections. With a police watch on the roads, those are just the sort of things that would be stopped and searched, surely? A heavy lump of stone that size isn't an easy thing to hide, on a vehicle. Most vehicles just wouldn't take it. So that searchers would be able to concentrate on those that could."

"It's being stuck to the roads that's the trouble," James Graham said. "If we could just keep off the roads."

"With the weight we've got to carry, we've little option. You know what it was like with the slype! We might possibly get it so far, over farm-tracks and by-ways, using a tractor and trailer—but the noise of a tractor by night would be hopeless. I mean, in covering any distance."

"I'm afraid so. And by day it wouldn't . . ."

"Quiet! Listen!" Jean interrupted. "Did you hear anything?

111

A car? I thought I heard . . ." She stopped. Plainly there came the sound of a car's brakes being applied. Jumping up, the girl ran to the window that faced into the yard. "It's the police!" she cried.

"Damn and confound them!" Patrick swore.

"Keep calm," James Graham advised, mildly. "No need for excitement. Gently does it."

His daughter had her own way of interpreting that. Hurrying over to Patrick, she grabbed him by the arm, and pulled him after her across the kitchen, to an inner door which she flung open. "In there," she directed, giving him a push. "And keep quiet. You mustn't be found here."

The man found himself stumbling down two steps, into a cool, stone-floored, whitewashed dairy, with the door closing behind him. It was a narrow chamber, with pails and bowls of milk on stone shelves, two sides of bacon hanging from hooks in the ceiling, a small window in the far wall, and no other exit. He sat down on the step.

He heard Jean and her father whispering, and then a knocking on the outer door. He heard the girl welcoming the visitors with a polite lack of enthusiasm, James Graham move to the door, and give a quiet greeting and an invitation to come inside. Two heavy sets of feet accepted. There occurred a sequence of ayes and uh-huhs, and a discussion on the weather developed out of it. A little small drink was suggested, sighed over, and regretfully declined.

"This is Sergeant Mackay, from Headquarters, Mr Graham," a voice introduced, almost apologetically. "He's just making a few enquiries, round about."

"Oh, yes?"

"About this Stone of Destiny affair, sir, just. A bad business it is—a bad bad business. Och, yes." The sergeant sounded sepulchral and very Highland.

"I should say it is! I've already had two reporters wasting a lot of my time this afternoon, over it."

"Is that a fact, sir? Och, I'm sorry about that. They're right borachs, the reporters. Nosey, as you might say. Och, but they have their job to be doing too, in a kind of a way,

I suppose. But myself, I'll not be wasting much of your time at all, Mr Graham."

"You're welcome, Sergeant. Sit down. Have a cigarette—if that's permitted? A cigarette, Constable? We've just been listening to all that nonsense on the radio. It all sounds highly improbable, to me."

"Improbable, yes. That is the word, just, Mr Graham. Och, the improbability of it all is just sticking out all round, as you might say. You wouldn't have any information that would be of help to us, would you now, sir?"

"I'm afraid not. Nothing that occurs to me, no. If there's anything in it at all—which I very much doubt—it all seems to have been confined to the other side of the river."

"Just that. You wouldn't have been seeing any strangers about?"

"Oh, plenty of them. But at a distance, that's not much of a help, is it? Over there, in the estate, the place has just been swarming with strangers these last two days. These Oxford people, I take it. Crawling all over the place. My grazing, too. I rent it. My daughter had a word with some of them, yesterday."

"Yes." Jean's confirmation was brief.

"Just that. Och, very nice ladies and gentlemen they are, too. But English—och, very English, of course."

"Quite. They can't really help that, I suppose."

"No, no. That is so. You will be after keeping your tractors well locked up at nights, Mr Graham, I'm quite sure? Och, yes."

"Tractors? No—we don't actually lock them up, Sergeant. They usually just stand in the cart-shed. We've three of them. But none of them are missing, if that's what you mean."

"Just so. Och, it's not to be expected, at all. And man, it wouldn't be like the thing for any borach just to be taking a loan of one, as you might say? Dearie me—you'd be hearing it, right enough. A noisy-like thing like a tractor! No, no." The sergeant sounded almost shocked at his own suggestion.

"Not necessarily," the farmer answered conversationally. "One's a noisy brute, but the other two are quiet enough. It

113

would depend on the way of the wind, and whether there were any noises going on in the house. The wireless, for instance. But you're not seriously suggesting that my tractors have been used without my knowledge, are you?"

"Mercy on us—not at all, Mr Graham! Would that be likely, now?"

"I'd say about as likely as the entire silly business! To tell you the truth, Sergeant," James Graham said confidentially. "Between you and me and the gate-post, I wonder at your superiors taking this whole affair seriously enough to send an intelligent man like yourself round enquiring into a fairy-tale of this sort. I do so."

"Och, Mr Graham—maybe you've got the right end of the stick there! A fairy-tale, just. You think it's a fairy-tale, then?"

"It certainly sounds like it, doesn't it? The whole thing. At least, what came over the radio. That, or the invention of a disordered mind. An irresponsible mind, perhaps. As I say, I'm surprised at the police taking it all seriously. All you've got to go on, so far as I can gather, that this Stone so much as exists, is the statement of one young student that he's seen it. On a dark night. Inside a car—somebody else's car. Dear me, it seems slender evidence to have built up all this excitement on, if you'll excuse my saying so, Sergeant."

"Of course, of course, Mr Graham. Slender is right, yes. Sort of corroborated it was, of course, in a kind of a way."

"Only by a slip of a girl—who'd be hardly likely to contradict her boyfriend!"

"Aye, aye. Just that. As you say, Mr Graham. A slip of a girl, indeed yes. You have the rights of it there." The sergeant sounded almost admiring. "Aye, you're the cute one to be knowing that it was a slip of a girl, just, that was with the student-man that time . . . when it wasn't saying so on the wireless, at all at all!"

In the dairy, Patrick bit his lip. That was a bad slip. The farmer's pause was momentary, barely noticeable. Then he went on, still in that calm reflective voice of his.

"It didn't actually say it was a girl, admittedly, on the wireless. But you and I know perfectly well, Sergeant, that

114

when they give only one man's name, and refer to him being accompanied by a companion, then it is to be inferred that that companion was a woman. And since the man was young, and a student, and he was taking the companion for a lonely country drive at night, it can be assumed that she was young. Am I not right? It was a girl, wasn't it?"

Patrick distinctly heard a fluttering sigh of relief from near at hand. Jean must be standing close to his door. "Surely, surely, sir. Och, there's no flies on you, Mr Graham—not a one! You're not that far out, either."

A knocking sounded clearly at the outer door. With it, the listener once again heard Jean's tell-tale breath, swiftly in-drawn this time. He cursed, to himself. If this was any of the Gregorach!

In the room beyond there was the faintest pause, and then James Graham spoke easily. "Somebody at the door, I think, Jean. It'll be Jock, likely. Tell him I'm busy just now. He'll find a bundle of new sacks in the stable. I'll see him later. These gentlemen won't be that long, I'm sure?"

"Och, no, Mr Graham—not at all." There was the scrape of chairs pushed back.

"All right." Jean's voice was not easy, like her father's, but tight, clipped-sounding. She walked quickly over to the outer door.

The farmer went on talking, unhurriedly, saying that he would have thought that Oxford University folk would have had more to do than to come away up here on a wild-goose chase of this sort, poking into something that didn't concern them—even if there was anything in it, at all.

Patrick heard only a faint murmuring at the other door, and then the girl's footsteps again, less tense now, somehow.

"Just a couple of tinkers. Wanting some milk," she declared—and the hiding man hoped that the relief in her voice did not sound so apparent to the policemen as to himself. He realised that she was coming into the dairy, and he retreated into a corner where he would be hidden behind the door. Jean came in, and down the steps, her eyes busy. She seemed about to shut the door behind her, and then

115

changed her mind, leaving it wide, and the man safely at the back of it. She carried a small battered and smoke-blackened pitcher, which she filled from a churn with rich yellow milk. She also picked up a couple of eggs from a great bowl of them. As she reached the doorway, her grey eyes sought Patrick's, met them and held for a moment. Then she went out, and the door closed behind her.

"It pays to keep in with the tinkers," he heard her father saying.

" 'Deed, aye—they're the boys!" the sergeant agreed. "Better give them an egg than have them take two."

"Maybe you could do with an egg yourself, Sergeant? And you, Constable?"

"Och, another time, Mr Graham. That would be nice, yes. We'll just be getting along now, and giving you some peace. Och, you've been real helpful—eh, Constable! Fairy-tales, eh? Just that. I'm not that much of a one for fairy-tales my own self! And maybe you're not that far out, too, about these English folk having no kind of a right to be taking this Stone, at all, at all!"

"I didn't say that, Sergeant, by the way," James Graham mentioned gently.

"Did you not, then?" the other said innocently. "Och, my mistake, Mr Graham. Of course not. Goodness me, no! Well, goodnight then, sir. Goodnight, Miss. I'm sorry to be after troubling you about such a silly business. I'll be up again, mind, one time—about the eggs. Goodnight to you, sir."

"Aye. Goodnight, Mr Graham."

"You're welcome. Goodnight."

There was quite a long silence in that pleasant kitchen as they listened to the powerful police car start up and go off down the farm road. Patrick, emerged from his refuge, broke in with a whistle.

"Whe-e-ew! Quite a narrow squeak!" he commented. "In fact, one or two narrow squeaks."

"I nearly died that time when the tinkers came to the door," Jean confessed, with a rush. "I saw visions of Roddie and his Glasgow friends marching in, all covered with axle-grease!"

"Roddie wouldn't have knocked!" Patrick assured. "But it was a sticky moment, sure enough. Though not so bad as when they jumped on you, sir, over that Oxford girl that the BBC hadn't mentioned!"

"Yes—that was a bad mistake. Very foolish of me," James Graham admitted. "I put my foot in it, there."

"You got out of it most adroitly, for all that. I thought, in fact, that the way you handled those policemen was masterly altogether, Mr Graham. Brilliant. You turned every question beautifully—without ever telling an untruth either! You had them held, all the way. Though, mind you—I don't think that sergeant was quite so daft as he sounded!"

"Daft! I'm sure he wasn't," the girl declared. "He gave me the creeps!"

"No, he wasn't daft, that one," her father agreed. "I'd say that he was a pretty astute man, in fact—like a lot of Highland men. He knew just what he was doing, I imagine—and I don't for a moment suppose that I pulled much wool over his eyes, either." The farmer pinched his chin thoughtfully. "I don't think that I was half so clever, Mr Drummond, as that one let me seem to be. I may be wrong, but I've a feeling that he could have tripped me up any time that he wanted."

"You mean . . . ? But why should he let you get away with anything?"

The other shrugged. "I may be mistaken, of course. But that's my impression. After all, he's a Scot himself, the same Sergeant Mackay—just as much a Scot, presumably, as you or I, Mr Drummond! He may have his own ways of showing it! He'll do his duty, of course, that one—but it's just possible that he may have his own ideas as to where the line of duty is drawn! But, as I say, I may be wrong."

Patrick Kincaid was looking out of the window. "That is an interesting thought, you know," he said slowly. "If the police should turn out to be not much more keen than we are on this Stone coming to light . . . then things might take on a rather different complexion, as far as we're concerned!"

"Perhaps. But it's not a thing you could rely on, I'd say," the older man cautioned. "All the police aren't likely to be

117

the same—like other folks. And I think you can accept that they'll do their duty. They have to. But you might be given a chance, here and there—given the benefit of the doubt, you know."

"Yes. I think that's possible. I heard a few stories about the police up here, during the last affair—when the Westminster Stone was being hunted. I heard it said that sometimes the Scotland Yard gentry didn't get quite as much co-operation as they'd have liked. In a thing of this sort . . ."

"In a thing of this sort, I think you'd be well to be warned, just the same—warned not to look for favours, lad. Just as the sergeant there warned me!" James Graham said.

"But *did* he warn you, Father?" Jean asked. "I didn't hear that."

"Of course he did, girl. That bit about coming back for the eggs. That was a perfectly clear warning, to me. That I'd better watch my step. That he'd be watching me. That he'd be back."

"Oh, dear!" his daughter exclaimed. "I hadn't realised that."

"Umm," Patrick Kincaid said. "I see."

IX

MORE cover-conscious than ever, now, Patrick made his wary, almost stealthy, way down to Kincaid Church. He had to knock both loud and long on the tower door, locked from the inside as it was, before he could gain admittance; obviously both young Glaswegians had been fast asleep. Not that he could blame them for that; their vigil must have been boring in the extreme. They informed him, somewhat grumpily, that apart from a fair amount of traffic in cars, there had been only two occasions when any interest had been aroused. Once, in mid-afternoon, when a policeman had ridden to the gate on a motorcycle, and come in to make a quick survey of the church and graveyard, trying the handles of all doors; and later, when two strolling individuals whom they took to be Pressmen, came from a car to poke around a bit. None apparently had noticed the rusty iron grating that indicated the presence of the crypt, hidden as it was at ground level by long grasses, nor had suspicious glances been directed upwards at the church tower. Patrick forbore to point out that there might have been other visitors during the watch's less wakeful moments.

Taking over duty himself, he told the other two, on their way back to the farmhouse, to wheel the three motorcycles deeper into hiding somewhere—not risking the noise of starting up the engines, of course.

Alone, in his lofty perch, Patrick sought to grapple with his problems. It seemed fairly clear that he must write off his car. With the roads watched, a towed shooting-brake with broken windows would just cry aloud its presence. But unfortunately, more than mere writing off was necessary; the wreck must not be found on James Graham's property. Again there was the difficulty that the Mains' tractors could at best only operate within a short distance and on, as it were, internal lines of communication. What alternative transport they could call upon, he just could not think, cudgel his brains as he would. It looked very much as though, after all their effort, they would be forced to leave the Stone somewhere hereabouts, and scatter—at least, for the time being. Even so, the difficulties would be serious; to try to ensure that the Stone was not found, and to avoid implicating the Grahams.

If these were the longer-term problems, the pressing short term one was, what to do with the Stone that night? Whether to shift it, or not? How safe was it here—remembering always that if they did not move it tonight, it would have to remain in the crypt all tomorrow, since it obviously could not be removed in daylight? Was the church likely to be thoroughly searched—not just casually glanced at, as apparently this policeman had done? For that matter, was there likely to be anywhere better, more secure, near at hand? All these and other questions chased themselves round and round Patrick's tired head as the sun sank over those green rolling uplands, with little in the way of solutions presenting themselves. With the dusk falling, and nothing vital decided, the man thought that he might safely terminate his watch, and return to the Mains. Apart from a police motorcyclist who passed back or forward along the road at approximately hourly intervals, and who was clearly on patrol, there had been nothing to report.

Patrick was not back at the farmhouse for more than a few minutes before Roddie Roy and the mechanics arrived. Depression was not a term that had any real application to the MacGregor's character, but he now owned to a mood of frustration and irritation. He admitted to being cheesed off, in fact. They had not been able to get the brake fully re-assembled before the light gave out—indeed there seemed to be some doubt about whether they were going to be able to get it wholly put together again at all, without proper tools. The whole sanguinary business was a wash-out, he declared— hotly rather than dolefully.

His temperature mounted quite notably as he listened to details of the BBC News, the police visit, and the word of the watch on the roads.

"My Goad!" he burst out, not waiting for Patrick to finish. "If it's a bluidy fight they're wantin', they'll get it! Jings, aye! I'll fetch a bunch o' guys oot frae Glesgy that'll knock the daylights oot o' thae polis! I will so!"

"No—not that! Whatever the solution to all this may be—that's not it!" Patrick declared wearily. "That would be just putting an extra weapon into London's hands."

"I agree," James Graham nodded.

"Kid gloves again, eh?" Roddie growled. But he let it go. "What do *you* reckon to dae, then?" he demanded.

"I must admit I'm at a bit of a loss," Patrick conceded. "It's the watch on these roads that's the big trouble. If we knew how effective, how complete it was . . . ? There's a lot of minor roads around here. The map shows a whole network of secondary roads, by-ways, and farm tracks. I suppose it does everywhere, in agricultural country. I was looking at the Ordnance Survey Map while I was waiting, down there. Surely they can't have them all watched, all the way? That would take an army of men."

"The trouble is, the crossroads," the farmer pointed out. "They can leave great stretches unguarded, so long as they watch the crossroads and junctions. Especially those that link up with the highways that lead out of the district. The others don't matter much, so long as you're trapped inside. It doesn't matter how much fish swim around *inside* the net, if they can't get out!"

"No—I suppose not."

"If you boiled it all down, I daresay you'd find that only about half a dozen strategically-placed road-blocks would serve to keep you bottled up in this area. That is, of course, if you are actually confined to the roads . . ."

James Graham's voice faded as his daughter made an entrance. She had not been in evidence since Patrick's return. Now she came into the kitchen, from upstairs, transformed. Gone the jeans and shirts, the overalls and jumpers. She wore instead an off-the-shoulder short evening-gown in crisp cotton, jet black splashed with large yellow roses, neat-waisted, full-skirted, with, casually thrown across her bare shoulders, a

121

stole of yellow silk. Her fair hair was groomed and gleaming, and make-up discreetly emphasised the excellence of her features. The rustle of stiffened petticoats, and the faintest waft of perfume, seemed to change the entire atmosphere of that workaday kitchen.

The girl's appearance came almost as a physical shock to Patrick Kincaid. And not only to him, judging by the gasps, exclamations and whistles of authentic Glasgow origin. Hitherto, of course, he had not failed to realise that she was attractive and good-looking. But now, suddenly, it hit him squarely that she was a very lovely young woman. And very *much* woman, into the bargain.

It was perhaps strange that, though Patrick was certainly no less appreciative of feminine quality and beauty than the next man, Jean Graham's metamorphosis before him there, produced no elation in him. The reverse, rather. He had grown to accept her as a colleague and companion, a useful ally and loyal fellow-conspirator—personable, comely, yes, and stimulating therefore. But this manifestation of sheer, potent, and dangerous femininity, seemed subtly but irrevocably to change everything. This was a new force to be reckoned with, somehow, and not one that any man could take for granted, a new and disturbing influence. One extra problem—and hadn't he sufficient problems on his mind already?

There was, perhaps, another aspect of the matter altogether, intimated in this transformation, that the man did not consciously acknowledge to himself, at all.

"Jings—whatna smasher!" Roddie Roy cried. "You hittin' the Town, Jeannie? Gi'en it big licks, the night? Wantin' company? You'll need a decent sort o' a figure o' a man to go wi' that ootfit!"

Jean laughed—and even her laughter was different, it seemed, silvery, tinkling, provocative. And well might she laugh, for the prospect, the contrast presented by this gallant offerer and her immaculate self was fantastic enough to be ludicrous. Though it might be said, admittedly, that they were almost equally eye-catching. The big fellow was still in his stained and ragged kilt, with his torn and buttonless khaki shirt hanging loose and open, his great hobnailed boots covered with mud, and all the bare red-furred brawn of him damp with sweat and smeared with oil. They all laughed. Except Patrick Kincaid, that is.

"I am going to town, Roddie—to Perth, anyway," the girl said. "To the monthly Young Farmers' Club hop. But . . . I'm afraid somebody's coming for me. Too bad! Another time, perhaps? Which reminds me—Bill usually comes for me about quarter-to-ten. That is, in about ten minutes. It might be sensible, save a lot of explaining and so on, if, well, if he didn't walk in on you all, here. I could meet him outside, of course. But it might look funny."

"Of course!" Patrick jumped up. "Out to the barn, everybody. Your, er, friend isn't likely to come wandering round there, is he?" That was rather abrupt.

"Oh, no. Of course not. Look—I'm not failing anybody, going off like this tonight, am I? Not falling down on the job?" she asked. "There's nothing vital on the boards tonight, is there? This is just a monthly dance that we run, for funds and to keep the members together during the summer. I'm on the Committee. Bill Ogilvie always calls for me. It might have looked funny to have put him off—when everybody knows I'm at home, and well."

"Quite. Naturally. We've interfered with your, your private life quite sufficiently as it is," Patrick asserted. "I hope you have a very enjoyable evening." He sounded almost as though he doubted that, however. "Come on, you fellows—time we were out of here. We don't want any more complications." And he led the way out by the back door.

"Say," Roddie suggested, as he passed the girl. "Get the lucky guy to fetch you the long way hame, Jeannie, in his car! Roond aboot, sort o'. He'll enjoy it fine! An' maybe you could spare a bit glance, noo an' again, to note whaur the dam' polis hae their road-blocks, see? No' to spoil onythin' for yoursel', mind!" The giant's good humour was completely restored, most evidently.

"Don't be absurd, MacGregor!" Patrick threw back sourly over his shoulder. "Hurry up."

123

"I'll see what I can do, Roddie," Jean promised. "And Bill's really very amenable!"

James Graham followed the others over to the hay-shed, presently, with a pitcher of milky cocoa and further provisions.

"You're not planning any move tonight, are you?" he wondered.

"We've been discussing that," Patrick informed. "About the Stone itself, nobody's very sure. I think the general concensus of opinion is to leave it where it is, just now."

"To hell wi' that!" Roddie denied. "That's *your* opinion, maybe. Me, I say grab one o' your tractors an' trailers, Mister. Say we pinched them, if you like. Load the Stane aboard, an' belt the hell oot o' here! Straight along the road to this Glen Almond place. One guy drivin', twa guardin' him on the tractor, an' three on motorbikes bashin' a way through for them. Breenge right along, I say, an' to hell wi' the polis! They canna be thick every place, an' there's six o' us. We'll can knock them flat, jist! An' once we're into yon hills, we've got them licked!"

"Your methods, MacGregor, are refreshing, at least!" the farmer acknowledged.

"But quite out of the question," Patrick added, heavily. "I've said from the start that that sort of violence is out—except possibly as a last desperate resort. That way we'd have the whole country mobilised against us, in no time. Anyway, the police are equipped with short-wave radio nowadays, and could whistle up reinforcements to intercept us long before any tractor could make the trip up Glen Almond."

"I should think that's true," Graham nodded.

"Och, to hell . . ."

"But what we *have* decided," Patrick went on, "is to try to get rid of my car tonight. Off your property. I'm just going to abandon it. It's had its day, anyway. It doesn't owe me a lot. They tell me that it's only the propeller-shaft that they can't get reassembled. The back axle is on. So the thing will actually run, if towed. Can we borrow a tractor?"

"Surely. But where are you going to tow it?"

"Somewhere off your land. It doesn't greatly matter where. Without going down on to the roads, of course. There must be some tracks up on the Muir there, still, where we could drag it? There's quite a few marked as dotted lines on the One-inch map."

"M'mmm. Well, yes. There's Forestry Commission land up behind there. Young trees, planted about eight years ago. The fence would be a bother. But once inside you could dump your car in there well enough, I should think."

"Good. Fine. Sounds pretty well ideal. It'll be found, of course—but possibly not for a few days, which is what matters."

"You leave the bluidy fence to us, Mister!"

"Gladly. But I'll guide you there. No, Mr Drummond—don't try to dissuade me. It's my land and my tractor, after all!"

So they got out a tractor, and all seven of them went with it, up to the Muir. There Jakey and Alicky spent fifteen minutes scraping off and defacing any maker's numbers and identifications on engine and chassis, while Patrick pocketed the Road Fund Licence. Then, hitching the forlorn vehicle to the tractor, they started to tow.

This one turned out to be quite the simplest of their operations, to date. They merely followed an old farm-track, grass-grown and almost smothered in bracken, westwards and climbing intermittently through very rough pasture, Jakey driving and the farmer leading the way with a torch. Behind, Patrick sitting at his own wheel for the last time, made a jolting, jerky journey of it. A gate in a drystone wall marked the edge of Graham property, but the track continued beyond. They were on the neighbouring hill farm of Pittenblair here, but by taking a right-hand fork through the bracken and scrub birch and climbing still more steeply, in a quarter of a mile they came to the tall fence of netting and wire that bounded Forestry land. Beyond it the serried ranks of the young trees were like a black barrier in the gloom.

But their track did not fail them yet. It had been there long before the tree-planters arrived, and had been utilised as a fire-break, with a gate where the fence crossed it. This was padlocked—but Roderick MacGregor had a short way with padlocks, which are ever only as strong as the staples or fastenings into which they are locked. This one had never been intended to resist the leverage which Roddie applied with two of the tractor's tools, and in a minute or less the staple fell loose and they were able to swing the gate open. They drove into the still, hushed obscurity of the plantation.

The trees, Douglas spruce, were about twice the height of a man, and grassy rides branched off the fire-break on either side. Passing the first two of these, they turned in at the third. Tractor and tow made much poorer going here, and they did not travel far before searching for a gap between the spruces large enough to insert the brake. They found one without difficulty, and, unhitching the tractor, manhandled the car in amongst the branches. A little assorted greenery draped over the rear, as camouflage, and they stood back, satisfied. Old cars have undoubtedly come to worse last resting-places.

Returning, they sought as far as possible to ruffle up and hide the tracks made in the long grass and bracken by the tractor's wheels—tough and resilient vegetation, fortunately. At the gate, Roddie hammered in the padlock's staple securely behind them. Only a keen eye actually looking for their traces would be apt to see anything amiss, by morning.

"Yon would be as guid a place to dump the Stane itsel' as any, would it no'?" Alicky suggested, on the way down.

Patrick shook his head. "No. That's different. I don't think we should kid ourselves. That car's going to be found, in a day or two. As I see it, this whole area's going to be searched as with a fine-tooth comb, to find that Stone. Mind you, the story hasn't really broken yet. Once it does . . ." He shrugged. "It seems to me that there's nothing for it but to get the Stone right out of the district . . . somehow. Shifting it from here to there isn't going to be any good. It'll be found. Don't you agree, Mr Graham?"

"I'm afraid I do."

"I do, my ain sel'," MacGregor asserted. "Am I no' sayin'— we should hae the thing on this bluidy trailer right noo, an' be bashin' along the road to Glen Almond wi' it!"

"We couldn't do that without the police being only too well aware of it—so what would be the benefit? They'd get us, and it, in the end."

"Aw, Jings!" the monosyllabic Tosh commented, in eloquent impotence.

"Exactly!"

The deep throb of the tractor prevailed.

It was when nearing the Mains again that Patrick touched Graham's arm, and pointed to where a pin-point of light still gleamed from one of the farm cottages.

"I'm not very easy in my mind about those people of yours—the farm-workers and their families," he mentioned. "Admittedly their cottages are a good way over to the south. But it's obvious that they can't have failed to notice our comings and goings. They'll hear this tractor, for instance."

"Aye—it's the first time, I think, that I've had reason to be thankful that the cottages are so inconveniently far from my house," the farmer admitted. "But you don't imagine, do you, that my folk don't know pretty well what's going on? Three of them, actually, including my steward, have come to me separately, offering to help in any way they can!"

"My goodness!"

"Why so surprised? They're not daft either, you know. And they're as Scots as the rest of us, aren't they? I think perhaps, my friend, that you haven't fully realised it yet, that in this business you'd have four out of every five of the population on your side—and maybe three of those four actually ready to help actively. Amongst the ordinary people, that is. It may be different amongst what we tend to refer to as the upper classes. I wouldn't know. It would be a pity if we began to think of ourselves as unique in some way—this little group of us!"

"Yes. You're right. That's rather a nice thought, you know—and comforting. Perhaps, despite all we hear about this couldn't-care-less age, and the state of spinelessness that the country's in, there's a kick left in Scotland yet!"

"I've never doubted it," James Graham said, in his quiet voice. "Given a lead we could be as good as ever we were.

Better than we were at the time when the Stone was buried certainly, when most of our quality signed Edward's inglorious Ragman's Roll—including Bruce himself! All we need—all we've ever needed, being a race of individualists—is a lead. Our MacGregor friend there, found that out six or seven years ago."

"That's true."

In the same unhurried tranquil tone, the farmer added, "Earlier in the evening I had a quiet word with each of my men. They'll be all right. They'll keep their mouths shut—and see that their families do likewise. But, of course, if the police actually start questioning them systematically, them and their families—that will be a different story. I can't vouch for what might be let out then. But, somehow I don't think the police will do that, go that far. Not the local constabulary, anyway."

"I hope you're right, there."

All this ought to have been enough, one might have thought, to smooth Patrick Kincaid's furrowed and weary brow, that night. But instead, he tossed sleeplessly, irritably, on his yielding aromatic couch of hay, long after his companions' snores resounded to the dusty cobwebs that draped the rafters of the hay-shed, his thoughts incoherent, irrational, but consistently sour. It was not until just after 2 a.m. when he heard the sound of an automobile engine in the yard, an interminable and objectionable wait of perhaps five minutes' silence thereafter, and then the slam of a car's door and the whirr of the starter, that he allowed himself at last to drift towards sleep.

Before leaden eyelids finally closed, however, he knew himself clearly to be several kinds of fool—not the least of which was for allowing any sort of emotional entanglement with somebody else's young woman, however incipient, to add itself to all the other clamant and grievous problems that beat around in his head like the pigeons in that doocot. Damn that Bill Ogilvie, anyway—whoever he was!

*　　　　*　　　　*

It was all wrong that Jean Graham, clad in her trim and colourful but workmanlike clothes again, should have been so notably the fresh, sunny and perky one, in the morning. Up before the men in the hay, she could not wait for breakfast but had to come bustling in on their bleary-eyed, hay-seedy semi-wakefulness to hurl the new day at them. Ignoring all signs and portents, she plunged into untimely eloquence. It was extraordinary, she said—the whole countryside was agog about the Stone. Everybody at the dance was talking about it. And nearly everyone she had heard had been hoping that whoever had taken it wouldn't be caught, that the police wouldn't get it, that London wouldn't be able to lay its hands on it, that it would remain in Scotland. It was the only subject of conversation. These were all young people, admittedly— but she did not think that such feelings would be confined to them. Bill's car had been stopped twice on the way to Perth, by the police, and four times on the way back. Yes, they had made a somewhat circuitous trip of it, as instructed! The police were nice enough. Quite apologetic, in fact. They had insisted on looking inside the car and the boot, with their torches—though it should have been obvious enough that there was no room for the Stone in Bill's Ford. Of course, perhaps they hadn't much idea of the real size of the thing. Yes, she could show them just where the stop-points were, on the map.

But that wasn't the main thing that she had to tell them. She had had an idea. It had come to her on the way to the dance. Those tinkers! Might not that be the answer?

Patrick's eye, like his voice, did not sparkle. "Tinkers," he repeated, dully.

"Yes—tinkers. Remember, they came to the door wanting milk last night when the police were here. Two of them. Well, they're camped down at the burnside between here and Redgorton. Two families of them."

"Interesting. But . . ."

"Don't you see? There they are, with their women and children, their dogs and garrons and carts. They're a gift. The police don't bother the tinkers much—they've more sense!

129

They come and go as they will, free as the wind—almost. At least, they don't stick to the roads."

"Carts . . . ?" Patrick said, more thoughtfully now.

"Yes. Pulled by ponies. Garrons. There's always a lot of them round about this district in the early summer. They drift about, doing seasonal labour, mending and selling things, attending the fairs. They're from the West Highlands mainly—Gaelic speakers. They have their own code of honesty, and they drink too much, but they have their points too. People leave them alone, don't like to get them wrong, and they more or less ignore the police!"

Roddie Roy had roused himself. "Say—maybe you've got somethin' there, Jeannie," he conceded.

"Are you proposing that we hand over the Stone to them. Pass the baby?" Patrick demanded. "In the hope that they could get it out in one of their carts?"

"No—not quite that. I thought, if we could join them—some of us? As tinks, ourselves. With a cart of our own . . ."

"Gee!" the big man exclaimed. "Noo we're gettin' some place."

"Three tinkers' carts. Almost a dozen men—some pretty tough. Some fairly savage dogs. Not to mention a few long-clawed females! I think it might take some bold policemen to force any search of those carts—don't you?"

"M'mmm. I see. Quite an ambitious project!"

"Not more so than we've tackled already."

"Perhaps not. I don't say that there mightn't be something in it . . ."

"Hell—here he's awa' again! Might not be something in it!" Roddie mimicked mincingly. "A right keen guy, you! Can you no' see, man Patrick—it's jist the job? The bluidy answer!"

"I can see a number of snags, too."

"I don't say that there aren't any," the girl cried. "But I do think it gives us a chance."

"The lassie's right," Alicky Shand made one of his infrequent contributions. "I ken thae tinks. They're the boys, right enough."

130

"Well . . . we can think about it."

"Perhaps a spot of breakfast will buck you up, Patrick," Jean said, with marked compassion. "Over in the kitchen, whenever you're ready."

They did a lot more than just think about it, of course. Throughout a noble breakfast of great quantities of porridge, bacon and eggs, and oatcakes and honey, nothing else was discussed. Patrick's request thereafter for hot water for shaving was met with a flat refusal—since he would look a better tinker unshaven. Only the arrival, by postman, of James Graham's *Scotsman* effected a change of subject.

The Scotsman is a substantial paper of much dignity, but it had quite gone to town on the Stone story. It gave it front-page treatment, two full columns with three-tiered headlines. It also devoted the fourth leader to the subject. The headlines were captioned—

STONE OF DESTINY CONTROVERSY:
REPORTED CLASH NEAR SCONE;
OXFORD SOCIETY'S CLAIM.

Underneath was, first, a calm and studiously factual account of the situation as seen from Edinburgh, mainly based on the same information as had been given to the Scottish BBC News, obviously, but as impartial as was possible considering that its compilers were conversant with only one side of the story. Then followed an interview with Dr Conrad Lister. The third section of the report was devoted to brief comments by distinguished persons, presumably reached by telephone.

Dr Lister expressed himself, in the sorrowful and slightly shocked indignation of the authoritative scholar, greatly grieved that anyone could have sunk so low as to this sort of thing, to wreck the results of an entire season's historical work, and to drag what was presumably national politics into what was in fact purely scientific and archaeological research. He appealed, however, to the better side of the miscreants to assert itself, so that they should hand back the Stone to his

131

Society—in which case he would be prepared to use what influence he had to cancel, or at least to mitigate, any proceedings which might be taken against them. He made this offer in the interests of national goodwill and regional amity and unity—though, of course, matters of archaeology and historical research should be right outwith and beyond all local and factional prejudice. In answer to questions as to his ideas on the ultimate resting-place of the Stone, Dr Lister said that it was only suitable that it should rest in some dignified public place, where all could have the opportunity to see it, if not in the Abbey itself, then either in the British Museum or perhaps in their own Ashmolean Museum at Oxford, which seemed peculiarly suitable in the circumstances. Further enquiry, by a Staff Reporter elicited that the Abbey to which Dr Lister referred was of course, Westminster Abbey.

"I say—just listen to these two!" Jean read out, over her father's shoulder. " '*The Lord Provost of Edinburgh said that while he did not wish to make any public statement at this stage, he felt that the whole thing was most unfortunate. He was sure, however, that sanity and common sense would prevail. He had every confidence that the authorities would handle the situation with tact and ability—unlike the previous occasion, when of course, the Government of the day was of a different political complexion.*' And then, hear Tweedledee: '*The Lord Provost of Glasgow, while not in a position to make any actual pronouncement, feared the worst. He felt that this was a matter which called for careful handling, and he was not convinced that the present Party in power was likely to take Scottish susceptibilities fully into account, unlike the occasion some years ago when perhaps the Government was more in touch with the people.*' Can you beat that?"

"Ah, but listen to the voice of our own democratically elected representative!" Patrick urged. " '*Colonel Sir John Ramsay-Smith, M.P. for North Perthshire, said that he thought the whole thing was a scandal, that guests to Scotland, distinguished guests like these Oxford visitors—his old University, incidentally—should be treated in this disgraceful fashion and made the victims of hooliganism. Personally he was satisfied*

132

*that the Coronation Stone at Westminster was entirely genuine,
and hallowed moreover by long association with the persons
of our beloved Royal Family, and that consequently this
Kincaid Stone was in the nature of a mare's-nest. That,
however, was no excuse for failing to accord the archaeologists traditional Scottish courtesy and hospitality. He hoped
that the police would do their duty unfalteringly, and called
on all who had the good name of Scotland at heart to co-
operate loyally.'* "*

"Baistard!" Roddie commented, in turn, succinctly.

The Moderator of the General Assembly of the Church of
Scotland, however, had sung a different tune. He declared
that he had long harboured doubts about the authenticity of
the Stone at Westminster. He hoped that, if the Perthshire
Stone proved to be the true one, it would be allowed to remain
in Scotland, where it belonged. He would be prepared to
suggest that the proper place for it would be in the High Kirk
of St Giles, in Edinburgh. It was quite probable that the
Church of Scotland could make out as good a claim to
ownership of the relic as anyone, as logical successor of the
original custodian, the Abbot of Scone. He urged whoever
had it in possession at the moment to treat it with reverence
and care, and trusted that no hasty action on the part of any
interests whatsoever would prejudice its safety.

"Excellent," James Graham said. "A thoroughly statesman-
like declaration. Good for the Kirk!"

"Ooh, aye!" the MacGregor said, and sniffed.

"That's interesting—about the Church possibly claiming
ownership," Patrick mentioned. "It would help a lot, if they
did."

"What's King John got to say about it?" Jean asked. "He's
next, I see. He'll give them the works, I'll bet." She read out:
" *'Dr John MacCormick, moderate self-government leader and
former Lord Rector of Glasgow University, said that he hoped
that the Scottish people would make their wishes known in
this matter in no uncertain terms. He urged the Secretary of
State to speak out for the Scotland that he was supposed to
represent for once, and not for the London Government that*

he did in fact represent—even at some small risk to himself politically. He proposed that a committee consisting of the Chancellors and Principals of the Scottish universities be set up to enquire into the authenticity of the newly-found relic, and in the meantime a moratorium should be agreed to by all sides, no move of the Stone outwith Scotland, and immunity promised to those who had taken it—almost certainly for patriotic motives.'"

"That's mair like it," Roddie approved.

The final short paragraph merely stated that the Secretary of State for Scotland had no comment to make.

The leader page, however, offered the paper's own comment. It treated the matter soberly, saying that here was a situation that, wrongly handled, could do grave harm to relations between Scotland and England. Whether or not the Stone newly uncovered in Perthshire was in fact the original Stone of Scone—and it was known that certain experts had long had doubts as to the authenticity of the Stone presently so well guarded at Westminster—its unearthing was bound to touch off the greatest interest and concern in Scotland, a concern that our friends south of the Border might well wonder at and even think to be overdone, but which nevertheless was part and parcel of the Scottish people's sense of history and pride of nationhood. And these were traits and characteristics to be encouraged, surely, in this press-button and humdrum age? It was to be hoped that the authorities would interfere no more than was necessary to see that the law was not flouted, and would ensure that any such intervention emanated from Edinburgh rather than London. In the end, this was a matter for the Scottish people themselves, and the comment of the Moderator that perhaps the Stone could be claimed as belonging to the Church of Scotland significant and timely. Certainly any attempt to take the Stone out of Scotland, at this stage, would arouse great and justifiable public resentment.

"Up *The Scotsman!*" Patrick cried. "Splendid! Could hardly have been better! That ought to strengthen the hands of our well-wishers. Even of the local police."

134

"Jings—wha wants to strengthen *their* hands, the baistards!"

"In one respect we do, Roddie," Patrick asserted. "We believe that, probably, they're not too keen on this job, at all. That they—or at least, some of them—are prepared to look the other way, now and again. Not at any actual law-breaking, of course—but at the sort of motive side of all this. Just now, you see, they're really only at the stage of making enquiries into an unsubstantiated story. They can't have anything actually pinned on anybody yet. We want to keep them merely at this enquiry stage, if we can."

"But that doesn't mean that there's any less urgency for getting the Stone out of this district and safely hidden elsewhere," Jean objected.

"Oh, no. I agree, entirely."

It was James Graham, folding up his paper and rising from the breakfast table, who noticed the sole item in the Stop Press space. Under the heading THE STONE, it merely said, "*A.P. reports from London, two Inspectors, Special Branch, Scotland Yard, left on Night Scot for Edinburgh.*"

"And there you have it!" the farmer commented quietly. "The mixture as before!"

Roddie Roy's great fist slammed down on the table, so that all the plates and cutlery jumped and clattered. "Goad save us a'!" he roared. "Mair strengthenin' o' the hands o' the polis, eh? So they're lookin' for a fight, are they? By Jings, then—they'll get it!"

By the time that they had calmed down the MacGregor, and discussed the implications of all this news, it seemed to have become accepted, not only that the tinkers project should be adopted, but that it should be attempted just as quickly as possible. That would entail quite a lot of preliminary work, needless to say. As far as material matters went, it seemed as though these preparatory difficulties would not be too great. James Graham, like many another farmer, had sundry old carts seldom if ever used in this tractor age, mouldering away in an old cart-shed. Amongst them was a light flat dray, better sprung than the heavy farm-wains. This probably would serve, with an old stack-cover tarpaulin hung over a frame, as hood. That was all that most tinkers' carts comprised. And Jean's garron could pull it—better than it had pulled that unwieldy slype it was to be hoped. That was fairly easy. The rest depended on other and less readily ascertainable factors—on their own adaptability, on the developing situation, on the police, and on the tinkers themselves.

To make a start, James Graham would show them the cart. Then he would drive in to Perth, and get a selection of the day's newspapers, to see if anything else of value might be learned from them—and in the going and coming, without making it obvious, try to get a fairly complete picture of the police arrangements for blocking and patrolling the road over and above what Jean had told them. Jean herself could go and interview the tinkers—it would be safer to leave the preliminary negotiations to her, probably—and the rest could get on with the job of converting the cart.

Patrick agreed with all that, but felt that he ought to accompany the girl on her visit to the tinkers. But he was dissuaded on the grounds that it would be foolish for him to risk showing himself till at least it was ascertained that the tinks were prepared to consider co-operation.

The cart, on inspection, appeared reasonably suitable to them all. The fact that it obviously required oiling and a certain amount of patching up, by no means invalidated it, for tinkers' carts were seldom in immaculate condition. The more string and wire that had to be tied to it, the better. There would have to be some strengthening and replacing of rotten floorboards, to carry the weight of the Stone, and a framework of willow wands and bits and pieces erected to support the hood.

Leaving the Gregorach to attend to this, Patrick made his way down to the church. Even before he reached the road, he heard the noise, above the chuckle and murmur of the stream. He heard the scrape of tyres, the revving of engines, the slam of car-doors, and upraised voices. Cautiously approaching through the thickest cover that he could find, he stared into the roadway. It was lined with cars, in both directions, as far as he could see. Policemen were stalking about, endeavouring to move people on, or at least to keep the highway clear and the parked cars to one side of the road only. Sightseers were milling about everywhere, and though most of them seemed to be pressing forward toward the vicinity of the Kincaid House gates, others merely stared around them with the vague and unfocussed interest of their kind. Some few might be Pressmen, certainly, but the majority were most obviously merely interested spectators, holiday-makers, tourists, and the like. Cars were parked in the access roadway to the church also, and undoubtedly people would be wandering about in the churchyard itself.

For a while Patrick waited in hiding, biting his lip. But the pointlessness of so doing soon struck him. Even unshaven as he was, there was no reason why he should be any more conspicuous in this crowd than anybody else. He might as well go rubber-necking with the rest. Choosing his moment, so that his emergence from the shrubbery would not attract the attention of the harassed police, he slipped out, and joined the chattering staring throng.

Hands in pockets, and strolling with marked casualness, he sauntered down towards the church. Two men sat on the padlocked gate, smoking and exchanging notes—and both had notebooks and pencils in their hands. Four or five people were wandering around the graveyard, staring at the building and the tombstones, trying doors, and seeking to peer in at windows. Everywhere the grass was trampled, and cigarette packets and papers lay scattered.

Patrick, climbing the gate, took a walk round, himself. He was thankful to see that all the doors were still securely locked. But rounding the tower end of the church, his heart went up to his mouth. Somebody had been sharp-eyed; the grating that let light into the crypt was revealed, with its concealing grasses pressed aside.

Glancing about him swiftly, he waited until a man and a woman moved away round the building, and then, he hoped unobserved, darted forward. He stooped, and peered in—and sighed in relief. Even though this was the east end of the

137

church, and the morning sun was bright, he could distinguish practically nothing in the gloom within. Hurriedly he sought to raise up and rearrange the grasses to hide the grating again—but found the result unsatisfactory. Casting urgently about for something more solid to screen it, he saw a small tombstone broken in two and lying flat nearby. Hastening over, and ensuring that he was not being watched, he picked up the top section, smoothed the long grass over the bare patch where it had lain, and came back with it, to stand it up against the church wall so that it covered the grating, seeking to make the grass round it appear as though it had been undisturbed for a long time. He was still at this when two young women came round the corner of the church. Pretending to be examining the lettering on the broken stone, he waited a few moments before straightening up. The girls, chattering and laughing, paid no heed.

He moved away, back to the gate. The journalists were still sitting thereon, looking bored. Leaning his arms on the top bar, Patrick remarked conversationally that this was a rum do. The reporters glanced at him, grunted something, and rather noticeably turned their shoulders on him, to address each other.

Uneasy as he was about the Stone and the church, Patrick realised that there was nothing that he could do here meantime. Any hanging about would only draw attention to himself. He moved on up the road, with reinforcements of sightseers. There was a sizeable crowd clustered around the lodge gates—which were shut, with a policeman on guard forbidding entrance.

"What goes on?" he asked, of a stout perspiring individual in open-necked shirt and sand-shoes.

"They're beating out t'woods and bushes in there, lad. T'police. Looking for these chaps as have pinched the Stone." His informant had a rich Yorkshire accent.

"In there? Do they think they're really in there?"

"Search me, lad. Better ask the copper. I know as much as you do."

"It's t'Stone itself they're looking for, Bert," a thin lady who was chewing sweets declared. She offered Patrick a chocolate, which he accepted gravely. "They say there's a big house up there. They've searched that. And now they're combing t'woods for it. Lots of them—hundreds. See all their cars, in there. You know, maybe I shouldn't say it, but I'm right sorry for those poor boys."

"Which? The police?"

"No, no. Them as took t'Stone. I mean. All these policemen after them."

"You don't think they've done much harm, then? These, er, boys?"

"Harm? What harm? Who cares who's got the silly old Stone, anyhow?"

"Well . . ." Patrick gestured at the surrounding crowd. "Lots of people seem interested, anyway." He considered this couple. "You're English, aren't you? Does it not matter to you who has this Stone?"

"Course not. Why should it? If they want it all that bad, let them have it, I say."

"All good clean fun," the fat man added, chuckling. "We can do with a bit o' fun now and again, lad."

"M'mmm. That's true. Well—thanks. I'll be on my way."

Patrick worked his way discreetly out of the populous area, and back to the high ground of the farm. In the yard he spied two strange cars drawn up—and hastily made himself inconspicuous amongst the barns and outbuildings. He found Roddie Roy and his friends lying low in the cart-shed, and cursing, complaining that they were unable to get on with their work. Those were newspapermen's cars, and their owners were waiting for James Graham to come back, and snooping around in the meantime. A right menace, they were. They'd near been on to them, twice.

Fortunately the farmer arrived back a few minutes later, and dealt with and noticeably expeditiously got rid of the Press—however unconvinced they seemed that he had nothing to tell them. He had been delayed because of the long queues of cars at the various police road-blocks. It seemed that the said police were nearly out of their wits with this great influx of visitors, that was making a farce of their blockade. Never had so many vehicles poured into this quiet corner of Perthshire, just when the authorities wanted the reverse. But the check-points could now all be plotted on their map—which was a help.

James Graham had brought a sheaf of newspapers back from Perth. None had failed to headline their story. Most were very considerably less restrained than had been *The Scotsman*. GREAT STONE SENSATION; TROUBLE IN THE GLEN; MYSTERY RAIDERS AT PERTH; they shouted. DRAMA OF TWO STONES OF DESTINY; CHALLENGE TO WESTMINSTER. One tabloid trumpeted, STONE SNATCH: OXFORD PLEA—GIVE IT BACK!

The farmer was most concerned with the *News Courier*, which evidently was the sheet whose minions had come to interview him the day before. Amongst other things it said that a Mr James Graham, tenant of a nearby croft, had declared that he was against Englishmen coming into their district and causing trouble, that the Stone belonged to Scone, and should stay there, and that it should be placed in the parish church. That was the place for it.

James Graham's somewhat restrained attitude towards today's batch of apostles of public enlightenment might have been in some measure influenced by this.

It was almost midday before Jean got back to the Mains. She had had to wait at the tinkers' camp for the menfolk, who had been out on some ploy of their own. Not being newspaper addicts or radio fans, they had been greatly mystified by the crowds of people and cars invading this quiet backwater—to say nothing of all the police. But when Jean had explained the situation, despite their very individual brand of English, they had very quickly understood and appreciated. Approved, too, apparently, of what was being attempted. Being not so much nationalists as instinctive anarchists, they were all for circumventing authority and demonstrating the freedom of men. Without being particularly interested in the Stone of Destiny, they were perfectly happy and agreeable to co-operate. The two men who had come up before, would come for the milk again, in the evening. That would not look in any way suspicious. The whole thing could be talked over then.

"Good," Patrick nodded. "That's as well. Though it will have to be more than talked over, I fear. We're going to have to move fast now." And he told the girl about the situation at the church.

"It's tonight, or never, then?" she put to him.

"I think it is."

X

WHEN the tinkers arrived up at Kincaid Mains that evening, it was to find a picturesque company awaiting them. Jean had spent much of the afternoon fulfilling the duties of wardrobe-mistress and make-up expert, scouring the farmhouse and certain of its cottages—it was suggested, even the field scarecrows themselves—for old and abandoned clothing. She had concocted also a brown stain—which some at least of the party hoped was not so indelible as it seemed—and practically bathed her victims in it. The results were quite extraordinary. Sir Patrick Kincaid, Baronet, clad in an ancient torn blue serge jacket, one side of which was largely ripped away, ragged plus-four trousering inexpertly patched at knees and seat in a different colour of tweed, that hung unfastened halfway down his calves, not quite meeting the tops of James Graham's oldest mud-encrusted farm-boots, the collar torn off his shirt and a dirty scarlet neck-rag substituted, looked quite the most disreputable and unsavoury tink in all Scotland, his dark knobbly features, two days' beard and tousled hair contributing. Jakey Reid and Alicky Shand had needed less touching up perhaps—but succeeded in looking as nasty a pair to meet of a dark night as might well be imagined. The two youths, Tosh and The Pluke, now appeared to be the acme of respectability, for it had been decided that, after tonight, their task was over, and that they should return to Glasgow and their normal life—while holding themselves available for recall to duty at short notice; six men in one tinker's cart would be just too much, anyway. It was Roderick MacGregor who had stumped the girl, his outsize proportions completely precluding an even approximate fit with any normal person's clothing, however stretched and burst as to seams. Fortunately, of course, he was far from conventionally garbed anyhow, and so he just continued to wear his old kilt

142

and boots and torn shirt, with the addition of the cut-down remains of a filthy old raincoat, the cuffs of which reached only halfway down his forearms, and a battered antique felt hat with the brim turned wavily down all round. The effect was far from humdrum, at any rate. All he needed now, he said, was a set of bagpipes.

Consequently, the genuine tinkers, when they were shown into the hay-barn, were something in the nature of an anticlimax. Without being actually dull, they had about them an air of normalcy and inoffensiveness. They were both youngish men, of markedly similar features—save that one had a livid scar across his mahogany-coloured temple and cheek-bone—long-faced, black-haired, with flashing eyes and teeth. Even in that aromatically-scented hay-shed, a strong odour comprising wood-smoke, malt liquor, horse, dog, stale perspiration, and sheer masculinity, was wafted in with them. Jean introduced them as the brothers Seumas and Dougal Macphail of Torridon, Wester Ross.

Patrick stepped forward, to shake hands. "Good evening, gentlemen," he said. "It is very kind of you to come up and see us, with the possibility of maybe giving us a hand. We are grateful, I assure you. Meet my friends."

"Och, yes—not at all!" the man Seumas, the one with the scar, observed, smiling brilliantly. The scar twitched upwards with the exercise, giving him a distinctly satanic expression. His companion nodded silently. But undoubtedly they both looked somewhat askance at the reception committee. Perhaps it was admiration.

"Aye, boys—hoo's tricks?" Roddie Roy greeted heartily, and slapped both visitors shatteringly on their backs. "Here's a right stramash, eh? Doon wi' the polis, an' up wi' the rebels—hey?"

It was doubtful whether the Macphails understood more than a word or two of Roddie's broad Glasgow Doric, but swallowing their choking breaths, they nodded with brave geniality.

The introductions over, Patrick wasted no time in getting down to business. Time was beginning to bulk over-large in

143

his mind, time progressing inexorably, time running out. He went over the situation again, briefly, emphasised the risks involved, and tactfully hinted at the unsuitability of anyone suffering financially over the business.

The tinkers listened politely, and smiled, and waited, summing the speaker up with eyes that were shrewd, however flashing. Evidently they were nobody's fools.

"You are prepared to join us, for a little, are you?" Patrick asked. "To take a chance on it? For a couple of days, perhaps?"

"Och, yes. To be sure, yes, why not?" That was the mephistophelian Seumas.

"Mother o' God, yes," his brother agreed. To this he added something in the Gaelic—at which they all looked suitably impressed.

"Good. What we had in mind was this. If we could join our cart, with the Stone hidden inside it, to your two, and move in convoy with you, by the safest route you can suggest, to upper Glen Almond, I think we've a chance of slipping through the police net. What do *you* think?"

"Surely, surely."

"Och, aye."

"Yes. But I mean, seriously. What do you think the chances are?"

"Och, fine. Fine. Why not, at all?" Seumas was the spokesman, evidently. He smiled. "The policemen, they do not speak the Gaelic, see you!"

"So I gather! You think the police would not search your carts?"

"I think not, no, my God," the other said quietly.

"M'mmm. I see."

"Already the policemen have been after speaking with us," the man Dougal informed. "A word, no more."

"You mean, since I saw you?" Jean put in. "This afternoon?"

"Yes, then. Three policemen. Very big." He grinned innocently. "Och, there was no harm in them, at all!"

"Asking about the Stone, were they?"

"Och, yes. They mentioned it, as you might say. But och,

we were not after understanding them, at all. So they went away, see you."

"And no searching?"

"Not a word of it, no. Och, we would not have liked that, at all," Seumas explained.

The Mains party exchanged glances.

"Just the job," Roddie nodded. "You're the boys, eh?"

"Sounds hopeful, I must say," Patrick agreed. "Now, look. We've got to move the Stone tonight. It's in a crypt, under the church. Now, things there are bad, and we daren't leave it for another day. It's safe so far—for Mr Graham is an elder of that church, and when he heard about all the people tramping around the kirkyard he phoned a complaint to the Chief Constable and got a policeman put on guard over the place during daylight hours. That's all right. Fine. But it's taking a major risk. The police themselves are bound to find the thing when they're finished searching the estate, sooner or later. We've got to get it away. And we can't shift it by road, at night, that's clear. Miss Graham tells me your camp is about half a mile downstream from the church—by road? But not much more than half that across the fields. We'll just have to carry the thing. That'll take some doing—seven or eight hundredweights of it! Can you be at hand, to help us, tonight? At the church?"

"Surely. Four men, yes. At the church. When?"

"Well . . . that depends. On when we decide to move off. In the carts, I mean. When do you usually make a start, Mr Macphail?"

"Och, any time," Seumas shrugged casually. "Any time in the morning, see you."

"You never move by night? In the dark?"

"Och, mercy on us, goodness me—no! Mary-Mother— there are other things to be doing at night!" The tinker laughed richly, eyeing all concerned significantly, especially Jean Graham. "Oh, well."

"I think he's right, anyway," the girl declared hastily. "I mean, I don't think we'd gain anything, travelling by night. It would just look suspicious. Asking to be searched. Let's just take our fate in our own hands. Travel in broad daylight, like honest ti . . . Macphails!"

"Sure—that's the stuff!" Roddie commended. "The lassie's right—as usual. Nae mair messin' aroond. Slam at it—an' to hell wi' them!"

"Still spoiling for a fight, Roddie?"

"Sure I am! If I can jist find some o' these guys to get a right crack at! I'm fair cheesed-off wi' a' this joukin' an' dodgin' an' hangin' aroond. I'm for a real bash at somethin', see!"

Patrick smiled. "I know how you feel. But mere having a bash won't solve our problems for us. All right, then—we'll wait till daylight. But first thing. An early start. Before everybody's too wide awake—before the police night shift is relieved by fresh men. Okay? Let's see—sunrise is about 4.45. We'd better all be at the church at, say, 3 a.m. All right? That ought to give us time enough. It will give us time for some sleep first, too."

That was agreed.

"One last thing. Will you two drive *our* cart down to your camp, now? We think that would be best, safest. Take the long way round—not the way you came up. Through the police check-point at the Redgorton crossroads. There's nothing in the cart yet but a pile of old clothing, sacks, and so on. So if you are stopped and searched, it will be all right. And it will get our cart safely into position in your camp, and establish it as part of your outfit. Will you do that?"

"You can have the cart, afterwards, as a gift," James Graham, who had just come in, added.

"Kind you are," Seumas Macphail acknowledged, with dignity. "Och, that will be fine, then. We will be doing that. Have you such a thing as a bit of a watch, now? Or a sort of a clock? So that we can be after telling the right time, see you. To meet you at this church. Not a clock have we, dearie me, amongst the lot of us, at all."

Patrick drew a hand over his tell-tale mouth. "You'd better have this one," he said, unbuckling his own wrist-watch. "In the meantime, anyway . . ."

146

*   *   *

Jean Graham, the possessor of an alarm-clock, came to waken the people in the hay, at the ungodly hour of 2.30 a.m. They had deliberately slept in their clothes, to make them the more tinker-like, and no attempts were made at tidying up or hair-smoothing. Since everything was done by the feeble light of a torch, in the interests of security, it was some little time before Jean's own get-up attracted any owl-eyed attention. It was the MacGregor who perceived the situation.

"My Gosh—look at Jeannie!" he invited, playing the torch on her.

His request was not unwarranted. If the girl's transformation of two evenings previously had shaken them, tonight's did no less. Somehow she had got her sleek fair hair matted, straggling, and soiled-seeming, locks of it falling over a brown and dirt-smudged face. Around her was a threadbare and stained tartan rug as a shawl, below which a ragged drooping hem skirt showed above brown-stained bare legs and split down-at-heel shoes. She scowled into the torchlight.

"My . . . godfather!" Patrick ejaculated, staring, quite overcome. "What on earth . . . ? This is . . ." He shook his head. "Good Lord!"

"Don't you like me?" she asked, in not at all the sort of voice that should have emanated from such a vision.

"Jings—you look a right second-hand tramp!" Roddie declared, but admiringly.

"Thank you!"

"What's the point of this?" Patrick demanded. "There's no need for you to dress up."

"Wouldn't I look rather strange in a tinker's cart, dressed the way I normally do—humble and undistinguished as that may be?" she countered.

"Maybe so. I mean, that's not the point. Nobody's going to see you tonight—we hope. And you're not coming with us in the cart, tomorrow . . ."

"That's where you're wrong, Mister Patrick Drummond! I am."

147

"Now, look here . . ."

"I won't look here!" Undoubtedly the young woman had come expecting trouble, and was all set to fight back. "I'm coming. That's final. It was my idea, in the first place. It's our cart. I'm going to see this thing through to the end."

"But, Jean—it's not suitable! It's . . . it's . . ." The man ran a hand through his carefully tousled hair. "You can't do this. Not somebody like you. I mean . . ."

"You mean you're just being stuffy and stupidly conventional! Why shouldn't I come? There's other women in the party, isn't there?"

"They're different. You don't seem to realise what it could mean." He frowned at her—and even in the half-dark he looked a very savage and alarming figure, himself. Not one for any young woman to argue with. "What does your father say to this?"

"He found the shawl for me—in the dog's bed!" she asserted. And suddenly laughed. "He's a lot more sensible than you are, Patrick, you see—not such an idealist, perhaps."

"I'm not an idealist."

"Oh yes, you are. It sticks out all over you. Anyway, you can save your breath—for I'm coming. What would a tinker's cart be without its tinker-woman, anyhow? Tell me that."

"You won't stop her, Drummond," James Graham's voice came from the deep shadow at the door. "Better capitulate with good grace—like I have done! I just wish I was coming with you, myself. But I'm better here, to cover up tracks, no doubt." He moved forward into the torchlight, to consult his watch. "I think you should be on your way, you know."

There was no more to be said, of course—not really. Though, as they took leave of the farmer, acknowledging his quiet good wishes, Patrick had one last shot to fire.

"What will Mr Ogilvie have to say to this?" he wondered.

"Mr Ogilvie . . . ?"

"Your Bill. Isn't he going to take a rather pale view of it?"

She looked at Patrick curiously. "What has it got to with Bill? Or anybody else beyond ourselves? Beyond myself!"

"Oh, well—you know best about that, I suppose."

"Och, nivver heed him, Jeannie—he doesna' dae wi' gettin up this 'oor o' the mornin'," Roddie advised. "C'mon."

They set off for Kincaid Church, some of them not too nimble in their ill-fitting footgear, their own normal clothing wrapped up in cloth bundles in their hands. The night was dark and chill again, with a faint smirr of rain.

Down at the road, they could just make out a subdued glint of light from up in the direction of the lodge gates—no doubt a parked police car. They crossed the highway and into the dripping trees again as silently as they knew how.

Like well-drilled ghosts four dark figures rose up from amongst the gravestones, as they reached the church. The tinker smell rose with them, the whisky content perhaps a little more pronounced. Patrick's luminous-dialled watch gleamed notably on Seumas Macphail's wrist. Greetings were brief and whispered. No, they had had no trouble with the cart at all, thank God.

Patrick, who had been carrying the crypt key about with him, for security's sake, made no delay. Opening the door they trooped down and within. All was as they had left it, the Stone sitting on its stretcher between the lead coffins. Already some enterprising spider had draped a cobweb or two across it. The sight of it, in the torch's beam, dark and handsome and so very ancient-seeming, so full of years and of history, had its own effect on some at least of the viewers. But not apparently on the tinkers—who seemed more inter-ested in the coffins.

A car, its powerful engine running only slowly, sounded from the road. Its headlights silhouetted the tracery of the trees between, but did not halt or falter as it drove deliberately southwards. Roderick MacGregor muttered something to himself, like a dog growling in its throat.

With no fewer than ten men on the job, raising the stretcher and Stone was not difficult. Indeed, in getting it out into the open and up the outside steps, the main handicap was from men falling over each other's feet. It was decided that six bearers at a time, with frequent graded reliefs by the other four, would be best. As Jean, carrying more than her share of clothes-bundles now, turned to relock the door and replace the key where it belonged inside the vestry window, her companions lurched away across the tombstone-littered churchyard, Patrick leading the way with shaded torch, heading for the broken-down wall into the turnip field. At least they need not worry about the grass, this time—it had been well trampled down for them.

A motorcycle, also running markedly slowly, came and passed in the opposite direction to the car. It stopped up at the lodge gates. Obviously, there were many sleepless folk around Kincaid, that night.

The Kincaid Water took a wide bend in its course here, on its way to the Tay, and, by cutting across the field, a considerable saving could be effected by stringing the bow of it—though it meant crossing the stream to get to the tinkers' present camp. But it all made a grievous pilgrimage, just the same. The drills of turnips, of course, ran the wrong way, and the sorely burdened men had to go stumbling and ploughing over and through them—which was hard on their equilibrium, tricky for the Stone, and sore on their shoulders. Jean assured them that it was only a quarter of a mile altogether—but no man believed her. Soon all were gasping and gulping painfully. And more than once the precious burden slithered on its suddenly canted stretcher alarmingly. If it fell, whoever it fell against would not forget the occasion.

It crossed Patrick's mind, during one of his relief spells, to wonder how his ancestor and colleagues had managed, exactly 659 years ago, shifting this thing in the opposite direction, no doubt on another similarly dark night?

Though they had hoped, with their relief tactics, to carry the Stone right across without having to set it down, they found this to be impossible. Twice they had to lower it to the ground, and wait, panting and sweating, to recover breath and strength. Only Roddie could have continued unhalting— and did not fail to say so, flogging the others with the lash of his tongue. By the time that they reached the far wall of that

150

interminable and shockingly corrugated field, however, none could care less what the giant MacGregor thought of them.

Patrick had feared that they might have to demolish the dry-stone wall to get the Stone across—for there was no gate at this side. But by four of the men climbing across and taking the end of the stretcher from their fellows, while two more got over to finish the transference, the thing was achieved smoothly enough. The crossing of the burn was not difficult either, compared with the turnip-field—getting down the low bank being the worst of it. Thereafter they just waded across the pebbly shallows, never actually over their trousered knees, and feeling their way with careful boot-toes on the slippery bottom. In the end, they turned downstream, while still in the water, at Jean's direction, for a further thirty yards or so, to find a suitably low bank to climb out of. Even so they were still further upstream from the camp than had been intended.

The staggering bearers had no breath left to sigh their thankfulness as at last the three dark shadows of the carts loomed up before them, with lower rounded shadows that were the tinkers' curious tents. A dog growled deep in its throat—and was quelled by a single snapped word. No other sign of welcome greeted them—whoever may have been peering from the tentage.

Somehow they got the Stone, still on its stretcher, into the flat Mains cart beneath its tarpaulin canopy, and leaned around in breathless quivering reaction. From somewhere, a lemonade bottle was passed round—and only Jean rejected it. Patrick almost choked on his mouthful—but offered no complaint. If it had contained less than proof spirits, he would have been surprised.

The time was barely 4 a.m. They would move off at about 6.30, leaving Tosh and The Pluke to wait till a more normal hour before they made their way to their hidden motorcycles, en route for Glasgow. Meantime, a couple of hours sleep would do no harm. The grass was dry under the carts and the Mains party lay down there, leaving Jean to keep the Stone company inside the vehicle, while the tinkers disappeared within their squat tents.

151

The faintest hint of grey was beginning to appear over the level lands of Tay to the east. Somewhere, the sound of a motorcycle engine throbbed slowly on the night air. In less than an hour the cocks would be crowing.

XI

IT was much later than 6.30 before any move was made—
nobody awoke till after that. Admittedly breakfast was not
an elaborate meal with either party—the tinkers indeed seemed
to start their day on cold porridge laced with lemonade-bottle
whisky, washed down by tar-like tea stewed on an economical
little fire of sticks. Where the supplies of the former beverage
came from was neither enquired into nor announced.

Neither then, nor later, did the Macphail company's com-
position become clear to the newcomers. Apart from the four
men—who may, or may not, all have been brothers, or possibly cousins—there was an indeterminate number of women
and children. Various counts produced varying totals, but the
most general assessment amounted to five adult women and
eight children—though this may well have been wrong on
balance as in total, for it was exceedingly difficult to tell the
approximate ages of the females, and some of those assessed
as juveniles may have been adult, and vice versa, owing to
the slight build of them all, wrapped up in wrap-around
plaids, non-fitting clothing, loose-hanging hair, and ingrained
dirt. Certainly there was one older woman, and two small
boys and a little girl. For the rest, ideas varied from time to
time. There was an even greater similarity of appearance
amongst the females than amongst their menfolk. And without
exception they all had lovely eyes, the softest of lilting voices,
and habitually scowling expressions lit by occasional brief
shy smiles.

Despite Patrick's impatience, they were in no hurry to
move off. The continued retention of the wrist-watch did not
seem to confer on Seumas, who was obviously the leader,
an enhanced sense of time. At Jean's suggestion, a faun-like
and incredibly dirty young creature, plus the little girl,
came to travel in the Mains cart, to bolster the impression of

153

genuineness. A dog, something between a collie and a grey-hound, attached itself to Roddie Roy, and would not leave him. Undramatic farewells were exchanged with Tosh and The Pluke, Patrick's little speech of thanks and appreciation rather tailing out in the face of acute and impiously expressed embarrassment. The MacGregor left them with vehement instructions as to looking after his motorcycle, where and how they were to be on call, and the fate that would overtake them if they failed him in any way. It was hard to know whether they were pleased to be thus dismissed, or otherwise.

The actual departure from the riverside haugh was a big moment. Seumas led the way, driving a shaggy skewbald pony with a dog running expertly between the cart's wheels. How many passengers were inside his vehicle it was impossible to say, but three females shuffled along on foot behind. Then came the Mains cart, with Jean at the reins of her own garron, the Stone well hidden inside under a heap of clothing, sacks and extra tarpaulin stack-covers, plus some old iron from the farm junk-heap that would help to give the impression of scrap collection. Roddie lay in there too, with the dog, at Seumas's suggestion; being of a somewhat eye-catching appearance, it was thought that it might be best for him to keep out of sight at first, ostensibly sleeping off some major drinking, a little whisky spilled about his person contributing to the right atmosphere. Patrick and Alicky and Jakey walked alongside or behind. The third cart was driven by the old lady, with a led horse at the rear, and Dougal and another man strolled some fifty yards behind. They made quite a noteworthy turn-out on that winding country road.

It was a mere six hundred yards or so to the Redgorton crossroads, and the first police check. According to Jean's watch, well hidden in an inner pocket, it was nearly 7.45. Would the night-shift picket have been relieved yet? Whether it had or not, a distinctly bored-looking young constable waved Seumas on. But the tinker jumped down, to say something in Gaelic, and then to ask in English for a light for the stump of cigarette that he produced from behind his ear, while his cart went on. Shrugging good-naturedly, the policeman

154

brought out a box of matches. Patrick hurriedly pulled out a cigarette from his torn pocket, broke it in two and gave a half to Jakey, and strolled forward to share in the light that was being provided, Jakey doing likewise. He nodded to the obliging constable, but said nothing, while Jean drove the cart on, and past, in the wake of the other. Seumas shouted something incomprehensible to the old woman driving the last cart, who answered in a gabble, ending in a brief screech of laughter and jabbing a pointed finger towards the second policeman. All the tinkers grinned, while the embarrassed officer first frowned, then rubbed his chin, then smiled back. The procession passed on, no cart having stopped, the men sauntering after.

That was easy. But then, these constables, being sited so near to the tinkers' camp, accepted them as part of the land-scape, probably knew that they had been questioned after a fashion already. That was no real test.

They had turned right at the crossroads, back up their own road. They passed the Mains road-end, crossed the bridge over the Kincaid Water, and passed the church entry. It made a strange sensation to be plodding along thus openly where they had hitherto skulked and crept.

Just before they reached the Kincaid House drive, an impatient horn-hooting behind them turned all their heads. Two large black cars were trying to pass. Jean hurriedly drew in, till her wheels were on the grass verge. But the tinkers were less eager to give place. These urgent travellers had to go slow for a good hundred yards before, edging up, they were able to get past the independently-minded Seumas. As, for a few moments, they ran level with the Mains cart, it could be seen that the first car contained a police driver and a brass-hatted senior officer, in front, and two lounge-suited individuals sitting at ease behind. The second car contained four constables.

"You see that?" Patrick said, almost whispered, walking close to Jean, as they drew ahead. "Plain clothes men. See their expressions? Authoritative as tin gods! Those are the Scotland Yard beauties, for sure."

"You think so? Oh, dear!"

"Baistards!" came growlingly from within the cart.

"Confound it—I don't much like the thought of *them* in front of us!" Patrick muttered.

But that precise worry did not remain with them for long. Where the lodge gates entry formed a widening of the road they found the two cars drawn up, and their passengers disembarking. There were four or five other cars there also that gave the impression of having been there all night—and a couple of motor-bicycles. One of the cars was a shooting brake, of more modern vintage than Patrick's, and outside it a man was using the driving mirror to aid his shaving. Press, almost certainly. The official newcomers' arrival had obviously made a considerable stir amongst the number of policemen and others present.

No attention was paid to the tinkers, as they passed.

Patrick let out a great sigh of relief, as they drew on, slowly, and rounded a bend. "You know—that was probably a stroke of luck, I think," he declared. "Those detectives arriving just then. They took all the attention. The big noises themselves, all the way from London! We were less than the dust!"

"Of course, they might not have been interested in us, anyway," the girl pointed out. "After all, they would know we would have passed through their road-block, back there, to get this far."

"All the same . . ."

About half a mile farther on, Seumas turned his cart off the road, to the left, and they followed him into a narrow winding country lane. This proved to be an unmetalled road between high overgrown hedges, skirting the northern edge of the estate, with fairly recently planted forest on the other side. Grass grew between the puddled ruts, and pot-holes were numerous. But the horses took it stolidly—even if the carts jolted and creaked more notably.

"I thought he'd take this route," Jean confided. "It runs westwards for almost three miles, giving access to three farms, and then more or less peters out in a deserted crofting area. There's a choice of tracks there, leading to fords over the

Kincaid Water, none of them good. Unsuitable for cars, anyway. As you can see, nothing can pass us on this road, either way, without a lot of bother—so I think we can say we're safe for the next three miles, at any rate. The trouble will be when we get to the other end. But the Macphails may know a way to get the carts through."

The jolting and pitching soon brought Jean down from her perch, and Roddie from his couch within, to walk at the garron's head—though their tinker passengers seemed content to remain in the cart and be tossed about. Unhurriedly they paced along.

"Relax," Patrick told himself, time and again. "Take the chance, and relax."

Certainly it all seemed most remarkably pleasant and uneventful, of a sudden—too good to be true. Only the scuffle and plod of hooves and the creaking of the carts competed with the singing of the larks and the occasional lowing of cattle. The scent of dog-roses and meadowsweet from their enclosing and protecting hedges was heavy on the morning air, the sun shone out of a cloudless sky, and ahead of them the blue line of the great hills beckoned. Roddie Roy, thankful to be stretching his long legs, began to sing in his curiously aggressive fashion.

Patrick and Jean walked on either side of her pony's nodding head. "The police must know of this road?" Patrick said. "They can't have overlooked it?"

"Oh, no. But, you see, it's impassable for cars. At least, the fords are, higher up. No car could get through. And then, once you're across the water, by whichever ford you take, you come to the main Glen Almond road again. And there's a road-block at the fork before Chapelhill, father says. We can't avoid it. So I suppose they feel that they can forget this bit."

"I see. So this is only a breathing-space?"

"I'm afraid so."

They had an hour of their gentle uncomplicated plodding without sight of another soul and only farmhouses in the distance, before their byway lost itself in a maze of weed grown tracks amongst small round hillocks, dotted with the tumbledown ruins of croft houses. Seumas led them, twisting and turning, by these tracks, now north, now south, the cart making heavy going of it but never actually having to halt. The last stretch, down a steep hill much washed away by floodwater, was the worst of it. But the Macphails instructed the Mains party to lead a rope through both rear wheels, and all drag back on it as the cart slithered downwards, to act a brake, and they got safely down. Before them then, the Kincaid Water ran over aprons of basalt slab, peat brown but clear, and though the approach to the ford was overgrown, uneven and bumpy, the actual crossing was smooth and easy. There was a ruined water-mill at the far side, and thereafter a similar stretch of grass-grown dirt road threading old woodland. Where this joined the main road there would be a police checkpoint.

When the three carts drew out on to the highway, sure enough there, at the fork, was a knife-rest barrier, a police car, and a couple of constables. A private car was just being allowed to go on, and a tradesman's van was being examined.

As the carts came up, a motor-lorry and still another car arrived behind them. Roddie was safely back beside the Stone, out of sight.

A constable signed Seumas to come up, and spoke. The tinker answered him in a voluble flow of Gaelic. The other shook his head, and pointed to the cart. Seumas countered with enhanced eloquence and vigorous gesticulation, certain of his passengers assisting. The officer drew back a little, and looked at his colleague, an older man, now signing on the van, for help.

The two policemen conferred briefly, and the senior frowning sternly, came forward and said, slowly but very, loudly, that he wanted to see inside the cart. Seumas shrugged, smiled brilliantly, but sat still. His womenfolk crowded forward within the vehicle, to stare and jabber, completely blocking the view within. The constable hesitated, and then spoke to his junior, who walked to the rear of the cart, lifted a loose flap of the hood, and peered inside. There can have been very little light to penetrate within, but after a moment he let the flap drop, and shrugged.

"Okay," he called.

Seumas, at a sign from the older man, led his horse forward a little, but left it and came back, as the two policemen bore down on the Mains cart. He resumed his monologue in Gaelic, too.

Patrick, Jakey and Alicky stood by, with varied expressions, but saying nothing. Jean scowled her hardest, in the driving seat, with the tinker girls at her side.

"Sorry—but we've got to look inside," the senior constable said.

Nobody spoke or moved, save Seumas, who touched the policeman's arm, said something at length, and laughed heartily.

The older man leaned forward, to try to peer in at the front of the cart, over Jean's hunched shoulders. His junior stalked round to the rear again. But this time the hood was much more securely laced down all round, and did not draw aside. The young constable's efforts at tugging and poking at the tarpaulin drew forth a vicious growling from within, that grew into a loud and high-pitched barking.

As though aroused and touched off by the dog's reaction, a great commotion arose within that vehicle. There was a loud and incoherent groaning, that rose steadily to a bull-like bellowing. There seemed to be a mighty heaving going on inside. An empty bottle came flying out at the front of the cart, over the heads of the women, to crash and splinter on the road. Roddie Roy heaved himself up, swaying and hiccuping, a fearsome sight. He aimed a swipe of his fist approximately at Jean, missed, and collapsed sideways against the hood. Sprawling thus, one arm thrashing about, and mouthing unformed and peculiar things that might have been Gaelic or might not, he grabbed at a blackened iron pan, swung it like a club, and struggled to his knees again, threatening all in sight. The greyhound-collie's barking rose to a crescendo.

Blinking, the policeman fell back. Seumas, a cascade of

Celtic oratory spouting from his lips, plunged forward seeking to push Roddie back deeper into the cart. Patrick and Jakey did likewise, falling over each other in their urgency. Great was the confusion, Jean began to shriek in hysterical fashion, the other females joining in. And from the rear Dougal came running, shouting, two leaping mongrels barking at his heels and snapping at the young constable. From away down the road somewhere an impatient motorist at the end of the queue pressed his klaxon steadily.

"Och, to hell—get oot o' this, the lot o' you!" the policeman cried, scarcely able to make himself heard. "Come on—get moving! Damned savages, that's what you are! Shut up, you! Get those dugs oot o' this! An' keep that big drunken stirk in there quiet, see—or I'll run you in for a breach o' the peace! Go on. Look lively. Scram!"

Quietly, Alicky Shand slipped forward to the garron's head and led the noisy four-wheeled battlefield on along the road.

The third cart and its appendages were shushed through that road-block like poultry that had somehow got into the drawing-room, with no suggestion of a desire for inspection.

Roddie and the dogs kept up their hullabaloo for a good seventy yards farther, till Jean's sham hysterics almost became real ones.

"Och, goodness gracious me—now wasn't that a bar!" Seumas asked the world at large. "Mercy to God—is the drink not an awful thing?" And he dug Patrick Kinkaid in the ribs.

That man was too far gone to reply.

It took some time and effort to restore a suitable aura of calm and responsibility to that entourage. Passing through the hamlet of Harrietfield helped, presently, to foster an air of sobriety—for there was a Police Station there, Jean said. But nobody challenged them—in fact, most probably the incumbent was one of those two heroes back at the checkpoint.

Safely on the open road beyond, Jean was able to assure her friends that they would now most likely have a clear run for the remainder of the lower Glen Almond. There was not another crossroads or major fork for four miles, till this road crossed the river and joined the one that followed the south bank of the Almond, at Buchanty, near the head of the glen. If there was another police trap anywhere in this direction, it would be there. Beyond that they would be on to the main Crieff-Aberfeldy highway, where surely they could not possibly be stopping all vehicles.

The Macphails were no believers in unseemly haste, and Seumas halted the cavalcade for a midday break, just before noon, on highish ground near the entrance to Glenalmond House, where they could look down on the bridge and road junction below, at Buchanty. Obviously there was no police or checkpoint there. It seemed as though they were beyond the net. Here there was wood and a little burn and greensward. What more could they ask? Patrick could, and did, ask for further progress, while the going was good—but did not press the point in the face of the tinkers' gentle stubbornness.

The women lit a fire, and brewed tea, producing large quantities of stale bread and, of all things, a couple of cold boiled fowls, sketchily plucked. Only Roddie Roy had the hardihood to ask where these came from—to be told, simply, guilelessly, that they came from a farm, just.

Patrick ate, chafing a little at the delay. Patience was a virtue that he much admired and coveted, but which was all too apt to elude him.

They were still at their meal, when, round a bend of the road behind them, from the eastwards, a car came, driven fast—a large black car, disturbingly familiar. It slowed down as it neared their verdant roadside halt, and came to a stop a mere dozen yards away. Patrick groaned.

Front and rear doors opened, and three men got out— the brass-hatted Superintendent and two plain-clothes men. They came forward, deliberately. There was neither time nor opportunity for any useful move on the part of the picnic-party.

The Superintendent nodded briefly. " 'Morning," he said. "You seem to be enjoying yourselves. These gentlemen would like a word with you." And he turned to his two companions.

161

"Och, good morning, yes," Seumas answered, courteously. *"Tha la briagh ann. 'S i tha soilleir."*

"Eh? Ah . . . h'rr'mm. Better stick to English, if I were you. We're not Gaelic speakers."

"Gheibh sibh bhur taghadh."

"One or two questions I'd like to ask you people," the larger of the two lounge-suited individuals mentioned in a Cockney voice. He was a heavy-featured man, remarkably pale of complexion, who kept his heavy-lidded eyes so nearly closed as to seem to have to hold his head back to see out of them. "I'm Inspector Dawson, Scotland Yard. This is Inspector Peters. I think you know, we're making investigations into this Coronation Stone business?"

"I am after speaking not good English," Seumas said, as with difficulty. *"Tha me gle dhuilich."*

"Nach bochd sin!" Dougal added, helpfully.

Patrick grunted.

"I think perhaps you know a little more than you'll admit," the Superintendent suggested. "Most tinkers do, we've found. I'd carry on, Inspector."

The man Dawson evidenced no change of tone nor expression. "Do you people know anything at all about this Stone?"

Silence greeted that.

He went on, evenly. "You passed us, with your wagons, at the entrance to Kincaid House, this morning just on 8 a.m. You did not pass through either of our two road-checks on this road, farther back. But you did at the last one, at the point called Chapelhill. Which means that you came by a very devious and difficult series of lanes and byways. We've checked up on that. Why, I wonder?"

Silence.

"Come, come," the other detective said, jovially. He was small and rubicund, red-faced and smiling, with quick darting eyes. By his voice. Patrick thought that he might be of Welsh extraction. "These are just routine enquiries. Nothing to be alarmed about."

Roddie Roy spat thoughtfully.

"That, by the description, will be the inebriate? The one who was so unfortunately drunk, an hour or two back," Inspector Peters mentioned, genially. "He has made a swift recovery, I'm happy to see!"

Seumas laughed, and pointed. "Trunk!" he said, and shook his head. " 'S uamhasach an galar i. Not good."

The MacGregor was now endeavouring to look as owlish as possible.

"I would like to know why you used that difficult side route?" the man Dawson reiterated—not a man to be turned from his theme, obviously. "We've had motorcycle patrols along there, and they tell us that you did not call at any of the farmhouses."

Nobody enlightened him.

"I put it to you that you might have been trying to avoid our road-checks?"

Blank incomprehension.

"You must have had some reason—three wagons going that hard way? Even fording a difficult stream. It may be quite unconnected with what we're after. But we'd like to know." There was a sort of steely patience about that.

"Not understanding," Seumas mentioned, conversationally.

The policemen exchanged glances.

"That driver of yours—he wouldn't know any of their lingo, would he, Super?" the detective Peters suggested.

The uniformed man shook his head. "I shouldn't think so. He is a Highlandman, yes—but there's not many know the Gaelic nowadays." He turned, and raised his voice. "You know any Gaelic, Maclean?"

In the driving seat of the car a young constable shook his head also. "No, sir. Sorry, sir."

"I believe these people know a lot more than they're pretending to," the Superintendent went on. "I'd say there's something mighty suspicious about them. They're a big party to be traipsing through under-populated country like this. Eight men. That size of party you'd be finding at fairs and gatherings."

Roddie Roy got uncertainly to his feet, leaned back against

a cart to steady himself, belched loudly, and then went lurching over towards the road and the car, muttering to himself. All eyes watched him. He reached the car, and leaned against it, peering in at the driver, and leering. He said something garbled, and hiccuped in the constable's face. The hand that held him up was gripping the socket of the car's lance-like radio aerial.

Patrick, for one, held his breath.

"Keep away from there, man!" the Superintendent said authoritatively.

Roddie, grinning, paid no heed. He began to sing, without words, the approximate tune of "Ho-Ro, My Nut-Brown Maiden", loudly, unmelodiously.

Seumas said something in his own tongue to Dougal, and that man, with the two other tinkers, got up and strolled over to Roddie's side, grinning. They laid hands on his arm and shoulders.

Immediately the singing stopped, and roars of rage replaced it. The MacGregor, glaring, began to swing one arm like a windmill, fist clenched—though with the other he still hung on to the aerial. He kicked out with his outsize boots also. One or two kicks struck the car's gleaming black paintwork. The driver got out, squaring his shoulders and looking as though he was prepared to die in the line of duty against any Goliath—but with the odd glance at his superiors. From under one of the carts the greyhound-collie gave tongue, and came to Roddie's aid, snarling. The old woman raised her voice to keen to the heavens, and all females present assisted, Jean included.

"Damn it all—this is impossible!" Inspector Peters cried, his joviality forgotten. "Shut up, everybody! Be quiet! Superintendent, for God's sake—can't you do anything with these people? Look at that drunken fool—he'll have that aerial broken in a minute!"

"I don't think this is all genuine," the Superintendent said heavily. "Looks like a put-up job to me." He had to shout to make himself heard. "I say—it looks like a put-up job to me!" He turned, and hurried over to aid his driver rescue the car and its fittings.

"Confound this—it's no good, George!" Peters cried to his companion. "Too many of them. And all these wretched women! We need a bunch of men."

"Agreed," the ponderously calm Dawson nodded. "And an interpreter. We'll get them. Don't panic!" And majestically, unhurriedly, head farther back than ever, he paced to the car.

Roddie was still creating uproar, with one hand firmly attached to that aerial. The constable was having to defend himself from the attentions of the dog, but the three tinkers were pulling strongly on the Macgregor's free arm. The Superintendent, coming up, aimed a blow at Roddie's wrist— and promptly drew the leaping dog's attentions upon himself. Seumas and Patrick came running—and so did the remainder of the tinkers' dogs.

With remarkable celerity and agility for such a monumentally dignified man, Inspector Dawson slipped into the rear seat of the car. Inspector Peters only just getting in behind him before the door slammed shut. From within they made pained and urgent beckoning motions to their brawling fellows outside. The Superintendent's fine hat had gone now, revealing a shiny pink bald head. He did not look half the man that he had been.

With a great final whoop of triumph, the MacGregor put all his strength into an explosive tug that burst the tapering aerial right out of its socket. Roddie, howling with laughter thereat, staggered back and back, lashing the thing like a whip all around, the three tinkers staggering with him. Aiming a shrewd kick at the angry dog, the young constable, looking from one thing to another unhappily, stooped and gallantly retrieved his superior's brass-bound hat for him. Then, at the imperative knocking and gesticulating that came from inside the car, he shrugged, nodded, and climbed back in beside his steering-wheel. With what dignity he could muster, lips very tightly closed—and an eye on the dog, on all the dogs—the Superintendent resumed his hat, edged round the bonnet of the car, and nipped in at the door that his junior swung open for him. With a loud and lordly roar the powerful engine

165

came to life, and the car jerked forward amidst a shower of roadside gravel and a puff of blue smoke.

Without a backward glance showing through its rear window, it swept away down the hill and was lost in the trees.

Roderick MacGregor surpassed all his previous whooping. "Jings!" he yelled. "Was yon no' great! Was I no' magneeficent? Bluidy wars—whatna cairry-on! An' they canna work their bluidy wireless, neither!" And he brandished his trophy as though it had a poached salmon on the end of it.

"This is where we jump to it!" Patrick Kincaid cried. "Everybody—at the double-quick!"

"The Lord Goad be praised!" Jakey Reid screeched. "Guid riddance to the hosts o' Midian!"

Even the Macphails could move swiftly, it transpired, when the occasion undeniably demanded it. In little more time than it takes to tell, the three carts were on the road again, and racing down the hill towards the bridge over the Almond— actually in the wake of the patrol-car. This time there were no walkers or stragglers.

As they had wheeled out of their halting-place, Patrick, with a shouted word to Jean, had sprinted forward and leapt up on to Seumas's cart. There, sitting beside the tinker, he panted.

"Look—the map says it's about four miles from here, through the Sma' Glen, to where the private road branches off up upper Glen Almond. How long will it take us to get there? Going as hard as we can?"

"Och, we'll be doing it in half an hour, maybe."

"There won't have to be any maybe about it!" Patrick returned, grimly. "Or else we're sunk. Those police will be back after us, just as quickly as they can. They've only gone for reinforcements. A squad of constables. And an interpreter. They'll get the men easily enough—though it may take longer to find a Gaelic-speaking policeman. But there must be quite a few of these in Perthshire? The trouble is, they may send a squad after us, to stop us, *before* they come themselves with the interpreter. Fortunately they can't use their short-wave radio, thanks to Roddie. But they've got a fast car—and the district's lousy with policemen."

"Aye," Seumas nodded equably. "But, och—they'll be needing the great lot of men to be handling the likes of us terrible wild devils! Eight of us. They'll not be finding eight policemen in Glen Almond in five minutes of time, I'm thinking."

"No. That's true. They may have to go quite a way to muster a posse. Right back to Kincaid House, perhaps. Ten miles. And they can't denude the whole area—for they don't *know* we've got the Stone. Roddie's an awful fool—but it was a stroke of genius to put their radio out of order. Let me see. Allowing for winding roads, explanations, and so on, it looks as though they're bound to give us our half-hour. Though of course they may meet up with another patrol-car, or a motorcyclist, and send them after us to keep tabs on us."

"Such would be wise men, whatever, and keep their distance, I'm thinking."

"Maybe, yes. But . . ."

They swayed and lurched across the bridge, and up to the road junction beyond, the ponies' broad hooves sounding a hollow tattoo on the tarmac. Considering their stocky build and short legs, the garrons were making a remarkably good speed, all three carts remaining bunched together as they clattered along. How the ancient vehicles held together was a miracle to Patrick Kincaid.

Where they joined the south road, and where the police-car almost certainly would have turned left, they slewed dramatically to the right, westwards, without slackening speed, their iron-rimmed wheels screeching alarmingly on the road. The Highland hills were marshalling before them now, range upon range. In a mile they would be into the Sma' Glen.

"No police check here," Patrick said. "If there's one in front, where we join the main Crieff road, we'll just have to drive straight through it!"

"That is so, yes," Seumas agreed cheerfully.

167

"Look—we won't have much time for goodbyes, when we reach our parting-place. I want to say thank you, now, for all you've done. We'd never have managed without you. You've been wonderful, all of you."

"Chust that," the other acknowledged, nodding agreeably. "Och, yes. You are for us parting, then? At Newton Bridge?"

"Oh, yes. We've got you into enough trouble already, I'm afraid. But once we're apart, I don't see that the police will have anything on *you*. You needn't have known anything about the Stone. I shouldn't think they could pin anything on you that you couldn't handle easily enough."

"Och, man—nobody is after worrying about that, at all."

"Maybe not. But we've got to think about it. Anyway, there'd be no point in you people coming up the upper glen with us. It's a dead end. *We're* going to ground there—but you'd be stuck. And three tinkers' carts up there would look mighty strange."

"Whatever you say . . ."

At a fast trot they breasted the hill up to the signposted triangle of grass that marked the junction with the main north-south road, A832, Crieff-Aberfeldy. In fine style they swung round to face north—to the marked admiration of two young men in a passing sports car, one of whom yippeed loudly. There were no police here, either.

And now the jaws of the mountains that had beckoned and enticed them for so long, engulfed them at last in the Sma' Glen. Stern and frowning they hemmed in the river, first in a narrow gorge and then into a dark and almost closed valley, V-shaped and rock-ribbed. The Highlands at last received them.

The Sma' Glen, in reality, is only a strange right-angled connecting link between the Lowland lower Almond valley and the fiercely Highland upper glen. For some two and a half miles it threads the harsh craggy shoulders of the mountains, and then, where the upper glen strikes off westwards, the road swings away abruptly to the north-east, to climb and climb up out of it on to the vast rolling heather moors. Along that twisting two and a half miles the three carts rocked and flounced and rattled, then, in a crazy stampede that would have been exhilarating had there not been so many possibilities of disaster—from pursuit, vehicular disintegration, collision with astonished motorists, falling horses, from the Stone itself crashing through the boarding of its frail cart, which became Patrick's immediate major worry. Most of the way, indeed, he leaned out of the cart, with his head turned anxiously to watch the progress of Jean's vehicle behind. In the watching, of course, he kept an eye on the road farther back still. But, no black police-car or motorcyclist appeared.

Then, with the road turning suddenly to cross the narrow old stone bridge ahead of them, at the start of its abrupt climb out of the glen, Patrick touched Seumas's arm, and nodded. At an open gate, where a rough road branched off to the left, a hundred yards farther, the steaming sweating horses were drawn up. After a quick glance back, down the road, with no sign of pursuit as yet, the people from the Mains cart came hurrying forward to congregate round the first vehicle, to be joined in a moment or two by Dougal and his colleagues.

"This is it, then," Patrick said. "It's thanks, again. And goodbye. And good luck! We daren't wait . . ."

"You have been splendid!" Jean declared. "Heroes! Any time you come to Kincaid Mains, you will be welcome, I assure you."

"Hell, aye! Up the tinks!" Roddie cried. "The MacGregors an' the Macphails'll show them, by Jings!"

"See—I said you wouldn't be the losers over all this," Patrick went on, hurriedly. "Can't go into that, now. But next time you call at the Mains, it will be waiting for you."

"And this cart, too," Jean added.

"Och, likely we will be seeing you before that," Seumas said. "Four miles on, there is a bit of a roadie goes off by Loch Freuchie, through Glen Quaich, to Kenmore on Loch Tay. Och, we'll be along there, see you. There is a bit we're after going to sometimes. At Shian, it is. We'll be there for two-three days. If you're after wanting help, maybe. Och, five miles across the hills from your glen, no more. You'll be finding us, easy. Near the bit of a school."

169

"Good. Grand. Bless you—all of you! We must be off."

"Goodbye, Seumas! Goodbye, Dougal! Goodbye, Kirsty and Ailie!"

"Up the rebels! Scotland for ivver!"

The Stone party piled back into their cart, with the exception of Patrick who, when Jean had turned the garron off the main road and through the gateway on to the gravel track, shut the gate behind them. It had not been closed before— but no harm in shutting it now, he decided. Large notices around it proclaimed the names of the hydro-electric contractors working up at the head of the glen, that the road was private, and that vehicles using it did so at their own risk. A signpost indicated a foot-track to Ardtalnaig on Loch Tay, seventeen miles away.

Amidst waving, the carts moved apart.

It was not until they were well on their way that the Mains cart's occupants discovered that the greyhound-collie was still curled up alongside the Stone of Destiny.

XII

IT was a bonny, long, narrow-floored glen between high rugged hills, and according to Jean it thrust fifteen miles into the great watershed of Breadalbane. Hundreds of empty square miles, of heather and deer-grass, rock and bog, peat-hag and running, tumbling, seeping water, lay ahead of them. Personally, once they deserted this ragged ribbon of a road, they were safe; it would require an army, and a nimble one, to hunt them down in that far-flung wilderness. Except for the Stone; that was a different story.

They passed a small farmhouse in the very mouth of the glen, with sundry pipes and contractor's gear lying around nearby—and after that, emptiness. There were four more places dotted over the long reaches of the glen, but Jean did not think that they were all occupied. Auchnafree, a former laird's house of the MacGregors, lay about six miles up. But the hills on either side were vacant, tenanted only by a few sheep and many deer and the buzzards and eagles of the high tops. Unfortunately, their cart could hardly have escaped observation at this first house, unless there was nobody at home.

It was more than time to make up their minds about intentions and prospects. The main question was—where to hide the Stone where it would be safe? Without that, the problem of their own escape would be simple. It had to be somewhere to which they could manhandle the thing, yet sufficiently out-of-the-way not to be found by searchers—for they had to reckon with the police tracing them up here and instituting such a search, eventually.

Patrick pointed to the vast litter of tumbled rocks that clothed most of the lower braesides. "Seems to me, we could dump it almost anywhere amongst these rocks, and it would never be noticed," he said.

"Yes. That would be all right for a bit," the girl agreed. "But not indefinitely. It's very dark, this Stone—almost black. In any really careful combing of the ground, it would stand out, I'm afraid, amongst all this grey and reddish stone. And we could hardly just leave it bare to the weather, anyway, could we? Mightn't that damage it, after being hidden away from the elements all these centuries?"

"I shouldn't think so. Not hard stone like that. But I agree that we can hardly just leave it lying about in the open, for all that. We'll have to bury it again. And in a place like this, almost anywhere will do—so long as it isn't obvious that something has been recently buried there."

"That's right. And since we mustn't be seen at the digging, it will have to be done at night. Which means we've got eight hours or so to fill in first—it's barely 2 p.m. now. Eight hours in which we mustn't be seen or caught by any police who may follow us!"

"M'mmm. That's the problem, yes. Though, of course, we could always dump the thing meantime amongst some of these rockfalls, and move on a bit without it. Then, if the police did come up on us, we wouldn't have it, and they'd have nothing against us."

"Yes. That probably would be best. The thing to do, then, is to look for a suitable place to put it temporarily. Anywhere. Only, it mustn't be obvious."

"Aye—an' it had better be sort o' near whaur we aim to bury it in the end," Roddie put in. "We dinna want ower long bummin' aboot wi' the cairt on this road, in the dark. They'll maybe patrol the road, jist, wi' motorbikes, if they're suspicious."

"That's true."

"I think we want some sort of a landmark to guide us— for the eventual resting-place," the girl said. "For ease of finding it again. For establishing its position. This is something precious, irreplaceable. We daren't risk losing it, ourselves— as we might do amongst all this stony wilderness. It's a great responsibility, really."

She made a strange picture, hunched there at the front of

the old cart, wrapped in her plaid, straggle-haired and dirty-faced, the rope reins of her garron held in stained fingers—but still somehow appealingly attractive.

"We can discuss all that later. I'm worried about police on our tail, right now."

"Yes—but it affects where we're going to dump the Stone for the moment, doesn't it? You see all these corries that open off on the left?" The south side of the glen was made up of a succession of thrusting shoulders running out of a great massif of ridge, with deep hollows between them, a series of hanging valleys tailing out into the vast flanks of the range. "The second one ahead has a cave in it. Away high up, at the head of the corrie. More than a mile back from this road, I should think. And possibly, 800 to 1000 feet above it."

"Heavens—we'd never get the Stone up there!"

"No, no—of course not! My idea is, that it might make an ideal base and sort of look-out post. Where we could overlook almost the whole of this end of the glen. I've had it in my mind all along. If we could hide the Stone somewhere in view of that, then we might be able to keep an eye on it, you see, till all this fuss dies down."

"That's an idea, yes. It's a proper cave? Where we could camp?"

"Oh, yes. At least, I've never actually seen it. I've tried to find it more than once, but never actually reached it. It's pretty inaccessible—but then, we'd want it that way, wouldn't we. We used to come up here for picnics, you know, when I was a kid. We never quite found this cave—it's very high up, you see. But an old shepherd told us about it. Actually, you'll see it marked on your Ordnance Survey map—though not in any exact position. Foolishly they've got it down as Thief's Cave. But that's a mistake. It should be Fionn's or Fingal's Cave, in Coire Chultrain, the Corrie of the Skulkers, or Caterans. MacGregors, no doubt! Fingal is supposed to have had a lot to do with this area, with Ossian his son."

But Patrick was listening with only half an ear. He kept peering round the side of the cart, back whence they had come. "Yes. Fine. But where are we to put the Stone?"

173

"I thought if we could get it across the river. Put it where the burn that flows out of that corrie joins the Almond? It would be readily identifiable. And we could keep it under observation from up at the cave. D'you think?"

Jean's voice was drowned in the loud rolling clangour of metal, as the cart went over the loose iron bars of a cattle-grid. This was the second of these that they had crossed—comparatively new-looking, and no doubt the work of the hydro-electric contractors, to save them having gates to open and shut, for stock, on this access road to their workings.

The thought made an impression on Patrick. "I wonder—is there apt to be a lot of lorry traffic up and down here? Contractors' lorries? We'll have to watch that."

The cattle-grid made a different sort of impact on Roddie Roy. "Say," he jerked, eyes narrowed. "Yon things are great for goin' ower—so long as the bars are in them! If they werena'!" He grinned. "If there were nae bars, there's mair'n a foot o' drop into the pit o' them. Lined wi' concrete. An' the bars are loose. You'd no' get a car past one o' yon!"

"By Jove—you're right! That's worth remembering."

"Uh-huh."

"All the same . . ." Patrick frowned, peering round behind again—as he did every other minute. "Plans are all right—but I'm not happy about all this plodding along. As though we hadn't a care in the world. It's an hour since those police left us. More. How far to this spot of yours, where the burn from the corrie joins the river, Jean?"

"Oh, it's more than a mile yet. Conichan's about half a mile farther still, I think. That's a sheep farm."

"Then I vote we get the Stone unloaded and dumped temporarily, right here. Look at all those stones, littering all the foot of the hill. It would be fine amongst these, for the time being. We can shift it on later. We might have the police on top of us any moment. *Probably* they'd follow the Macphails up the main road—but not necessarily. Anyway, they'd soon see there was a cart missing from the outfit, and maybe come back to look for us."

Though all felt that it was a pity to have to make two bites

174

at the cherry, with the Stone having to be moved again at night, the wisdom of Patrick's suggestion was accepted. They pulled up, with the stony hill-skirts close on their right, and the steep slope down to the river on their left, and began to uncover the Stone from amongst its rags and sacking.

They had got the thing half out of the cart, still on its stretcher from the graveyard, when Roddie Roy burst into profanity. All eyes turned on him, and then swung to follow his stare. Down the road that they had come, perhaps three-quarters of a mile away, two black cars had appeared around a bend, running close together.

"Lord—that's torn it!" Patrick exclaimed. "Quick—we've got to get quit of this thing! No time to cart it across the road and up amongst the stones. They'd see us at it. Have to just pitch it down this bank. Nothing else for it. Hurry!"

Working feverishly, almost superhumanly, the four men got their heavy burden drawn out from the cart, staggered the two or three paces to the edge of the bank with it—and paused, reeling.

"Not down there!" Patrick gasped. "It'll go straight down into the river! Never get it up again. Along there. Farther along. Quick! The slope's not so steep. It'll maybe catch in those tree-roots and boulders."

Drunkenly they tottered sideways along the very lip of the bank, fifty feet above the river, Jean doing her best to help. Then Roddie, his great muscles bunched and bulging, tripped over the dog which clung to his legs. The stretcher canted abruptly, and the Stone slid. The MacGregor, by an amazing contortion, only just managed to hurl himself out of the way in time, as the great mass of stone crashed downwards, struck the bank with a ground-shaking thud, and began to slip.

For a moment or two they all stared, panting. All expected the Stone to plunge right down the slope and into the water. But it did not do so. Its very weight, plus its squared edges, seemed to restrain it, to dig itself into the soft topsoil. The roots of the birches and alders that grew there undoubtedly helped. After sliding a mere slow yard, it stuck, and hung there, poised, not ten feet below the road, bottom up.

"Good heavens!" Patrick cried. "Damn and blast it! We can't risk shifting it now." He glanced away down the road. The two cars were not driving fast on that pothole-strung track, but nevertheless had halved the distance from them. "We'll have to leave it. And pray they won't look over, or snoop around. Maybe we can think of some diversion? Quick, now! Roddie—you'd better get out of sight. Keep right out of it. They'll look for trouble from you. They needn't know you're with this party, at all. Down at the river, somewhere. Jakey—you can be collecting sticks for a fire. Down the bank, there. Come up with them, soon after they reach us. We're camping. Got it? The rest of us—get this stretcher back into the cart, and stuff on top of it. Hurry for Pete's sake!"

When the two cars, mud-spattered now, came rolling up to their position, and there halted, Jean was leading the garron and cart off the roadway to the right, on to the rock-strewn grass of the hillfoot, with Patrick preceding her, a heap of old sacks and blankets in his arms. They hoped that they looked as though they were selecting a site to camp. From the cars, many faces considered them—nine in all, including their old friends the Superintendent and the two Scotland Yard sleuths. No greetings were exchanged.

The cars disgorged their occupants—four constables and a sergeant from the rear vehicle, the three senior officers and a new driver from the front one. At a shout, and beckoning gesture from the Superintendent, Patrick turned, his reluctance by no means affected, to face them. Alicky Shand watched gloomily from the rear of the cart. The cars' drivers got in again, and began the complicated manoeuvre of turning them on the narrow road.

The Superintendent waited patiently for his driver. Then he turned. "You!" he called peremptorily to Patrick. "Come here. You'll answer our questions now!" The driver said something unintelligible, presumably repeating the statement in the Gaelic.

Unhappily Patrick moved nearer. Suddenly he sensed Jean moving close at his back, and smiled to himself.

176

"Where is your drunk friend now?" Inspector Peters asked and had it interpreted for him, likewise.

Patrick's quandary was no light one. He could not go on playing dumb—and yet he had no word of Gaelic. Anything that he said would have to be in English. There was no getting out of the predicament, this time.

"None of your dumb insolence, now!" the Superintendent said sternly. "Or do you want to be charged with obstructing the police in the execution of their duty?" Curiously, that sounded almost lyrical the way that the driver translated it.

"Och, no—naethin' o' the sort," Patrick said then, in the broadest Doric that he could make himself pronounce. "Fire aheid, Mister."

"Confound it—you speak English, then? After all! Well, I'm damned!"

"Och, I ken it a wee," Patrick conceded, shrugging.

"Then why didn't you answer when we spoke to you before? Come on—out with it, man."

"Och, whit way should I? It wasna' me you were spierin' at? It was aye at Shamus. An' he speaks the Gaelic."

"Rubbish! What nonsense! What impudence! You knew perfectly well that we were speaking to you all, not just to one man. You were just evading our questions. You watch yourself, my man—I warn you!" He turned to the detectives. "You see—it's as I feared. They could speak English all the time!"

"D'you call that English!" the man Peters said, sourly.

At this stage, Jakey arrived on the scene with an armful of birch twigs.

"Another English-speaker?" the Superintendent barked at him.

Jakey looked venomous, seemed as though he was going to spit, shrugged instead, and went unspeaking over to the cart.

"My man," Inspector Dawson said, just as weightily as before. "What is your name?"

"McSporran," Patrick lied, without a blink of the eyelids. "Mick McSporran."

"Well, McSporran, tell me why you and your friends took that difficult route by the ford, this morning?" A persistent man, this.

"Och, whit for no'? It's a free country, is it no'?"

"I see. And why did you separate from the other gypsies, back there?"

"Wha're you callin' gypsies—eh? No' me, I hope? An' there's nae crime in goin' your ain road is there? They're goin' some place else than us—that's a'."

"You'd better watch how you speak, McSporran," the Superintendent warned. "Keep a civil tongue in your head!"

"My tongue's my ain, is it no'? I've committed nae offence. Whit are you, er, geysers chairgin' me wi'?" Patrick found it a distinct trial to keep up his unaccustomed accent in time with his racing thoughts.

"Smart fellow, eh?" Peters commented. "I think we might short-circuit this. What do you know, McSporran, about this Coronation Stone? I want a full answer. And it will be noted, mark you, for future reference!"

Patrick drew back his shoulders a little. "Jist the same as yoursel'—whit I read in the papers, Mister. Onythin' else?"

The Superintendent glanced round at the interested ranks of the attendant constabulary. It was obvious that he felt that this was not proving a very useful lesson for them on the slick handling of suspects. He cleared his throat strongly. "This is a waste of time, gentlemen," he said, turning to the detectives. "I know this kind—standing on their rights. We'll take them in for questioning. He'll change his tune at the office, they always do. In the meantime, no harm in having a look in their cart." He motioned his men forward. "Search that cart," he ordered.

All six uniformed policemen strode forward to the assault. Perhaps they feared resistance. Perhaps they feared that the terrible drunkard was still lying inside.

They found out differently. Hardly had they tossed the odds and ends and old iron out of the cart, their superiors coming forward to watch interestedly, and Jean, Patrick and Alicky standing sullenly by, when suddenly all eyes were turned elsewhere. The starter of the first parked car whirred, and the powerful engine roared into life. Roddie Roy was sitting in the driving-seat, the dog beside him. The door slammed shut, and with a leap like a bucking bronco the vehicle jerked forward, to go zigzagging down the road.

From an open window the big MacGregor yelled out at them, "Scram! Scram!" and gestured back up the glen.

There was a moment or two of appalled and perhaps forgivable confusion and loud-voiced if unprofitable fury, and then training and discipline reasserted itself, and the police dashed as one man for the remaining car. Indeed, so unanimous and consistent was their reaction to this outrageous challenge that all ranks acted identically, and only the fact that the seniors were older and less spry on their feet than the young constables, prevented them leading the chase in the waiting vehicle. As it was, the sergeant, Superintendent, and two detectives were the last to reach the car, in that order, and found it already filled. Some slight difference of opinion about who should go and who should stay thereupon developed.

Not that the pseudo-tinkers had eyes for much of this. As soon as the constabulary started to run, Jakey was tugging at the elbows of Patrick and Jean, uttering urgently something that might be described as a whispered screech.

"Quick—bolt for it! Up the glen!" he cried, dancing about in his agitation. "Roddie says bolt for it. In the cairt. He tellt me—doon at the watter, see. Och, dinna stand there—aff wi' us! Like he said. Us it is that's to scram!"

Patrick's mind worked swiftly. This might be the worst of folly. And again it might not. And it was no time to stop and argue. The Superintendent had said that he would take them in for questioning. That must not happen. And they had to get these policemen away from the vicinity of the Stone. Maybe Roddie had the rights of it . . .

"Okay!" he cried. "Into the cart."

Alicky had already anticipated the order, and Jean did not question it. Bundling in anyhow, they abandoned such of their gear as was outside the cart. Jean grabbed the reins, and jerked the garron into motion. They had no whip, but using the

179

ends of the rope, she whacked the beast's hindquarters. Straight into a startled trot the pony broke—at precisely the same moment as the second car plunged off furiously in the wake of the first, in the opposite direction to themselves.

As they swung on to the road, lurching wildly, they could hear shouts behind them. Patrick peered round the side. Two neatly lounge-suited gentlemen stood alone and abandoned in the middle of that bonny Highland track, as lost-looking and out of place there as tinks would have been in Piccadilly, one looking up the glen and one down.

"The Babes in the Wood!" Patrick Kincaid chortled, with a quite unsuitable glee. "This . . . this is utterly fantastic, and quite crazy . . . but, up the Gregorach!"

They careered on up that gravelly winding road at full and spectacular bone-shaking speed—unnecessary too, probably, since undoubtedly there was no pursuit at this stage. Soon Scotland Yard was lost to sight.

Sternly, grimly, Patrick took himself in hand, seeking to discipline his over-stimulated mind to useful constructive thinking. "We'll have to abandon the cart, and take to the hills," he declared, breathless with their bumping progress. "Only thing to do, now. Lie low somewhere. Or, better—make for that cave of yours, Jean. Out of sight. Roddie knows about it. He'll make for it. The only place that *was* mentioned."

"Yes. Yes. You think he'll be all right? He won't be caught?"

The girl's voice was high-pitched, excited, only just short of the hysterical. She was having her own battle with her wits, obviously. Her brown-stained knuckles showed white as she gripped the reins.

"That one will be all right," Patrick assured. "He can look after himself, if anyone can."

"I hope so—oh, I hope so. But, for us—we can leave the cart anywhere. It doesn't matter. But Garve—my pony. That's different. We can't just abandon *him*!"

"We can't take a horse with us! We'd be spotted a mile off!"

180

"No. But . . . probably he'd try to follow us. Even if we loosed him from the cart. Look—Conichan's on in front. A mile from here, perhaps. We could stop this side of its nearest field. Push Garve into the field, and leave him. They'd look after him—the farm people—if we couldn't rescue him for a while. And then we'd cross the river and take to the heather."

"Fair enough. But *is* there such a field?"

"There always is. It's a decent-sized sheep farm, and they've got to have fields along the valley-floor to grow their winter feed. Nowhere else for them. I don't actually remember the layout, but there's almost bound to be some enclosed pasture."

"All right. That sounds the best thing."

As they rattled along, crossing one more cattle-grid, the road now high above the river, now down at the waterside, the great scoop of the chosen corrie, Coire Chultrain, began to open across the stream to their left, lofty, crag-ringed, over a mile deep and half that across, much larger than either of the two corries that they had already passed.

"Right up at the head of that—a few hundred feet below the skyline. Somewhere under those cliffs you see—that's where the cave is," Jean pointed. "We should be all right there, don't you think?"

It crossed Patrick's mind that that would depend on what was meant by all right. But he nodded. "Grand," he approved. "Could hardly be better—as to situation, anyway."

Rounding a bend of road and river, Jean exclaimed. "There you are. Cattle. And, look—two or three horses of their own. That field will do fine for Garve. And see—over there is the burn that flows down from the corrie to join the river. Where I thought we'd bury the Stone. Though, of course—if we abandon the cart, we've no transport to bring the Stone up here."

"No. Of course not. I hadn't thought of that. It can't be helped. You know—I think that field is just *too* convenient. If we put the horse in there, and leave the cart nearby, it's going to be pretty obvious that we took to the heather hereabouts. And that corrie up there is just about the first thing to take the eye. We might as well put up a signpost! I think we'd better drive on, past the farm, and come back on foot. Inconspicuously."

"Perhaps you're right. A pity—but it would be safer."

They trotted on, passing the farm of Conichan, embowered in its old trees, without challenge or incident. Patrick was at his backwards-looking again, now. About half a mile beyond, at a little roadside gravel-pit, they drew up, unhitched the garron, and took the clothes bundles and such food as was left, abandoning the rest. The steaming pony they led back a few hundred yards to the last of the little fields of reeds and rough grazing, and there turned it in, Jean a little conscience-stricken. Then, leaving it, they hurried down to the riverside, seeking a place to cross.

The Almond was only half the river that it had been last time that they crossed it, fortunately, and they found shallows to splash across without difficulty, Jean scorning assistance. On the other side they hastened for the cover of a steep narrow burn-channel that scored a wedge down the hill-side, lined with ferns, dwarf birches and rowans, and that should offer them a reasonably well-hidden stairway to higher ground. They had to get up to a level where the swell of the mountainside would allow them to move along the contours out of sight of the road—and from the configuration of this slope, they would have to mount fairly high to do so. They began to climb.

Soon Jean cried a halt. She was nimble-footed enough, but could not climb in the sloppy old footgear that she had affected as tinker-woman. She had a perfectly serviceable pair of brogues in her bundle.

Patrick nodded. His own borrowed boots were not proving too comfortable for this sort of thing. "No reason why we should play tinker any more, is there?" he asked. "That phase seems to be over. We might as well get back into our own togs. We'll be a lot better equipped for the hill."

It was agreed. Jean climbed on ahead a little farther, for privacy's sake, and the change was effected.

The alteration in their appearance, especially Jean's and Patrick's, was extraordinary, however crumpled they were,

182

and still brown-stained. The two Glaswegians looked different too, but surprisingly little more respectable—though their companions did not tell them so. They decided that it might not be wise wholly to discard their tinker gear meantime. It was something of a burden, but they carried it along.

Climbing on, they kept an eye on the road that dwindled and dwindled below them. No traffic of any sort passed up or down. Patrick remarked on the fact that the hydro-electric people did not seem to be very active, and Jean reminded him that it was Saturday afternoon—a thing that he had overlooked.

At last, after perhaps 600 feet, the hillside began to level off to its first major shelf, providing the desired dead ground, invisible from the valley far below. It would not offer them anything like consistent cover, on their way down the glen, of course—but at least it would help greatly, and there was an unlimited supply of boulders, great outcrops, and tall heather to lie low behind, in between.

They left their burn-channel, and started their eastward traverse.

It was on a thrusting shoulder of the hill, the westernmost bastion of their Cateran's Corrie actually, above a row of steep rocky cliffs which the map marked as Eagle's Rock, that they halted at gaze, pointing. Away down the glen, at least a couple of miles off, were two dark specks, close together and stationary. They looked like two tiny black beads strung on the thread of the white road.

"The police cars, for a bet!" Patrick said. "I wonder what that means? How far is that below the point where they caught us up?"

"Not far. No more than half a mile, I'd say," Jean answered. "I think I can make out where we were. You see where the river's glinting in the sun—at that sharpish bend? Well, it was about there, I'm sure."

"Yes. Well, you'd have thought Roddie would have bolted farther than that with his stolen car. He'd have plenty of start."

"Maybe they're on their way back, after recovering their car? I think . . . I'm not sure, but I think I can just see figures moving about just in front of the cars. Or it may be behind them, of course, depending on what way they're facing. This side, anyway."

"They wouldn't be searching for the Stone? If only we had a pair of glasses with us . . ."

"Say—d'you yins see whit I see?" Jakey demanded. "Na, na—no' doon there. Up the hill yonder. See—dodgin' aboot amang thae stanes." And he gestured farther down the glen on their own side, on the opposite shoulder beyond the corrie.

"You're right. It's him—it's Roddie! He's a great lad, that! What a character!"

"Ooh, aye," Jakey agreed. "But he's a right backslider an' blasphemer tae, mind you." He sighed. "Och, the Lord lets him awa' wi' an awfu' lot!"

It was too far actually to identify MacGregor—but it could hardly be anyone else up there, moving along and obviously keeping out of sight of the road. They could see the dog now, too. Assured that they were unobserved themselves, they waved, Jean flapping her tinker's plaid. And presently the distant figure was waving back.

Roddie Roy joined them in mid-corrie, breathless, perspiring, but his red face grinning from ear to ear. He had got rid of his ridiculous raincoat and battered hat. The greyhound-collie nearly wagged its disreputable tail off.

"Hiya, folks!" he cried. "Jings—you're awfu' posh an' smert! Oh, boy—what a caper! Did you see me? Och, you should of seen me, doonbye, though. I fair gi'en them the works. Aye, an' d'you see thae polismen doon there, the noo? Dookin'!" He slapped a hairy knee, laughing heartily. "They're at their Hallowe'en, jist—dookin' for iron bars!"

"We saw the two cars. Halted . . ."

"Sure they're halted! It's a cattle-grid, an' I threw a' the bars into the river! They're dookin' for them, noo—tryin' to fish them oot so's they can get their bluidy caur across. Paddlin' in the watter, wi' their breeks rolled up!" The MacGregor hooted his mirth. "Want to hae a look?" And he slung over to Patrick a powerful pair of prismatic binoculars in a handsome leather case.

"Good Lord, Roddie—these are . . . this is . . . damn it, you shouldn't have . . ."

"What for no'? Better we hae them than them, by Hokey! They were lyin' on the back seat o' yon caur. Scotland Yaird! Bonny ones, tae. Jist hae a wee peek. Climb yon wee knowie, an' you'll see them, likely."

Patrick had his wee peek, and duly saw five constables, tunics off and sleeves and trousers uprolled, plowtering about in the River Almond, with impatient-looking senior officers pacing the road above. It looked as though they had so far found only about half the iron bars.

"Very fine glasses," he acknowledged, coming down from the knoll. "We could do with them, too. All the same, I don't like you taking them. Other people's property. Up to now, we may have obstructed the police a bit—but we haven't done anything to be ashamed of, anything actually illegal."

"Aw, come offit, man Patrick. Be your age!" the MacGregor requested. "We're no' playin' games, noo. It's them, or us. You're right stupid aboot some things. Is he no, Jeannie?"

"Well . . ." She smiled. "I've a certain amount of sympathy for both your points of view. It's done now, anyway. We can send them back to London later, with a nice letter."

"Will we hell!"

"Tell us what you did with their car, Roddie?"

"Och, naethin' much," the hero said, shrugging, a little offended. "Jist breenged doon the road wi' it, dumped it in the river one place, whaur there was a kind of bit ford, an' scrammed it up the ither side. An' hid. Och, they were that worried aboot gettin' their fine caur oot the watter, they didna' come seekin' me at a'. Sae I wheechled off up the glen, jist."

"Out of sight? To the cattle-grid?"

"Sure. No' jist one cattle-grid, neither. I jiggered two o' them. Och, I'd plenties o' time—I'd let the air oot o' one o' their tyres, see."

Jean swallowed audibly. "You had! I . . . I see, yes."

"The first grid I jist sort o' bunged the irons awa'. But the second, I'd mair time, so I doused hauf o' them in the burn,

185

an' hauf poked awa' in roots under the bank. It's them they're no' findin' noo, I guess. Then I jist came on up here." The giant yawned, and stretched hugely. "Gee—I could eat a hale cooper-ative store!"

"We'll eat up at the cave," the girl promised. "Though we're not what you'd call well endowed with provisions. We might as well go there now."

"I want to see if they start looking for the Stone, where they stopped us first," Patrick said.

"Oh, yes."

They had nearly twenty minutes to wait before the cars came hurrying up the glen again. They drew up where the cart had been overtaken—but only for a momentary halt, with obviously no idea of searching for anything save the tinkers themselves. On up the road they sped.

"I wonder what they're promising us, in those cars?" Patrick commented. "I wonder what sort of report the BBC is going to be given to broadcast, tonight! I rather think that restraint will be the watchword!"

In another fifteen minutes a single car came down the road, fast. Roddie, with the glasses, said that he thought that it was probably the top brass. It made no halt at the spot where the Stone lay—or anywhere else.

"Had enough, for the time being," Patrick interpreted. "The other car will have been sent on up the glen for a look around. I think, my friends, that we can relax for a bit. Lord—it's nearly five o'clock! Where's this cave of yours, Jean?"

XIII

THE Corrie of the Caterans was like a great tipped basin gouged out of the mighty side of the Hill of Auchnafree, by glacial action no doubt, spawning a hundred burnlets that coalesced and ran together to form one sizeable stream that cascaded down the centre of the bowl in a series of rushes and pools and quite substantial waterfalls, till it lipped over the lower rim and spilled down the remaining 500 foot drop to the Almond itself. There was much high old heather in the bottom of the corrie, a vast amount of fallen stone from the cliffs that rimmed it, many pieces as large as houses, and innumerable outcrops large and small. But there was also much green grass on the sides of it, and since it was sheltered and cradled within the very arms of the tall hills, it obviously would be a place that the deer loved. And, sure enough, as the fugitives climbed steadily up into the heart of it, a herd of fully thirty hinds drifted out from its upper recesses, were outlined against the skyline for a brief moment or two, all ears and necks, and then were gone with the sailing cloud shadows.

They found their cave, eventually, after no little searching—for there were scores of possible sites in crevices of the crags, hollows under fallen rocks, and so on—high amongst the skirts of the topmost range of small cliffs. It proved to be a fine high dry place, perhaps 20 feet deep, with a dog's-leg bend in the middle, and no musty smell. And from its entry they could look down right to the road, so high were they. They could even see, without having to move, the patch of roadway below which the Stone lay. Even the undemonstrative Alicky admitted that it was no' bad, considering.

They settled down, to make themselves at home—and Patrick found himself quite the least expert at the business. Roddie and his two associates, of course, had lived in the heather for weeks, on their famous freebooting adventure, and Jean—who, it was to be suspected, had always longed to do just this—seemed to have some experience of hill camping. They pulled great armfuls of heather to cover the floor of the cave. Roddie searched about and found a crevice in the cliff-face nearby, that went right up like a chimney, suitably overhung and overgrown—which meant that they could light a fire there in safety, with the smoke dispersing itself so that it would not be visible. Water presented no problems, with two burns at hand. When Patrick wondered about fuel, up here so far above the tree level, it was pointed out to him, scornfully, that there was bog-pine practically everywhere in the Highlands—the roots of the ancient giants of the Caledonian Forest that had once clothed all the land up to a thousand feet and more above the present level that trees would grow. Had he not noticed the jagged fangs and stumps of it, jutting out of the bare peat, on the way up? And it burned like a torch, full of resin.

Jean chose the inner section of the cave for her private accommodation—and bore patiently with Roddie's less than subtle assertions that he'd come through and hold her hand for her whenever she got scared of the dark. She had her plaid still, but the rest of the blankets had been left down in the cart. The MacGregor's easy announcement that they would collect them later, when they were down seeing to the Stone, raised one or two eyebrows.

Food was now the over-riding preoccupation. Their total stock from all sources was not impressive. There were two loaves, some biscuits, mainly broken and crumbled, nine hard-boiled eggs, some slabs of chocolate, and a packet of dates. There had been quite a lot more, together with an old blackened kettle and some broken-handled cups, in a grocer's carton in the cart—but these had been ravished by the constabulary, and left lying on the grass, with the old iron, when they had bolted.

It was while scratching their heads over their less than substantial provisions—though assuring each other that it all might have been much worse, really—that Jean gave a little cry, and pointed. A dead bird lay on the pulled heather, in the very mouth of the cave—a half-grown grouse.

"Where on earth did that come from? It wasn't here before. It couldn't have been. Is it dead?"

Patrick picked it up. "Yes. But it's quite warm. A cheeper. An immature grouse."

"Och, there's lashings o' them on the hill. I put up hundreds," Roddie declared. "Did *you* no'?"

"Yes. But how did it get here?"

"Och, they're no' awfu' good at flyin', yet. But the hell wi' that. I'll cook it. It's no' very big for the five o' us, but . . ."

"But we don't know what it died of!" Jean complained.

"Yonder's what it died o'!" Alicky said, pointing. They turned. Across the heather the greyhound-collie came loping, in its slightly furtive fashion, in its mouth another young grouse, still flapping feebly. The dog ran with it, straight to Roddie's feet, dropped it, wagged its tail briefly, and turned to slip away unobtrusively as it had come.

"Weel—cooper me! Isna' yon a right sensible dug!" the big man cried. "It kens its stuff, yon one. Leave it alane an' we'll feed like bluidy kings!"

"I hadn't realised before the full benefits of owning a tinker-trained dog!" Patrick commented. "I've heard though, that gamekeepers seldom love tinks—perhaps with some reason. No doubt this is also how the chickens we had at lunchtime arrived!"

Jean nodded. "It makes you think, doesn't it! But . . ." She smiled. "Never look a gift dog in the mouth!"

Roddie was already plucking the feathers from the first offering. "One each'll dae us just fine for oor suppers," he declared. "There's plenties mair whaur these came frae."

That was proved to be true. It was June, and the plentiful grouse coveys were largely comprised of half-grown birds, heavy on the wing and slow at taking off. The dog—which MacGregor, for obscure reasons of his own, had named Pieface—brought in only these immature flappers. Before long they had seven of them. It was a shame to see them killed Patrick observed, as in duty bound—a point of view that only the girl supported, and that half-heartedly. And later, with the glorious aroma of roast game, however immature, over-laying the scents of heather, bog-myrtle and wood-smoke, where Roddie Roy toasted Pieface's victims skilfully on spits above a fiercely hot little fire of bog-pine, a watering mouth effectually drowned further objections. If the resultant delicacies were just slightly underdone, the fault lay entirely with the eager diners, Patrick included, and not with the cook. The flavour was as delicious as the smell.

As they ate, they watched the road so far below them. For an hour or two there was no traffic, save for two motor-cyclists. Then three black cars came up from the east, going slowly, to pass on without stopping, up the glen. One of them, the binoculars, revealed, was a kind of van. Later, two of them came down again—and the van was seen to be towing the Mains cart incongruously behind it.

The comment from the cave-mouth was vigorous and to the point. Their blankets, and the stretcher for carrying the Stone, amongst other things, were still in that cart. There was nothing to identify any of them, however.

Though there was no great enthusiasm for the trip, it was agreed that it would be wise to go down, when it was dark, to have a look at the Stone. Though it was stressed that there was no need for Jean to go, she insisted on accompanying them.

They waited until it was as dark as a clear northern June night was likely to be, and then set off downhill, stumbling and tripping with depressing regularity amongst the tall heather and over the broken ground. This enforced slow going, and it took them almost an hour to reach the confluence of the corrie burn and the Almond. It was extremely boggy, down on the lower slopes, and all were duly soaked about the legs and feet before ever they reached the river. There was no need to remove their footwear, therefore, when they crossed by wading the shallows, Roddie sounding their way for them with a stick.

On the far bank they did not climb up on to the road, but turned downstream, beside the water. Twice on their descent they had seen the single powerful headlight, of what was no doubt a police motorcycle patrol, go slowly up the glen, and down.

Scrambling and slipping along the riverbank, with its holes, its hazels and birches, and its wet patches, was not pleasant, either, but at length they reached the point where the Stone had fallen. A cautious reconnaissance of the area around revealed no trace of watchers. It also revealed that the old iron and junk from the cart lay where it had been dumped by the police searchers. The food was gone, but the ancient kettle and handleless cups had been left. These were gladly retrieved.

The Stone itself lay as they had left it, about ten feet below the road level. Inspection with the carefully shaded torch made two or three things clear. One was that any least bungling in moving the Stone from its present position would be almost certain to end in it crashing down into the river—which here formed a series of deep pools. Another was that it would be next to impossible to move it any way save downhill, without the use of some sort of stretcher or rope tackle—certainly by a mere four men. Also, it was evident that, owing to the slight overhang of the road directly above, the relic was unlikely to be noticed unless an actual search was being made of the bank. There were many other stones around, of all sizes and shapes.

They had really no choice, therefore, but to leave the Stone where it was, meantime. What they might do, however, was to try to camouflage it a bit, so that its noticeably dark colour and squared angles would not be so apparent.

It was while they were pulling the required heather-clumps and lumps of turf and collecting stone to heap up against the sides of their precious charge, that lights from down the glen alarmed them. It was no motorcyclist this time, obviously; there were three sets of twin headlights. Hurriedly the party made for the foot of the slope to hide at the water's edge.

It was a still night, and they heard the noise while yet the vehicles were far off. Considerable noise. They heard a distant rattling and banging. They heard the drumlike roll of a cattle-grid crossed at speed, thrice. They heard heavy engines coughing and snorting. And lastly, they heard singing, loud, hearty, and not very melodious. Relieved, they relaxed.

"Jist the hydro-scheme boys comin' back frae a night oot at Crieff," Roddie interpreted. "*They'll* dae us nae harm. Hark at them!"

"A noisy lot."

"It's Saturday night," Jean reminded again, in extenuation.

"It's nearly Sunday," Patrick amended. "In fact, it's ten past twelve." And he yawned, cavernously. They were all suffering somewhat from lack of sleep. They did not do much more to the Stone. Shortly after the three truck-loads of navvies had roared and rattled past, a single motorcyclist followed them slowly up the glen. The watchers decided that they had had enough. Seeking to hide any traces of their activities, they moved back upstream, crossed the river, and started the long and weary climb back up to Coire Chultrain, taking the kettle and cups with them.

There was talk, on the way up, about making a brew of some sort out of hot water and melted chocolate, but in the event, after what seemed an eternity of benighted stumbling, slipping, and sweating, when they reached the sanctuary of their cave, only sleep held any invitation for them. Even Jean's request that her "room" round the bend in the cave should be inspected by torchlight, to ensure that no adders, bats or bogeymen had taken up their abode therein, produced little of the reaction that might have been anticipated. Roddie did mumble something about coming to tuck her in, but that was as far as it went.

The couches of heather received all the men, just as they were—whatever dispositions for the night the young woman may have made around her corner.

Some time during what was left of the night, Patrick wakened, and listened to the rhythmic breathing of his companions, the murmur of running waters, and the faint whisper of a night wind over endless leagues of heather. He felt rather than heard, too, something between a sigh and a tremor, comprehensive, all about him, as though the hills themselves had turned over in their sleep. He shivered. He was cold, admittedly, with only the ragged tinker's jacket for extra warmth around his shoulders. But not cold enough to stay awake. His eyes closed again.

In the morning Jean was up first, as usual—though not very early, at that. She was washed and looking as fresh as any daisy—save for the somewhat streaky effect of the stain that still lingered about her features—when the disreputable, bleary and unshaven male side of the company came abruptly to life.

It was her cry of alarm that did it—that, and the curious throbbing sound of motors. Sitting up, blinking, yawning, and rubbing heavy eyelids, the men peered about them.

"Look! Quick! Wake up!" she cried, running into the cave amongst them. "Look what they've got now. An aeroplane!" And she pointed—but downwards, not up.

It was a helicopter, flying low and slow, following the turns and twists of the glen floor, fully a thousand feet below them. At what could only be a bare couple of hundred feet above the river it flew, zig-zagging from one side of the valley to the other, for all the world like a giant dragonfly searching closely, methodically, for somewhere to alight.

"Damn it—I don't like the look of that!" Patrick exclaimed, staring. "I never thought of a helicopter."

"Jings—what next?" Roddie demanded. "Can you beat it? Got the bluidy R.A.F. oot noo!"

"Do they expect to find the Stone with *that*?" the girl wondered.

"I daresay it's not so much the Stone as us, that they're trying to locate, in the first place. After all, they can't actually know that we ever had the Stone. As well we're in this cave, and not camping somewhere in the open heather. We'd better keep well in, out of sight."

That hovering inquisitive aircraft gave the fugitives an anxious Sunday morning. Up and down the glen it flew, at varying heights, now just above road and river, now halfway up the hillsides, now up above the summits. It explored every flank and shoulder, threaded each side valley, nosed its way into every corrie, the buzz of it filling all the morning air, echoed and magnified by the enclosing slopes. It was not in evidence all the time, of course, since it had a fifteen-mile glen to cover. But the throb of it was never entirely absent, from their high eyrie—and undoubtedly it devoted more time to their end of the glen than to the remoter upper fastnesses. It meant that they dare not venture any distance from the cave-mouth—and half a dozen times one or other of them had to come scrambling back to cover in a hurry. The dog, too, had to be kept in, after giving them an initial scare. They dared kindle no fire, either. Once, in mid-forenoon, the wretched thing was away for almost an hour; but since they were not to know that it would not be back at any moment, they could not take advantage of this break. Heartily they cursed the bumbling contrivance. The only bright spot was that it did not seem to show any especial interest in either their corrie or the spot on the road where the Stone lay.

The Glasgow contingent wisely went to sleep over it all, eventually.

Had it not been for the helicopter, it would have been very pleasant, of course, to laze the day away up there on the roof of the land, with the great sun-bathed panorama of hill and valley spread around and below them in smiling colour and gentle grandeur. It was a lovely day of balmy breezes, with vast white cloud galleons sailing proudly across an azure sky and trailing their attendant shadows lightly over the uplands.

Patrick Kincaid would have asked nothing better—especially with the company he was in—had his mind been at rest.

It was in the early afternoon, however, that irritation with the situation changed to something not far from alarm. Jean and Patrick, sitting in the mouth of the cave, became aware of it almost simultaneously—though it was the girl who cried out.

"See there!" she said, pointing.

Just coming into view, round a bend in the glen away downstream, was a party of people, walkers. But not ordinary walkers. They were spread out, in line abreast, at perhaps five or six-yard intervals, from the road to part-way up the hill on the other side of the valley. Unhurriedly, steadily, they came on, thirty or forty of them at least—and they spelt menace, every one.

Patrick grabbed the glasses. "A mixture of police and civilians," he reported. "About half and half. Confound it—they're doing the thing thoroughly, I'll say that for them!"

"This is . . . serious, isn't it," the girl said, biting her lip. "Thank goodness they're on *that* side of the glen, at least! They are, aren't they? I mean, only that side?"

The man did not answer at once. He was scanning the lower slopes of their own side of the valley, carefully, as far as the lie of the land let them be seen. "No," he said, at length. "I don't see any sign of them on this side. Not yet. If they think we've got the Stone, they probably imagine we'd have difficulty in getting it across the river. As we would. So they may stick to that other side, at first. That's reasonable. What is a blessing is that they seem to be ignoring the short belt between the road and the river. It's steep, of course, and generally fairly obvious. I daresay they think that nobody would be fool enough to hide anything, or themselves, quite so close as that!"

They awakened the Gregorach to acquaint them with this new danger. It was Roddie Roy, thereafter, who spotted that there were women amongst the searching party—and at least one man with a beard. "Bluidy Oxford's on the job, again!" he cried.

"That settles it," Patrick nodded grimly. "They're sure we've got the Stone, then. Or these people wouldn't have volunteered to help. I wonder what made them so sure of it? After all, tinkers fighting shy of the police is no new thing. We might have been up to anything—peddling illicit-still whisky, poaching, petty theft, anything. There's nothing specific to link us directly with the Stone."

"Och, they dinna need onythin' specific, man," Roddie declared. "We're the only caird they've got, an' they're playin' it for a' their worth."

"The fact that the floor of the cart had been recently strengthened, may have told them something," Jean suggested. "And that stretcher."

"Yes—that's true. Circumstantial evidence."

The searchers were coming on slowly, but surely. It was clear, now, that they were confining themselves meantime to the north side of road and river. The question was—for how long would that content them?

"If they're going to work right up that side, it's quite on the boards that they'll eventually cross over and work back down this," Patrick said. "The thing is—how far will they go up, before they decide to turn?"

"It's a long glen," the girl pointed out. "And they're not going very fast. They can't be doing more than two miles in the hour, if that. They could be all day at that side."

"They could. But will they? After all, they know where we abandoned the cart. They know that the Stone must be pretty heavy. The chances are, surely, that we wouldn't have carried it very far. Certainly nothing like up to the head of the glen. I'd say they might keep on two or three miles up, farther, and then turn. Not much more."

"Likely they wouldna' come up as high as this, on their way doon," Roddie claimed.

"Probably not. But we're bound to have left footprints on muddy patches and peat-hags. Fresh prints. Pointing up and down this corrie. Close searching might find them. Just as close searching might find that Stone below the road there."

"What . . . what on earth are we to do then?" Jean exclaimed. "We can't just wait here, for all that to happen!"

At the note of despair newly come into the girl's voice, Patrick mustered a grin. "Chins up, the Grahams!" he told her. "The flag still flies! We're not done yet—not by a long chalk! It's all a question of time. And I think time may well be on our side, yet. These folk are still more than a mile off, aren't they? And it's more than another mile up to where we left the cart. And say that they go on another two or three miles beyond that. That gives them up to six miles to go yet, before they turn." That was highly hypothetical, and an overestimate, at that. But the cause was good. "That should take them another three hours, at the rate they're going. And it's turned 3 p.m. now. That ought to take them till after 6.

I should think they might pack up then, for the night. The Oxford types, anyway. I know I'd be inclined to. They're only human—and remember they've probably been at it for an hour or two already."

"Sure. They'll be saft. The polis, tae," Roddie concurred. "You can bet your life on that."

"Perhaps. But even if they do carry on later than that, remember it will take them more time to get back this far. Another couple of hours, or more. I don't really see them keeping it up as late as that, tiring work like that. My own feeling is that they'll put off doing this side till tomorrow. Which means we'll have to shift both ourselves and the Stone, tonight!" Patrick hoped that he sounded more confident than he felt.

"Aye, then. You've said it," Roddie agreed, loyally. But he favoured the speaker with a rather peculiar glance, just the same.

"How? And where?" Jean demanded. "The Stone, I mean. We ourselves can cut and run, easily enough. But the Stone?"

"The only thing I can think of is to shift it over to where they've already searched, somewhere."

"Oh! I never thought of that. But, even so . . ."

"Yes. We'll need help. We'll need to call on the Macphails again, I'm afraid. I don't see anything else for it. And that's where this confounded helicopter complicates things. How we're going to get over to where they are, in Glen Quaich, without being seen?"

"Och, you leave that to me," the MacGregor announced cheerfully. "I'll dae it. I'll gie yon lang-nebbit hurdygurdy a miss! Me and Alicky. Better there's the twa o' us, separate in case one is spotted an' has to lie low. See—when yon plane goes past, on the way up the glen, its' aye awa' for ten meenits an' mair. Oot o' sight. We'll let it by, next time, an' then we'll mak' a belt for the skyline up there. Och, we'll dae that in less'n ten meenits. We can aye lie low behind a rock till it's by again, onyway. An' once ower the top, we'll be fine. We'll awa' doon behind the hill, an' work roond, an' cross this blasted glen lower doon—when that bluidy crate's no' pokin' aroond."

197

"It will be a slow process, Roddie. And tiring work. A long long way round."

"Och, aye—but we'll dae fine. An' once we're ower the skyline on the ither side, we're weel awa'. Easy then, to this place the tinks are at, in Glen Quaich. Shian, it was—near a bit school? Naethin' in it—except my belly's gey empty!"

"Aye," Alicky Shand confirmed heavily.

"Yes. The food position's getting serious. With this heather-hopping business we can't do much on empty stomachs. What's left, Jean?"

"Practically nothing. Only a few dates and some crumbs of biscuit."

"Well, food's a high priority, obviously. Where's the nearest shop?"

"The Post Office at Amulree, I should think. But it's Sunday. It won't be open."

"M'mmm. I wonder, could we risk trying at a farm or a croft, somewhere? Not here in this glen, of course."

"The hydro camp—we'd dae better there," Roddie proposed. "Thae boys'll no' be a' that suspicious—or be a' that keen on the polis, neither. They'll hae lashin's o' grub. If Jakey was to mak' his way up roond to there. Act like he was on the tramp. He'd get some grub frae them, sure—an' no' that many questions asked. He could aye gie them a sairmon in return!"

"Dinna you scoff, Rod MacGregor, if you want the guid Lord to feed your great fat face!" Jakey warned. "Hasna' He fed us fine, a'ready? Thae bit birds, the dug brought. Like manna frae Heaven. Or quails, leastways."

"Ooh, aye. Fine that. But wha's scoffin'? I bet thae hydro boys could dae wi' a sairmon or twa—an' they'd likely gie you a right sackload o' grub, jist to get rid o' you!"

"Hud your tongue, you great muckle lump o' depravity!" the little man cried. "I wonder the A'mighty doesna' strike you doon deid!"

Patrick and Jean intervened, to restore peace.

So it was decided. Roddie and Alicky would depart, to fetch the Macphails, just as soon as the helicopter had passed on its next trip up the glen. Jakey would go with them, as far as the skyline of the hill behind, when he would leave them to turn right, instead of left, heading west to make his long detour to the contractor's camp. Jean and Patrick would stay where they were, to keep watch on the Stone and on the progress of the line of searchers. It was 3.30 p.m. With all the dodging and the hiding that they would have to do, going, and possibly also returning, it was not anticipated that Roddie and the Macphails could be back before nine at the earliest.

Jakey would not be much sooner. In all their minds was the thought that a lot might happen in those intervening hours.

They waited for the helicopter to come on its monotonously regular westward flight.

XIV

THE Gregorach were gone, apparently unobserved either by the airmen or the line of diligent searchers far below—who now were beginning to pass out of sight under the swell of the hill directly beneath. Roddie and his not very enthusiastic colleagues, with Pieface in skulking attendance, had made their unobtrusive way towards and over the summit ridge to the south, using every scrap of the fairly plentiful cover, but going hard, just as soon as the deplorable helicopter had passed on the westward leg of its patrol. By the time that it had come back, nearly twenty minutes later, all three men had been safely over the skyline for fully seven of those minutes.

Patrick felt a little foolishly self-conscious about having so clearly been left to play the waiting role. There was no doubt that, despite his vaunted deer-stalking experience, the Gregorach considered him to be a mere babe on the hill. His male ego was just slightly injured, however irrationally—for he was the obvious one to leave behind with the young woman. The strange part of it was, that frequently in the past few hectic days he had wished that he *could* be alone with Jean, now and again, and not always in the somewhat overwhelming company that he had been keeping. He was an inconsistent and moody man, it was to be feared. He demonstrated that now by pacing up and down and around that cave and its entrance, rather like a caged lion.

Jean Graham stood it patiently for a while, eyeing him thoughtfully on occasion. But presently she spoke up.

"Do sit down, Patrick," she suggested. "Or else run along after the others, if you feel so cramped and out of it here. I'm sure you could make up on Jakey, at least. He'd probably be glad of company—he didn't seem over-keen on his trip to the hydro camp. I'd be perfectly all right here alone, you know."

"Nonsense. Of course not," the man returned. And then, a little less brusquely, "I mean, no sense in doing that. But, well, it's a long spell of inaction, isn't it. So much to be done, so much hanging in the balance, and we just have to sit and wait."

"The woman's role, oftener than the man's, I'm afraid! Perhaps it takes a little getting used to."

"You're a fine one to talk that way, aren't you? Not much sitting back with folded hands and patient waiting, about you!"

"You think not? You think I'm just an interfering female, pushing my way in where I'm not required, and complicating matters for you practical and well-doing men? Is that it, Patrick?" Perhaps something of the long spell of stress and strain was to be sensed in the woman, too.

"Good Lord—no! Nothing of the sort," he denied. "Don't be ridiculous. You've been wonderful. Magnificent."

She changed her tune, with truly feminine capriciousness. "You don't act as flatteringly as you speak, Mr Drummond! Some young men I could think of would be quite happy to be left to keep a girl company in a cave high amongst the mountains! So, so romantic and all that sort of thing, you know."

"Like your friend Ogilvie, for instance!" That was said sharply, accusingly almost.

"Well . . . I suppose so. In a way. Bill would quite appreciate the opportunity, probably. But . . . no more than others."

"Others! I see."

Jean eyed him a little askance. "This is a quite ridiculous conversation," she declared. "I think you must be hungry. I know I am. They say that a hungry man's an angry man!"

"I'm not in the least angry," Patrick denied stiffly. "Far from it. Only distressed to be a disappointment. I wouldn't like to fail you, you know. Especially in matters romantic."

"Oh, don't be an ass, Patrick! You know perfectly well that was only a silly joke!"

"Was it? What a pity. I'm sorry about that, you know.

The fact is, I *could* wax quite romantic about you, you see. Quite. Indeed, I have frequently had to stop myself from doing just that! Been quite difficult, sometimes."

"Oh, Patrick—please! Do be quiet!" The girl got up abruptly, and went to stand in the cave's mouth. "This has gone quite far enough."

"I'm sorry. That is what I was afraid of. That's why I kept quiet, before. I shouldn't have mentioned it now, either, I suppose."

"Not . . . not if *that* is how you feel about it, thank you!"

"No. Well, as I say, I'm sorry. Forget it. I certainly don't want to embarrass you. To spoil anything." He sighed, and shrugged. "You've been so splendid. So kind, and staunch."

She turned to face him, wonderingly, frowning. "For a man so, so nimble with his tongue, you can be curiously clumsy, I think. Un . . . unperceptive!" she said.

"I daresay. I never thought that I was nimble. Quite the reverse, in fact. But we'll say no more about it. Though it's probably just as well that you should know how I feel about you."

"Just as well?" she echoed. "How you feel about me! Dear Lord—is it you that's crazy? Or me? You've flung at me that you could feel romantic about me, on occasion. Just like that! Whatever that means?" The young woman shook her head. "Do you realise, Patrick, that though we've been living closer than, than brother and sister these last days, I really know nothing about you at all? Nor you of me, either, for that matter!"

"I know enough to be sure that I love you, at any rate," the man answered levelly, doggedly.

"Love?" She swallowed, silenced for the moment.

"Yes. Love. What else? Is that so strange? I've loved you from the very first, I think. I don't see how any man could do otherwise. But . . ." He paused, "Oh, well—let it go. I've said I'd say no more."

"But, Patrick—don't you see, this is different!" she cried. "This isn't what you said before."

"Eh? Why not? What did I say different?"

"Oh—everything! You didn't say that . . . you said . . . oh, well—it was all quite different."

"Well, you know best, I suppose. But it's what I meant, anyway. That I loved you. Adored you."

She shook her head again. "How can you say that, Patrick? We've only known each other for less than a week."

"A week! A day! A lifetime! What's that got to do with it? What's so important about time? Mere minutes and hours and days? I know you better, I believe, than I know anybody else in the world."

"Do you?"

"Yes. I think so. I hope so. I'm sure of it. You don't feel, yourself, that I'm just a stranger, do you, Jean?"

"No. Oh, no. But . . . it seems that there's a great deal I don't know about you just the same!"

"That's true, of course. In a way. An unimportant way." He laughed, shortly. "You don't even know my name, if it comes to that!"

"Your name?" She wrinkled her brows.

"My full name. My surname. It's not just Patrick Drummond, you see. There's more than that. It's Kincaid. Patrick Drummond Kincaid."

She stared at him, lips parted. "Kincaid?" she breathed. "You mean . . . *Kincaid*? The same . . . as the farm? As the estate?"

"The same, yes. That's why I didn't broadcast it, at first. Much too kenspeckle. Too readily identified. Just asking to be connected with the whole Stone business. I saw the effect it had on Roddie, when I told him. He's the only one who knows. We agreed to keep it dark—in case it got talked about. From everyone. I should have told you, I agree. I mean, before this. I've begun to, more than once. But . . . well, it didn't seem to be important, after a bit."

"Not important? When you were masquerading under a false name!"

"It wasn't exactly false, you know. Patrick Drummond *is* my name. I was just missing out the Kincaid. I was uncomfortable about it, Jean, I assure you. At first. But having

203

started out, well, I suppose I was sort of reluctant to bring it up again. I suppose I had something like a guilty conscience."

"And well you might!" she said severely. "It's a very curious coincidence, isn't it?"

"Not really, it isn't. I wouldn't really say it was a coincidence, at all. It was just *because* I'm Kincaid of Kincaid that I felt bound to involve myself in the whole affair. The Gavin Kincaid who brought the Stone from Scone, in the first place, was my ancestor, you see. 'Guard Weel', our motto, refers to the Stone, and . . ."

"You're Kincaid of Kincaid, now!" Jean interrupted. "This gets worse and worse! But—just a minute. Haven't I heard somewhere that Kincaid of Kincaid is a titled man? A baronet? Sir Somebody-or-other Kincaid?"

He nodded ruefully. "That's right, too, I'm afraid. Sir Patrick Drummond Kincaid of Kincaid, Bart., himself—poor devil!"

"But . . ." Biting her lip, she turned away. "Oh!" she said.

"So you see why I was keeping it quiet?" he asked, almost pleaded indeed. "A title sticks out—a fearful handicap, really."

"You should have told me," Jean said, tonelessly, without turning round, her voice set, stiff. "It's . . . it's put me in an entirely false position."

"Oh, it's not so bad as all that, surely? I mean, it's not important."

"Of course it is. I should have been informed. Father, too. I would never have . . . well, anyway—it was most unfair of you!"

"I don't see it. What difference does it make?"

"A lot of difference."

"Why should it? The title's an empty one. It means nothing—except that I'm my father's son. I've no money, no property. I earn my living, like anybody else—only less so than most!"

"When Sir Patrick Kincaid of Kincaid comes to Kincaid, he should be treated differently than he was," she declared, still with her back to him, with a strange obstinacy. "In . . . in the doocot, that time! When first I spoke to you. Oh, it was ridiculous! And in the crypt. That was *your* family vault.

Those were your ancestors' coffins. Why couldn't you have told me? Didn't you trust me, or what?"

"Of course I trusted you. Good Lord, I . . ."

"The Grahams have been tenants on Kincaid for generations. We have a, a feeling for the place."

"Quite. Then you're a deal more closely connected with Kincaid than I am. Especially since you now own Kincaid Mains. For my family haven't owned a stick or a stone of it since the Forty-five."

She said nothing—but her back looked most rigidly uncompromising and unforthcoming.

"Look, Jean," he said. "I'm sorry if I seem to have deceived you. And to have hurt you in consequence. Heavens—it's the last thing I wanted to do! I love you, I tell you. I . . ."

"I think you could spare me talk about love, at any rate, in the circumstances!"

"But, why? You seemed prepared to listen to me a few minutes back. Why the change?"

"If you can't see that for yourself, you're less intelligent than you've appeared."

"I must be, then." He stopped. That helicopter was back again, and heading into their corrie to fly rather nearer to their cave's level than heretofore. "I think we'd better lie down," he said abruptly. "These chaps are getting a bit close for comfort."

As he sank down on the pulled heather, his companion turned and walked past him, back deeper into the cave, and rounded its corner and out of sight.

He waited some considerable time after the buzz of the plane had faded away up the glen. Still she did not reappear.

"It's gone," he called. "No need to hide in there, any more."

After a moment's interval, she replied, "I'm not hiding. I'm resting. Lying down. I . . . I didn't sleep very much last night."

"Oh. Umm. That means . . . well, be quiet, I take it?"

"Probably that would be best, yes."

"I see."

The man sat there in the mouth of the cave for a long time, silent, his thoughts a chaos and of no pleasure to him. More than once he opened his mouth to speak to her, and once he half rose to go through to her—but he did neither. Nor did the young woman emerge or make any sound.

The afternoon passed at its own pace. The helicopter appeared twice more, and then the noise of its engine died away towards the east, and it came back no more.

At long last frustration and restlessness got the better of the waiting man. He rose to his feet.

"The helicopter's away. I think for good," he said, low voiced. "I'm going to have a look up the glen. See, if I can, how the search-party's getting on. I may have to go some distance. I may be a little while."

He was not quite sure whether or not there was a faint murmur of acknowledgment to that. She might indeed be asleep.

He strode out into the open. It was good to stretch his legs, at least—to be doing something, anything.

Patrick had spoken truly when he said that he might have to go some distance. Owing to the configuration and contours of the Hill of Auchnafree, and the fact that he must all the time ensure that he could not be seen from the low ground, he was forced to work his way round two distinct subsidiary shoulders of the hill, and right to the edge of the next corrie, Coire Garbh, before he could see any way up the glen beyond. He had to cover the best part of two heather miles, indeed, and owing to the need for inconspicuousness, to do it mighty slowly. At least, however, on the way, he had the satisfaction of seeing three black cars and the police van going in convoy down the road, eastwards, and through the binoculars ascertaining that they were filled with civilians. The Oxford contingent no doubt had had enough for one day.

But his satisfaction was short-lived indeed. When, at last, from a rocky knoll, he was in a position to spy out the farther reaches of the glen, it was to make a shattering discovery. The search was not over for the night. The police section of the line was made of sterner stuff—or subject to harsh orders. And it was not bothering about the upper valley. It was working down again, a wavering but inexorable black line of perhaps a score of uniformed men, less than a mile above his present vantage point. And worst of all, it was split into two now, with the majority across on this south side of the glen, but five constables still on the far side, combing that vital stretch of bank between the river and the road.

For a few moments Patrick watched, appalled. There was no question about it, any more; unless by some miracle they decided to pack up within the next couple of miles, they were bound to find the Stone. He had no watch nowadays, but he judged that it could not be much more than six o'clock. There was plenty of daylight left to get the searchers farther than that. The issue was crystal-clear. This was it.

The watcher's mind raced. What was left to them? What could he and Jean do, alone? Roddie and the others could not possibly be back for a couple of hours yet, at the earliest. Too late to be of any help. Could they manage, desperately, to cover up the Stone somehow, with soil, heather, turfs, and so on? Not in time—and not without it being obvious to close searchers that such had been going on. The police were no fools. And they couldn't move the thing, between them. Unless?

There was no time for detailed thought, and the weighing of pros and cons. Backing away heedfully, so as not to show himself to any eyes that might be upturned down there, Patrick turned and ran.

It was a long run, back to their cave in Cateran's Corrie, and the terrain was not made for running over. Tripping, floundering, stumbling, falling, he raced on, ploughing through the heather, leaping the burns, splattering across peat-hags. Soon he was panting, then gasping, and presently sobbing for breath. His practically empty stomach did not help him. What a fool he had been when he had said, even in an endeavour to encourage Jean, that time might be on their side!

He reached their sanctuary at last, scarlet-faced, dizzy, and trembling, pain like an iron band across his chest. The girl was in the mouth of it, watching for him—for it was over two hours since he had left.

"Quick!" he croaked. "The police! Working down . . . between river and road. Only a mile away. The Stone!"

The sight of him coming at the run had prepared the other for trouble. "Yes," she said, not demanding details. "But what can we do?"

"Get down to it. Move it. Before they come . . . in sight."

"But how? Just the two of us? It won't move."

"It will. Downwards. Into the river. Only thing we can do. Into one of . . . deep pools. Come on!"

She did not hesitate, but started to run at his side.

XV

HOW they ever got down that long and wet and slippery hillside, Patrick never knew. When he started, he felt that he had scarcely the energy left to place one foot before another, or sufficient breath to carry him farther. Yet, in fact, he had not more than begun to tap his physical reserves; the human body being a remarkable mechanism, capable of infinitely more than its controlling mind is apt to give it credit for. In this instance the minds of neither of the runners imposed any limiting influence on their physical efforts—for the good reason that both were entirely preoccupied with a different issue altogether; the dual problem of how long it would take the police to get near enough to see what they planned to do, and how they were to do it. The thought that their descent could be seen from the road, should anybody pass up or down there in the meantime, did not fail to occur to them, either.

Somehow, then, they reached the bottom of the hill, and went staggering and splashing straight across the river's shallows, clutching each other for mutual support amongst the slippery stones of its bed.

Down the farther bank, they had almost half a mile to cover to reach their goal. Their dragging unsteady steps along its tree and stone-littered course were but little aided by continual backwards glancing.

At last they came to the three deep pools. The Stone was poised some forty or fifty feet above the lowermost one. Up to it they dragged their way, largely on hands and knees now. Distressed, open-mouthed, their eyes refusing to focus properly, they reached the Stone. The floor of the glen was visible for the best part of a mile up. No movement, other then the glitter of running water, showed there, as yet.

The girl was leaning against the Stone itself, for support,

209

one hand on her breast, her breathing chaotic. Patrick was glad to sink to his knees as, without pause, he began to scrape away the soil and rubble that they had heaped up around it the previous night. He could scarcely see what he was doing, through a heaving red mist.

The girl joined him. They had no time to be really careful over keeping the displaced soil and turf inconspicuous—but the larger divots and pulled heather they threw down into the river.

Feverishly they worked, and presently the Stone was as clear as when first it had fallen. Still there was no sign of the police.

Patrick pointed to the lowermost edge of the Stone, where it had dug itself into the soil of the bank for five or six inches. "If we . . . could clear that," he panted. "Think it would . . . roll clear."

She nodded.

Casting about, the man found two flattish pieces of stone that they could use to scrape and dig with more efficiently than with bare fingers. Kneeling below the relic, they started to undermine it.

"Have to watch. If it moved—came down on top of us. Could kill us," he pointed out.

They scraped away quite a cavity under the Stone—but it showed no sign of moving.

"If we'd something . . . to act as a lever," Patrick jerked. He glanced around him—but could see nothing that would serve. There could be but little time left, surely?

"Round here. And push!" he cried. "You'd think . . . dam' thing would go . . . easier than this!"

He tried to get his shoulder down to it, but it was too low for him to obtain full purchase. He turned, and sitting on the bank above, set his feet against it, and, gripping a tree-root to anchor him, pushed with all his might, the girl using her hands. And it moved; an inch or two only, but it moved.

"Stick it! Again," he grunted. "She's going."

The next push did it—and more swiftly than they had bargained for. Presumably the point of balance had been reached. For suddenly the Stone came alive. It did not move

210

away, so much as leap away. For better or for worse, they had done what they set out to do.

The Stone leapt straight downwards for a few feet. Then it struck the jagged stump of a tree that some spate had broken. It did not stop it—nothing would stop that hurtling mass of rock now—but it deflected it, changed its course. Instead of crashing straight down, it plunged away to the left. And there, as luck would have it, a dry burn-channel scored a wedge in the braeside—a tiny thing, but enough to deflect the Stone's course still farther to the left. In a shower of pebbles and grit it slewed away, and bounded on to a small shoulder.

Rooted to the spot in consternation, the man and the girl stared. The river took a bend away from them, directly after the last of the three pools, to flow wide and shallow through a stretch of water meadows. At least, the ground on the south side was water meadow of a boggy sort; that to the north, on their own side, was obviously a crescent of sheer quaking marsh, emerald green scum overlaying the black peat-mire. Protected by a natural bank of bleached pebbles and rubble brought down by innumerable floods it lay, a half-moon of reedy treachery perhaps eighty yards long. No doubt it had been waiting there, like that, for a long time.

There was never a moment's question but that the Stone would go right into it. Bouncing out from the little shoulder, it only struck solid ground once more before it plunged down directly to that bright green surface. And with an obscene sucking smack the swamp received it, and heaved up curiously, repulsively all round it in a shuddering yet lazy-seeming crater. For a moment or two the Stone appeared to sit there, like a great black jewel on an emerald cushion, and then, quietly but steadily, it sank, and the walls of its enclosing crater subsided, flowed in towards their centre, and closed over it. Only a narrowing dark circle of peat-mire showed where Scotland's Stone of Destiny had gone.

"Good Lord!" the man groaned. "Heavens above—what have we done?"

"It's . . . it's gone!" Jean cried. "Oh, Patrick—it's gone!"

"Yes, damn and confound it—it's gone! We've lost it.

211

We've lost the Stone! After everything . . . all we've done!"
He wiped the sweat from his brow with a trembling earth-
covered hand. "This—to be the end of it all!"

"You think it's lost, for . . . for good?"

"You can see as well as I can!" he answered roughly,
unhappily. "You can see all that's left—a little patch of bare
mud, that's almost closed over already." That thought checked
him. He pointed. "See—we must know the exact spot. Fix it
in our minds. Where it went in. While the mark is still there.
Look—in line with that quartz-shot outcrop across the river.
To here. We'll not forget this spot we're standing on, by
George! Now, a cross-bearing. That birch, in line with the
bend in the river. No—that's too distant, too vague. Make it
that jagged rock. That, and the birch tree. You got that? We
mustn't forget that, come what may. We'll fix it on a large-
scale map. You got it?"

"Yes, yes. Where the lines cross between us and that white
quartz outcrop, and that rock and the birch. Yes. I have it.
And look! The mark's gone. It's covered over."

"Aye. Just in time." Patrick shook his head, staring at the
spot where their hopes and their country's relic had foundered.
"But it's, it's crazy, isn't it? Almost unbelievable. I mean,
that it's all finished. That there's nothing more to be done.
After all these days of effort and struggle and risk. I can hardly
take it in, really."

"No," the young woman agreed, dully. "It doesn't seem
possible. So unfair, somehow. But, at least, the police won't
get it either."

"The police—hang it, I'd almost forgotten the police! They
mustn't find us here. Come on, Jean—nothing more we can
do now. Except make sure that the police don't get us.
Quick—down there, and through the first of the shallows.
Up that burn-channel at the other side. Some way, at any
rate. Can you make it?"

She nodded, unspeaking.

He took her hand, and squeezed it. They threw a last glance
at that fateful quagmire, and side by side went down to the
river again.

XVI

THEY got three or four hundred feet up the burn-channel across the Almond, going heavily, but watching carefully that they left no footmarks on soft ground, before the line of policemen came in sight round a bend in the glen. They were able to continue some way farther, too, in the slightly sunken staircase that their burn made for them, before there was risk of them being spotted. So that they had time to find a little hollow where they might sink down unseen, hidden by a heather bank from view from below.

It was a very small sanctuary, and if one of them was not to be soaked by the splatter of the little waterfall that had formed it, they must crouch very close together indeed. They sank down thankfully, gasping. The young woman, in fact, was racked with convulsive sobs, her shoulders heaving sorely against those of the man. He put his arm around her, instinctively, protectingly, and held her close. Apart from the labour of her respiration, she did not stir.

They crouched thus, speechless, while the worst distress of their breathing died away. That they found some mutual comfort in their close proximity and contact was certain, and not strange. It was indeed with some reluctance that, presently, Patrick left her side to move over to a spot where, by peering round, he might see down into the valley. Jean did not.

"They're just below us, now," he reported softly. "The nearest one, on this side, isn't more than three hundred yards away. They look pretty tired and fed up, I must say."

She did not answer.

"Nobody's looking up this way. In fact, I'd say that none of them are looking very hard, any way. I expect they've had just about enough, for one day. There's a couple of cars coming slowly down the road, just behind them. Our London friends, no doubt. Probably, if it wasn't for them . . . Damn it there's two chaps stopped, just where we were! On the other side, where the Stone was lying before. They're looking about, and pointing. They can see, I'm afraid, that something's been going on. We're bound to have left some traces—marks in the raw earth, footprints. They're casting about, confound them! Two young constables. They're pointing up to the road, now. They seem to be more interested in the road area. They're climbing up. I wonder? Oh, I see—it's the cars, of course. They're going to report, blast them!"

At the constables' wave, the two slow-moving cars drew up with them. Getting out the binoculars, Patrick watched anxiously. The Superintendent and the two Scotland Yard men got out. The younger men pointed back down the slope. The three seniors came to look down. The Superintendent turned, and gestured across the road. He indicated a line, quite plainly to be seen, as though following the path of somebody who had come up from the river, crossed the road, and gone on over the grass to where the Mains cart had been ravished. The two detectives nodded. Then, casually, they waved the younger officers away, and returned to their car. The constables shrugged, and hurried on to catch up with the wavering line of their colleagues.

"Well, I'm blowed!" the watcher gasped. "They've been brushed off—given the bird. Their bosses aren't interested. Or else . . . yes, I think I see what's happened. It was Jakey's doing—bless him! When we were unloading the Stone, that time, and we were interrupted, Jakey went down to the riverside with Roddie. Remember? To gather wood, ostensibly.

Then he came up, and crossed the road to us, later, with an armful of sticks, passing the police. They questioned him. They've remembered that—and taken the marks we left as being made by Jakey in his stick-collecting. That must be it. What a stroke of luck! The line has moved well on, now—and the cars are going on, too."

Jean nodded, listlessly.

He came back to her. "We'll let them get well on their way down the glen, before we move," he said, and sat down beside her. And, as of its own accord, his arm went round her again.

She did not show any resentment. In fact, she turned, after only a moment or two, and buried her brow against his shoulder.

"Oh, Patrick—we've made an awful mess of things, haven't we!" she said, miserably.

He had been feeling momentarily more cheerful, over the police blunder and their apparent escape. Now, the gloom of the longer view flooded back over him. The feel of her within his arm, pressed against him, only served to accentuate the dimensions of his failure.

"Yes—I'm afraid we have," he admitted. "At least, *I* have. Over the Stone . . . and everything else!"

"Why you only?"

"It was my idea that went wrong, wasn't it? All my ideas. Even . . . even those that I didn't ask for!"

Suddenly Patrick Kincaid was feeling very sorry for himself, indeed—even more sorry than for poor old Scotland, whose precious relic he had lost for her. Perhaps his weariness, perhaps the sudden relaxation after intense strain, perhaps that young woman's head against his shoulder, the scent of her hair in his nostrils, was too much for him.

She seemed to perceive it, to sense the different note in his voice—and rallied her own drooping spirits in consequence.

"None of it has been your fault, Patrick," she said, raising her head. "You have worked so very hard—worked wonders, really. Nobody could have done more."

"Roddie Roy could. Roddie would never have let this happen," the man declared bitterly. "He may be more brawn than brain, but he would have foreseen what would happen down there. What he'll say when he hears, I won't anticipate!"

"What he says doesn't matter. He couldn't have done anything more himself, anyway—with all his strength. It was just rotten bad luck."

"Bad luck! Isn't that always the excuse of the bungler?" He would not be comforted.

"You are no bungler, Patrick. I could call you a few things, perhaps—but not a bungler."

"And yet you did call me that, not so very long ago! You told me that I could be very clumsy."

"No! No—that was different. That was just in words—not deeds. Anyway, it's not true, really. I didn't mean it. I was so surprised, taken aback."

"I blundered then, just the same—to my cost! The . . . the Stone fell the wrong way then, too, with a vengeance!"

He felt her stir within his arm, but she made no comment.

"I have set my sights too high, I'm afraid. All along. Aimed at targets beyond me. Both of them."

"Both?" she echoed.

"Yes. You. And the Stone. Both I was foolish enough to aim at—and miss!"

"I see," she said then, slowly. "But they are not quite the same, are they? Your targets. You may get a . . . a second shot at one of them, perhaps!"

He swallowed, audibly. And though he did not realise it, his fingers gripped her arm so fiercely that she had to bite back a wince. "You mean . . . you mean . . . ?"

"Just that your aim might be better a second time. Who knows?"

"Jean! You're saying that you might give me another chance?"

"Perhaps it is myself that I'm offering another chance to, Patrick!" And she turned to face him. "I think it is, really."

"Jean—can it be true? That you could care for me? After all?"

"I'm afraid so, Patrick. I've . . . I've tried to get out of it, but I can't, my dear!"

"Oh, my darling, and my love!"

His other arm swept round to enfold her now, and her lips came up to meet his own eagerly.

For how long they sat there in the tiny hollow beside the waterfall, they neither knew nor considered. Nor was it material. They had much to learn about each other, about their love, about the mutual prospects before them—all of which they would go on learning for many a year to come.

216

But at least they made a start there amongst the ferns and the heather. Leave them to it. Let it suffice to say that the busy police, and even Scotland's Stone, no longer wholly preoccupied them. They had a destiny of their own to consider.

When, at length, they rose stiffly, and laughing at their aches, it was to face a different world altogether—a world where the sun shone unclouded, the mountain sides were no longer harsh ramparts against them but kindly welcoming breasts of heather. The larks trilled more sweetly, the bog myrtle smelled more fragrant, and the bees hummed a praise to match their own. That is the world that they were in.

The man said, laughing, "So you're prepared to wed a bold bad baronet who deceived you—penniless though he may be?"

"Well, I don't mind the penniless bit. And I'll forgive you for deceiving me—though it must not happen again, mind. But I'm not so happy about this baronet-business, I must admit. I'm only a farmer's daughter, you know."

" 'She was only a farmer's daughter,' " he quoted, " 'But her calves brought in the bacon!' "

"Be quiet! I'm serious. The thought of being Lady Kincaid appals me!"

"I'm serious too, my dear—and the Lady Kincaid bit of it is essential. Now that you're securely promised to me, and can nowise wriggle out of it, I can let you into a secret. It's been incumbent on me to marry an heiress, all along. It's always done by impoverished baronets. However, by getting hold of you, I've gone one better than that, you must admit. Since you are your father's only child, and presumably will inherit his farm eventually, I'm marrying back into Kincaid land! I'll really be Kincaid of Kincaid, with a minimum of trouble and expense! The moment I set eyes on you—or, at least, the moment you divulged your identity I stroked my luxuriant black moustaches and perceived most clearly my course of action. I would have married you, my love, had you possessed the appearance of one of your own comfortable milk-cows! I would so!"

217

"You . . . you dastard!" she cried.

"Exactly. So isn't it fortunate for me that, instead, you are quite the loveliest, fairest, most shapely and delectable young person in all bonny Scotland? I might even go further, and include Northern Ireland in that!"

"Well, well! And to think that I hinted, one time, that you might be a little clumsy with your tongue, Sir Patrick!"

"Wait you—you haven't heard anything yet!" Patrick Kincaid was a man transformed. Gone the gloom, gone the tension, gone the slight diffidence of speech. "But in the meantime, my bride-to-be, I think that we ought to climb this hill. It just occurs to me that Jakey Reid the Godly may be getting back. The time must be getting on. Good heavens— it's a quarter to nine! How on earth did it get to be that? Even Roddie MacGregor may be back by now. Come on, lassie—race you to the cave!"

He held out his hand to her, and she took it. They started to climb, without so much as a glance up or down that glen of policemen.

Roddie Roy MacGregor was indeed back, and the Macphails with him. Also Alicky, and Pieface the dog. And Jakey Reid, too. The climbers saw them, up at the cave-mouth, as soon as they entered the corrie, seven men all told. All came hurrying down to meet them.

"Hell—you fair gave us the willies!" the big man cried, reproachfully. "Whaur you been? We were feart the polis had got yous."

"Not them!" Patrick asserted, breathless but assured. "I don't think they're trying very hard. They're getting tired of it—it's only those dam' detectives keeping them at it." He turned to the Macphails. "So you came, Seumas. And Dougal. As good as your word. Stout fellows. A lot of trouble we've been to you."

"Och, dearie me—there was no trouble in it at all," the tinker declared, with his most villainous scar-faced smile. "Sleeping we were, nothing else."

"They were that," Roddie confirmed. "The hale bang-jing

o' them. Deid to the world—and a right fierce smell o' liquor aboot the place! But, say—what you lookin' sae pleased wi' yoursel' aboot, Jeannie?"

"I'm not pleased with myself, Roddie MacGregor. Nothing of the sort."

"Sez you! You tae, Patrick man—you're like a dug wi' twa tails! What you been up to, the pair of yous?"

"Nothing. At least . . ." Patrick cleared his throat, and sought to adopt a suitably sombre expression. "Quite the reverse, actually. I'm sorry we've troubled the Macphails—bringing them all this way, on a wild-goose chase. The fact is, we've . . . we've lost the Stone."

"You've *what?*"

"Lost the Stone. It's gone. Sunk. The game's up."

"You mean, the polis've got it?"

"Oh, no. Not that. It might have been better if they had—I don't know! The thing's lost, I tell you. In a bog. Sunk. For good." He gestured helplessly. "I'm sorry."

"Jings!"

"Maircy on us!"

"You're no' kiddin', man?"

"Och, my goodness gracious me—is that a fact?"

"I'm afraid it's true. I made a mess of it."

"Oh, you didn't, Patrick!"

"I did. No getting out of *that*. I meant to push it down into the river. To get it under water, out of sight. The police were making their way downstream, searching the banks. No time for anything else. We had to do something. They'd have discovered it, for sure. We worked it loose, and pushed it over. But it didn't go straight. I'd never have believed that it could take such an angle. The idea was for it to drop into one of those deep pools. But instead, it slewed away to the left, and plunged bang into a stretch of marsh—flood-bed, where the river took a bend. Sank like . . . like a stone! We couldn't do a thing—except note just where it had gone in."

"It was hopeless," Jean confirmed. "We couldn't do any-thing about it. It was nobody's fault, really."

"It was *my* fault," Patrick insisted. "My idea. I should have thought of that."

"Say—what you belly-achein' aboot?" Roddie interrupted. "You say it's in a bog, an' covered ower? An' you ken *whaur* it is. What mair d'you want, man?"

"Eh . . . ?"

"Is that no' what we were aimin' to dae? Get it dumped some place safe—whaur it'll no' be found?"

"But, Roddie—I tell you, it's at the bottom of a bog!"

"Look, man Patrick—use your loaf," the big MacGregor requested patiently. "I reckoned you were a sort o' bright-like guy? You say yon bog's at the riverside? Must be, for the Stane to hae rolled in. Weel, then—the bottom o' that bog canna be deep. Nae deeper'n the river bed. Less, see. Stands to reason. Bedrock canna be far doon—no' if it's alangside the river's bed."

"By Jove—I never thought of that! And me, an engineer!"

"It's right obvious, man. The Stane'll sit doon there fine—till it's wanted. Till bluidy Scotland's ready for it—worthy o' it! Jings—you couldna' hae found a better place, likely!"

"Good Lord!" Patrick turned to Jean. "You know—I do believe he's right," he cried. "It never occurred to me—but the marsh *can't* be deep. Not there. It's where the river widened and shallowed, after those pools. The river bed there can't be four feet below that level. And of course rock-bottom under the bog will be less—the water not scouring it. It's right enough—the Stone could be got out of there. It's not lost. It would take a little doing. But any contractor with earth-moving machinery could get it out in a day. If he knew where it lay. But *we* know—exactly. The Stone's safe—safe as houses. After all."

"Of course! Of course it is. What idiots we were! Oh, Patrick—I'm so glad. So happy. This . . . this just makes everything wonderful, doesn't it!"

"Yes. Yes."

"Gee—you twa been up to mair'n heavin' stanes into bogs, I guess," Roddie commented, grinning. "You're right on top o' things."

"I've . . . well, I've got myself a wife," Patrick confided—since he could by no means contain his news.

"Not yet!" the young woman amended, but gently.

"Och—you've jist fund that oot?" the giant wondered, scornfully. "I could of tell't you that days ago!"

"Indeed?"

"Och, aye—it was stickin' oot a mile."

"What rubbish you talk, Roddie," the girl said. "You know nothing about it."

"Ooh aye? You ask Seumas, then. I tell't him you twa were for it, yon night at the kirk!"

"Aye, he did that," the tinker agreed, from behind them. "Och, very nice, too."

Jean did not meet Patrick's eye. "Oh," she said, small-voiced.

"Umm," the man agreed, examining his fingernails. "Well, well."

"At least," she added, brightly, making a quick recovery, "it seems to go to show how wrong you were, saying that you were a blunderer, Patrick! You seem to have succeeded in . . . in both your undertakings, don't you!"

"It almost looks like it, doesn't it?" the clever man admitted, modestly smug. "It just goes to show you can't keep a good man down!"

Alicky Shand, that silent realist, spoke up, out of his communion with himself. "Fine that. What do we dae, noo?"

They all looked at each other, somewhat blankly. It was Roddie Roy who answered. "Jings—we pack up an' awa' hame, I reckon. Naethin' else to dae, is there?"

"I suppose there isn't, really," Patrick shook his head, uncertainly. "It's all come about so suddenly. But . . . our job's finished, isn't it? All that remains is to disperse and get away from here as quickly and discreetly as possible. Without running into any policemen. That shouldn't be difficult for the Macphails, at any rate. For the rest of us—well, it won't be long before it gets dark."

"Och, we dinna need to wait for that. Back ower this hill, an' doon the ither side, an' in three-four miles we strike Glen

Turret. It has a bit roadie that'll bring us doon to Crieff. Frae Crieff we'll can get a bus into Perth—an' there we are!"

"As easy as that?"

"Sure—what for no'? It's a free country."

"I suppose so. The police can't be watching everybody in a place the size of Crieff."

"Better than that—we can get off the bus at Lochty, and can be back at Kincaid Mains in less than an hour's walking," Jean declared. "Over the Muir. And then—supper."

"Lead us to it, Jeannie lass—for my belly's flat as a burst tyre!"

"Good," Patrick nodded. "Then there's nothing for it but to say thank you to our good friends the Macphails, apologise for troubling them—and go."

"It was a pleasure," Seumas assured.

"Och, yes—any time you are after needing to be wiping the noses of the policemen, see you, just be letting us know," Dougal agreed.

"A handsome offer, indeed! I'm afraid you've lost the cart you were to get—the policemen took that. But I'll make that up to you, I assure you. Next time you come to Kincaid Mains."

"Aye—an' mind you take the dug back wi' you," Roddie added. "Me, I could dae wi' it fine—but, och, its capabeelities would be fair wasted in Glesgy!"

They shook hands all round.

Jean sighed. "So this is the end of our adventure, our saga of the Stone?" she said, almost regretfully, looking back down into the trough of the glen, now filling with the lilac shadows of the summer night. "It seems funny, just to be going away and leaving it there—after all the excitement we've had with it."

"As good an end as we could have hoped for," Patrick pointed out. "Besides, it's not quite the end. There's still a letter to be written. To the Press. To *The Scotsman*, probably would be best. Explaining approximately what has happened. Letting the people of Scotland know that their Stone is safe. That's incumbent on us, I think."

222

"Yes. After all the fuss there's been in the papers and on the radio, we can't just leave the thing entirely up in the air. But you'll have to be terribly careful what you say, Patrick—not to get implicated in any way. You mustn't risk anything."

"Oh, I'll be careful, all right. I'm not worried about that. What does worry me, though, is the interview I'm going to have with your father tonight—or, rather, tomorrow morning!"

"I shouldn't get too upset about that, you know," the girl informed him, judicially. "As fathers go, he's no ogre, I think."

"If he's anything like his daughter, especially on the subject of the decadent aristocracy!"

"You leave him to me, Patrick man," the MacGregor advised. "Me an' Mister Graham's jist like that!" And he linked two large fingers. "I'll hae a bit word wi' him, for you, before I skelp back to Glesgy on the bike wi' these two misbegotten critturs."

"You are very kind."

"It's naethin'—naethin' at a'. I'll dance at your weddin', tae. Bring a' the boys. Frae Glesgy. The Gregorach'll be there. Whoop it up. Gie it big licks. An' damn the polis!"

"You know," Patrick said mildly, "I think this is approximately where we came in! Don't you? How about Crieff? And supper?"

"Goodbye, Stone," Jean Graham murmured, with a tiny catch in her voice.

"Say, rather, *au revoir*, my dear."

Postscript

FOUR days later, a letter addressed merely from Scone, Perthshire, was given pride of place in *The Scotsman*'s Points of View column. Headlined by the Editor THE VOICE OF SCOTLAND?, it read:

THE Stone of Scone, Scotland's true Stone of Destiny, is safe. It is securely buried in the Highland hills, where no Scotland Yard detectives, or earnest Oxford researchers, or even reluctant local policemen, shall lay hands upon it. It is hidden, and cannot be stumbled upon, yet it is fairly readily accessible for disinterment, when the time is ripe, its position mapped accurately to a foot.

Since it is unsuitable that the location of this precious relic should be known only to one or two private individuals, the exact position has been worked out and plotted in a detailed map reference, the figures of which have been split into three, and sent, at the same time as the posting of this letter, to three well-known, distinguished, and patriotic Scots, whose integrity is undoubted. These gentlemen have been charged to retain inviolable each his own third of the secret until such time as a 75 per cent vote of the General Assembly of the Church of Scotland (which probably has the clearest claim to ownership, or trusteeship, of the Stone) shall advise the Stone's disinterment, when they shall each render their portion of the map reference to the then Moderator of the Assembly, who will act, it is confidently believed, in Scotland's best interests.

The writer wishes to make it known beyond all doubt that he and his colleagues have acted from patriotic motives throughout, have no animus against the people of England in general or Oxford or any other university in particular, belong to no political party, are peaceful law-abiding citizens, and staunchly loyal supporters of the Crown. Their sole objective throughout this entire incident has been the retention in

Scotland of a precious relic, part of the Scottish regalia, that indubitably belongs only to Scotland—and as indubitably, had it not been for their actions would have been lost to Scotland.

In case anyone should cast doubts upon the authenticity of this statement, let him approach the Chief Constable of Perthshire, who will vouch for and verify the identity of the undersigned—and also the ownership of a pair of high-powered binoculars at present in the post to New Scotland Yard, London.

(Signed) *Michael McSporran Drummond*

God Save The Queen!

Other Nigel Tranter titles from B&W:

FAST AND LOOSE

Beginning in 1704, *Fast & Loose* is a tale of treachery and revenge in the Highlands, telling the turbulent story of Clan MacColl and the bitter feud that develops between the heirs of the Chief as they struggle for control of their ancestral lands.

> *'It has long been Nigel Tranter's habit to take a slice of Scottish history and breathe believable life into it'*
> DAILY TELEGRAPH

ISLAND TWILIGHT

Set in the Inner Hebrides in Napoleonic times, *Island Twilight* tells the story of Surgeon Major Aeneas Graham's return from the wars. Wounded at Waterloo he comes home to convalesce, but is soon involved in the desperate struggle to save his native Island of Erismore from a legacy of ancient evil.

> *'He has a burning respect for the spirit of history and deploys his characters with mastery'*
> THE OBSERVER

BALEFIRE

Balefire is a gripping story of courage, honour and divided loyalties set during the Border warfare that raged at the start of the 16th century. In the chaos following the massacre of the Scottish army at Flodden in 1513, the life of Simon Armstrong, a young Scottish Laird, is spared only upon his promise of a huge ransom. Yet this is only the beginning of Armstrong's fight for survival. . . .

> *'A tale of border warriors, blazing homes, heroism, vengeance, and a lust for ransom'*
> MANCHESTER EVENING NEWS

THE QUEEN'S GRACE

Set in the north-east of Scotland during Mary, Queen of Scots' visit in 1562, as two powerful nobles struggle for control of the Kingdom, *The Queen's Grace* is a superb evocation of the intrigue and drama that characterised the life and violent times of Scotland's most celebrated monarch.

> *'Nobody does it better'*
> DAILY TELEGRAPH

THE FLOCKMASTERS

The Flockmasters tells the story of Lieutenant Alastair MacRory, who returns home wounded from fighting with the Highland regiments in Spain, only to find that the families of his men are being evicted by the ruthless flockmasters. This veteran of foreign wars is soon forced to take sides in the tragic and desperate struggle for his own land.

*'Tranter lives with the story of Scotland's past
as if he were a witness to events of only yesterday'*
THE HERALD

THE GILDED FLEECE

Set in the Western Highlands in 1809, this novel tells the story of Adam Metcalfe, a young Englishman who travels north to become deputy factor of a large Highland estate and is soon involved in the tragedy and drama of the infamous Highland Clearances.

*'This is a strong and stirring story,
beautifully written'*
MANCHESTER EVENING NEWS

HARSH HERITAGE

The story opens in the western Highlands of Scotland in 1817. The Highland Clearances have begun, and everywhere land-owners are brutally evicting their tenants, condemning them to a grim future of starvation and despair. One particularly terrible act of cruelty leads to a dreadful curse being placed on the family, lands and descendants of the man responsible— Edward Macarthy Neill. From that moment on, Neill's family will never be out of danger, as the curse pursues them relentlessly down through the generations. . . .

KETTLE OF FISH

The Tweed Fisheries Act made it illegal to fish for salmon off the mouth of the River Tweed. The ban infuriated local fishermen, and poaching was rife on dark nights, until local schoolmaster Adam Horsburgh decides that the Act should be challenged openly. When poaching gangs from the cities and even the Royal Navy join in, Adam begins to feel out of his depth—but by then things have gone too far. . . .

'He is a magnificent teller of tales'
GLASGOW HERALD

TINKER'S PRIDE

When a Highland estate changes hands, there are difficult times ahead for Alastair MacIver, living off the land in the remote valleys of his ancestors. A story of wealth and privilege set against one man's pride in his native land, this is a nostalgic and moving tale of West Highland life before the Second World War.

> 'Tinker's Pride skilfully evokes the
> atmosphere of the Highlands'
> THE SCOTSMAN

BRIDAL PATH

Bridal Path charts the adventures of Ewan MacEwan, a young crofter living on the remote isle of Eorsa, who leaves his native island and journeys to the mainland looking for a wife. But his arrival in Oban is swiftly followed by a catalogue of mis-understandings and misadventures which land him in deep trouble—with the police, poachers, dynamite and numerous young women.

One of the finest novels of Scottish island life in the 1940s, *Bridal Path* was made into a highly successful film in 1959, starring Bill Travers, George Cole, Annette Crosbie and Gordon Jackson.

THE FREEBOOTERS

Nigel Tranter's prophetic story of the daring theft, from Westminster Abbey, of the Stone of Destiny—published months before the Stone was in reality 'liberated' by Scottish students. A tale of intrigue and mayhem, as a group of Scottish adventurers strive to keep one step ahead of the English authorities.

Available from all good bookshops,
or direct from the publishers:

B&W Publishing,
233 Cowgate, Edinburgh,
EH1 1NQ.

Tel: 0131 220 5551